The car 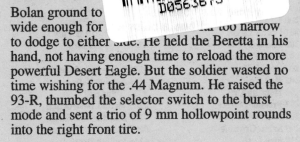 the Exec

Bolan ground to wide enough for too narrow to dodge to either side. He held the Beretta in his hand, not having enough time to reload the more powerful Desert Eagle. But the soldier wasted no time wishing for the .44 Magnum. He raised the 93-R, thumbed the selector switch to the burst mode and sent a trio of 9 mm hollowpoint rounds into the right front tire.

The tire blew. The Executioner swung his weapon toward the left tire, but had no time to pull the trigger. By the time he found his target, the vehicle was ten feet in front of him and still hurtling forward at fifty miles an hour.

Having no choice, Bolan bent his knees, then vaulted as high as he could, straight up into the air.

DON PENDLETON'S
THE EXECUTIONER®
ROGUE TARGET

A GOLD EAGLE BOOK FROM
W☉RLDWIDE®

TORONTO • NEW YORK • LONDON
AMSTERDAM • PARIS • SYDNEY • HAMBURG
STOCKHOLM • ATHENS • TOKYO • MILAN
MADRID • WARSAW • BUDAPEST • AUCKLAND

First edition September 2001
ISBN 0-373-64274-1

Special thanks and acknowledgment to
Jerry VanCook for his contribution to this work.

ROGUE TARGET

Simply to kill a man is not murder.

> —Thomas de Quincey
> *On Suicide,* c. 1847

...and they loved murder and would drink the blood of beasts.

> —The Book of Mormon (Jarom 6), 1830

There's a very definite line between killing and murder. The two are not the same. One is morally wrong, the other sometimes necessary.

> —Mack Bolan

To Becky

Prologue

He was a trained professional, and running and hiding were part of that profession. Over the years he had added experience to education, and his intuition was finely honed. But every man had his breaking point—a point past which, no matter how superbly talented or tutored, the imagination creeps in to taint insight.

Hugh Pollard knew he had been running and hiding for so long now that he could no longer fully trust his instincts. Distinguishing the real from the imagined had become increasingly difficult over the past few weeks, and he could no longer be sure if the red warning flags that popped into his head were genuine or simply stress-induced paranoia. His mood swung from total terror to a sort of forcefully rationalized peace of mind, then back again, at a rate that threatened to turn him into a feeble-minded idiot.

Pollard's emotions were in constant contrast, much like the city through which he now drove the battered old Ford pickup. Yes, Pollard thought, the landscape and architecture of Rio de Janeiro were indeed as contrasting as the sensations in his heart and soul these days. Much like his vacillations from sanity to near dementia, Rio's modern, European-style Municipal Opera stood almost on top of archaic peasant huts of mud and bamboo. In the same sudden and dramatic way that high mountain peaks like Hunchback, Two Brothers and Sugar Loaf suddenly dropped to flat beaches like Copacabana, so did Pollard's rare moments of peace—seconds during which he was actually able to convince himself he was safe—suddenly reverse themselves into a frantic trepidation.

Pollard slowed the rusting pickup as he neared the intersection of Avenido Rio Branco. A parking space appeared along the street and he pulled in. For a moment he sat frozen behind the wheel. Then he forced himself to look behind him to the busy street, at the cars whizzing by in the rearview mirror. It wasn't the fast-moving traffic that he studied—it was no threat. But each vehicle that slowed as it neared him was a shot of pure adrenaline injected directly into his heart. Each of the slower-moving cars and trucks that finally crept past without stopping brought a moment's relief during which he was afraid he might burst into tears. Then each brief respite ended when he spotted another flagging vehicle.

His fingers still clenched around the steering wheel, Pollard forced himself back to rational thought. Yes, Rio had its share of drive-by shootings. But such acts of violence were the work of gang members, drug peddlers and other criminals. None of the various groups of men seeking Hugh Pollard would shoot him from a moving car. They all wanted him alive, and they would take him on the street, more than likely overpowering him with the force of numbers rather than at gunpoint. Yet, Pollard knew, they would have guns with them. If they couldn't take him alive, they would kill him to insure none of the other groups got him.

Pollard dropped his eyes from the rearview mirror to the sidewalk in front of him. Through the windshield he watched an old woman limp across the broken pavement, her arms wrapped around a paper sack. Cucumbers, peppers and other vegetables could be seen at the top of the sack. But what was at the bottom? A submachine pistol? The sack was large enough.

The woman walked by, muttering incoherently to herself.

Pollard's eyes moved to a middle-aged man seated on a bench beneath the shade of a brazilwood tree. The man held a folded newspaper across his thighs, occasionally circling items on the page with a ballpoint pen. Was something hidden beneath the newspaper on his lap? A mini-Uzi? A 9 mm Ingram perhaps? Was the man prepared to leap from the bench as part of an abduction team that might even now be moving in unseen from other areas?

A woman carrying a package came out of a dress shop and headed toward the man. The man stood, folded the newspaper under his arm, and the two walked away.

Pollard took a deep breath, then forced himself out of the Ford. His legs wobbled slightly as he started down the block in the opposite direction the couple had gone. When he reached the corner he turned onto the sidewalk paralleling Avenida Rio Branco, his eyes still scanning ahead with every step. Two blocks later he turned again, this time onto a side street too cramped for vehicular traffic. Another of Rio's sharp contrasts, he thought. Modern eight-lane thoroughfares were crossed by ancient walking paths. The narrow lanes branched from the broader streets like tiny creeks twisting away from a mighty river.

The crowded, snakelike street Pollard now took led him past street hustlers, open-air craft shops and fruit-and-vegetable stands mobbed with customers. But for every human being there were ten thousand flies, and he found himself swatting them constantly from his face. He stopped at one of the stands, feigning interest in wooden gifts and other novelties, while his peripheral vision studied the raggedly dressed men and women around him. Satisfied—at least partially—that he wasn't being watched, he moved on.

The street opened abruptly onto another modern avenue, and Pollard turned right onto another sidewalk. Now he mingled with men and women in business suits who carried briefcases made of soft leather or exotic reptile skins. Two blocks ahead he saw the sign: Wayne Axe Imports. With a final glance over his shoulder, he quickened his stride.

Where was Axe? Pollard wondered as he watched the reflections of the people behind him in the office windows to his side. Wayne Axe had agreed to meet him at the Blue Mongoose Café at one-thirty, and he had known how important the meeting was—if not what the actual subject of discussion was to be. He knew Pollard's situation, knew the constant peril in which Pollard had lived during the past six months. And Axe had agreed to help. He was Hugh Pollard's friend.

Wasn't he?

The double glass doors leading into Axe Imports were tinted, but through the smoky glass Pollard could see the reception desk. Empty, the chair behind it had rolled back against the wall. For the thousandth time in the past fifteen minutes, a cold shot of fear rolled up and down his back. Why? Why did the empty chair bother him? The sanity that still remained within his brain told him the receptionist had simply gone to the ladies' room. Or she was off on some other errand just as innocuous. But the paranoia that was also now a very real part of Pollard screamed.

Pollard's hand trembled slightly as he forced it into the side pocket of his jacket, his fingers curling around the handle of a cheap lock-back folding knife. In the old days, he thought, he could have scored any gun of his choice thirty minutes after arriving in Rio. But now he had only one contact left on the continent whom he trusted, and that man had been unavailable when Pollard had suddenly decided to come to Rio to see Axe. The knife was the best protection he had been able to obtain without drawing suspicion.

With his other hand, Pollard opened the door and forced himself to enter the reception area. He took a cautious step forward, wincing as his weight caused the wooden floor to creak. The folding knife came out of his pocket. He left it closed and hidden in his palm but gripped it tightly with his fingers, ready to use should the need arise. He moved faster now. If his footsteps had been heard, there was nothing he could do about it. Quickly, he dropped his head to check behind the desk and in the chair well. Empty.

The only other door in the reception area was set in the wall opposite the glass entrance. It was closed. Pollard stopped in front of it, pressing his ear against the cold metal. He heard nothing. Another surge of fear crept from the small of his back to the nape of his neck. He should have heard something. Wayne Axe employed at least a dozen people as office staff, and there should have been some kind of sound behind the steel.

Pollard glanced at his watch. It wasn't even three o'clock. The middle of the working day. Siesta? No, not with the front doors unlocked. And the Hispanic tradition of siesta in Brazilian business had died with the arrival of Americans and air-conditioning.

Opening the knife now, Pollard moved slowly, doing his best to muffle the click as the four-inch blade popped into the locking notch. With the weapon clutched in his hand, he opened the door.

The hall led straight ahead for perhaps thirty feet, dead-ending in windowless brick. Open office doors could be seen along the walls. But the hallway was as silent now as it had been when the door was shut. No voices met his ear. No sounds from adding machines, computers or any of the other equipment one might have expected to be in use within a thriving Brazilian import-export business in the afternoon.

One thing, however, was vastly different with the door open. The smell.

Pollard had encountered death many times during his career, and he knew that there was no one single smell of death; the stenches came in stages. Later, whoever was dead down the hallway would reek of rot and decay, but what he smelled now was recent death, and the odor of human excrement was still the overpowering scent. Whoever had died had released his bowels along with his soul.

Pollard hesitated. Should he go on or flee? For a moment he teetered between the two decisions, then realized he had no choice. He had to meet with Axe. But in addition to that fact, Axe had been his friend. For that reason alone it was imperative that he learn whether or not it was Axe's body that produced the nauseating aroma.

The hallway floor was made from the same wood as the reception office, and he knew it would squeak just as loudly with each fall of his feet. Checking the rear offices with stealth wasn't an option. Speed was what was called for now. After the first step into the hall there would be no turning back. He guessed that Axe's office would be the last one, at the end, insulated from pesky solicitors by both the receptionist and his other employees.

With a deep breath Pollard readied the knife and sprinted through the door toward the end of the hall. His eyes flickered right and left as he passed each open doorway along his path. All looked empty, but the fact that the rooms were in disarray raced through his mind as he neared the final doorway and the stench of death grew stronger. Two steps from the office, he raised the knife in front of him.

Pollard turned into the opening.

Into a scene that might have come from Dante's *Inferno*.

Hugh Pollard froze just inside the door. What he saw threatened to drive the last remnants of sanity from his brain. This office, too, was empty of human life. But it was hardly empty of human bodies. A dozen men and women lay strewed around the room. Each body had fallen forward onto its face, and what looked like a small-caliber bullet hole was visible in the back of each head. Some of the bullets had stayed inside the skulls, and only the residual blood from the entry wound was visible. On others, however, the lead missiles had penetrated through the front of the face, leaving gaping exit wounds. These bodies lay forward like the others, but they were surrounded by multicolored pools of blood, brain matter and other body fluids.

Pollard turned his eyes to the large mahogany desk in the center of the office. Behind it he could see Wayne Axe. His friend sat silently, his wrists secured to the arms of the leather desk chair with silverish-gray duct tape. His shirt had been torn back over his shoulders, and blistering red welts covered his chest, neck and face. Whatever monsters had done this had spent extra time on the face, and the only features that still looked human were the eyes. They stared, wide open in pain, horror and death, at Hugh Pollard. In those eyes. whether real or imagined, Pollard could also see the accusation. In his brain he heard Wayne Axe scream, It's all your fault!

A whooshing sound from down the hall pulled Pollard out of shock and back to reality. The front door—the same front door through which he had entered—had opened again. Footsteps squeaked toward him across the wooden reception-area floor. Pollard whirled away from them, toward the window set in the wall behind Axe. The curtains had been drawn open, and through the glass he could see an alley. He raced forward, lifting the window and wondering if the noise could be heard down the hall in the reception area. But a moment later his arms had pulled his body up and through the opening. He fell to the alley floor as the footsteps behind him started down the hall.

Pollard struggled to his feet and stumbled forward like a drunken man suddenly awakened from sleep. Each step he took brought a little more feeling back to his traumatized limbs. Soon he was sprinting away from Wayne Axe Imports with a strength only possible through complete and total horror.

And each time one of his shoes hit the dirty concrete of the Rio de Janeiro alley, he wondered if the screaming he heard was real or only in his mind.

The big man wore black cross trainers and khaki pants beneath his yellow shirt. The pants and shoes helped him blend in with other American sightseers on the streets of Rio de Janeiro. So did the shirt. But the baggy garment served another purpose, as well. Its loose fit eliminated printing—a term used by police officers, military personnel and covert operatives the world over for the outline of a weapon pushing through its cover. The same men and women also knew that the larger a weapon was, or the more weapons one attempted to conceal, the harder it was to avoid such printing.

And the weapons Mack Bolan carried were both large and numerous.

Bolan, better known as the Executioner, pulled his rented Chevy into a parking lot across the street from Wayne Axe Imports. Rolling down the window, he handed the attendant the keys and a handful of Brazilian coins, then got out and waited while the man wrote out a ticket. He had arrived in Rio de Janeiro less than an hour earlier, flown in by his good friend and longtime pilot, Jack Grimaldi.

His mission was simple—at least on the surface: find Hugh Pollard, the former director of the Central Intelligence Agency, then bring the man back to the United States.

The parking attendant tore the ticket from his pad and handed it to the soldier. Bolan turned away, his mind returning to the intelligence file he had reviewed during the flight from Washington, D.C. Over a year ago Pollard had been accused of selling highly classified intel to the Chinese. Senate hear-ings had been held. As they progressed, it became more and more evident that the CIA man was indeed guilty, and that charges of treason would be brought. While he was under house arrest and twenty-four-hour guard by both the FBI and CIA, the age-old jealousy between the two agencies resulted in a communications mix-up. The reason was long and complex, and insignificant to the Executioner's purposes. The bottom line was that the night before the Senate verdict was to be rendered, and a decision made as to whether or not Pollard would be indicted on criminal charges, a hole was created in the guard. That hole was the only window of opportunity Pollard needed.

The former CIA director disappeared. He'd been missing for nearly six months now, and the American government and intelligence community hadn't stopped sweating during that period. Then, he was spotted in Rio. Bolan's Grimaldi-flown Learjet was in the air within thirty minutes.

Bolan stopped at the street, waiting as several cars raced by. Besides reviewing Pollard's file during the flight, he had stayed in radio contact with Stony Man Farm—the top secret counterterrorist installation out of which he often worked. Aaron "the Bear" Kurtzman, the Farm's computer wizard, had been busy tapping into CIA files. Kurtzman learned that it was a CIA field operative, currently working out of Rio, who thought he had seen Pollard. The agent had tried to tail the former director but lost him. As far as the CIA knew, none of the other countries eager to capture and pick Pollard's brain—and that meant every country in the world, friend or foe—knew of the sighting in Brazil. Kurtzman had also dug up the information on a friendship between Pollard and Wayne Axe. Axe had served under Pollard in South America before retiring from the CIA to open his import-export business.

Finally spotting a break in the traffic, the Executioner zigzagged his way across the street. As he jogged, both the 9 mm Beretta 93-R machine pistol and his trademark .44 Magnum Desert Eagle bobbed up and down inside his belt. Because a jacket would have drawn unwanted attention in the warm weather, his usual shoulder rig and belt holster were locked in the Chevy's trunk. Both guns now rode securely in Bianchi inside-the-waistband holsters. The Desert Eagle was on his right side. The Beretta sat cross-draw fashion opposite it. Both guns could be reached by either hand if necessary.

Bolan reached the curb on the other side of the street and stopped, looking briefly through the tinted glass doors to Axe Imports. The chair behind the desk that faced the doors was empty—which could mean anything, and probably meant nothing. But it was enough to remind him that in addition to his pistols, he carried two additional weapons. A tiny but wickedly curved and serrated Spyderco Cricket knife was clipped inside his underwear at the small of his back. The Cricket's blade was less than two inches long, and would never be Bolan's first choice as a fighter. But it cut deeply, and hid well. His primary edged weapon for this mission was a new knife that had caught his eye in John "Cowboy" Kissinger's Stony Man armory. The Szabo Rad folding dagger was actually two knives in one. The blade was longer than the handle, and even when the knife was closed, three inches of razor-edged steel extended from the grip down into the Concealex sheath. It could be drawn with lightning speed in an ice-pick grip, and employed immediately as a short dagger. But if there was time, a thumb stud opened the folder and transformed it into a deadly fighting knife with seven inches of double edge. The Rad was aptly named, Bolan thought as he reached out to grab the handle of the door to Axe Imports. Rad was the ancient Viking rune that stood for, among other things, "transformation."

When the Executioner opened the glass door, the smell hit him. He recognized it immediately, and without consciously drawing it he found the Desert Eagle in his hand. His eyes quickly scanned the empty reception area, then moved to the open steel door across the room. Through the opening he could see a hallway. It was from this direction that the stench came.

Staying close to the walls to minimize the squeaking wood beneath his feet, Bolan made his way to the door. Unless the hallway led to a sewer, there was a recently dead body some-where on the other side of the door.

Bolan stopped at the open door, peering around the corner. The lights were on in the hall, but the entire rear of the build-ing was quiet. *Dead* quiet. He was about to round the corner when he suddenly heard footsteps ahead. Then a sudden whoosh met his ears. The Executioner frowned, unable to identify the sound. But it, and the footsteps, meant someone was there. He waited, listening, and heard several more un-identifiable noises. Then the building lapsed into silence once more.

Still hugging the walls for silence, Bolan made his way down the hallway to the first office. Through the door he could see a desk littered with papers. But several pages had fallen haphazardly to the floor. He moved on, and through the next open doorway he saw a desk chair overturned on its side. Again he felt his eyebrows lower. The people who had been in these offices had left in a hurry. Either by choice or coercion.

Three more empty offices showed evidence of sudden de-partures, and as he made his way toward the final open door, the smell of excrement became almost overpowering. He had seen no one in any of the other offices, which meant the foot-steps and other sounds had to have come from the final room at the end of the hall. The combination of empty desk chairs and the volume and intensity of the odor told him something else, as well.

There wasn't just one dead body on the other side of the wall he now walked along. There must be several.

Raising the Desert Eagle slightly, the Executioner peered around the corner. He took the sight in quickly, his eyes mov-ing from the bodies on the floor to the one behind the desk. What had happened was obvious now. Whoever had done all this had come after Wayne Axe and his knowledge of Pol-lard's whereabouts. The other dead men and women had been nothing more than unfortunate office workers in the wrong place at the wrong time. Rounded up like cattle and summarily executed—perhaps in front of Axe as a means of persuading him to talk. Which also told Bolan that Axe hadn't known much about Pollard's whereabouts. The murders would have taken place before the torture, and few men would have held out while so many died before their eyes.

So what had Axe known? Anything? That was the big question. Of one thing, however, the Executioner was certain. The CIA had been wrong. The U.S. wasn't the only intelligence agency that knew that Pollard was in the area.

Bolan turned his attention to the open window behind the desk, and suddenly what he had heard became clear. The footsteps belonged to someone walking to the window. The sound had been the window rising, and the other unidentifiable sounds had been that same person climbing out of the office. With the Desert Eagle leading the way, Bolan hurried around the desk. He had little hope that whoever had been in the office was still outside the building; the gap between the time he heard the sounds and the present had been too long. He was right. The alley behind Axe Imports was deserted.

The Executioner holstered the Desert Eagle. There was only one thing to do now. Search the office. Perhaps he could find something that might connect Axe and Pollard and give him another direction in which to take his search.

The obvious place to start was Axe himself. Ignoring the revoltingly desecrated body in the chair itself, Bolan began to go through the man's pockets. Against the right hip he found a billfold. It contained a Brazilian driver's license, a permanent-resident card and other ID. But there was nothing of interest that connected the man to his former CIA boss.

A suit coat matching the slacks hung from a nob on the wall, and Bolan moved toward it. In the right pocket of the jacket he found a key ring. From the inside breast pocket he pulled a small red leather day planner. Opening it to the day's date, he saw "P. 1330 BMC."

Did the *P* stand for Pollard? Bolan had no idea, but he stuffed the small book into his own pocket.

Back at the desk the Executioner shuffled through a stack

of invoices and other paraphernalia. At the bottom of the pile, he saw a desk calendar. Within the square for the current date, Wayne Axe had scribbled, "Blue Mongoose-1330." Bolan recognized the name. And the time, and initials *BMC*. The Blue Mongoose Café. A quiet little out-of-the-way bar and restaurant where a clandestine meeting might well take place. He raised his wrist to his face. It was now almost 1530—two hours later than the time on the calendar and in the day planner. If Axe had planned to meet Pollard there for lunch, he had missed the meeting. It was also unlikely that Pollard would still be waiting. In fact...

Bolan's eyes shot back to the open window behind him. He frowned. If Pollard was desperate for Axe's help, and Axe hadn't kept their appointment, the former CIA man's next logical step would have been to come here to find out why.

Silently, the Executioner nodded. It was Pollard whom he had just heard in this very room. Pollard who had come and seen the same human carnage Bolan now saw littering the floor. Pollard who had escaped through the window, probably thinking the sounds he heard when Bolan entered the reception area were the killers returning.

Bolan rounded the desk again. He started for the hall when he heard the front doors open again. The sound of heavy feet made the wooden floor creak, and a voice cried out in Portuguese, "This is the police! Anyone in the building must freeze!"

The Executioner turned toward the open window.

He arrived just in time to see the flash of a blue uniform and feel the barrel of a 12-gauge shotgun press into his forehead.

As a soldier during wartime, he had fought for freedom. And since striking out on his own after his war duty was over, he had blazed a path of freedom for the oppressed.

But during all those years, Mack Bolan vowed never to kill an innocent man or woman, or a police officer who was doing his duty. Even when it was at his own personal peril, the

Executioner would lower his gun rather than shoot a cop. He didn't intend to change that pattern now. And so the Desert Eagle slowly fell to the windowsill and Bolan let it be taken from his hand.

The Rio cop on the other side of the window was sweating as he jerked the big .44 Magnum from Bolan's fingers. At the same time the Executioner heard the footsteps of other officers as they entered the office. Questions and exclamations filled the air in Portuguese—close enough to Spanish that Bolan could pick up a few words, yet far enough from the neighboring language to keep him from following verbatim. But no one would have needed any mastery of the vernacular to comprehend the mood of the room.

The Rio cops were shocked and outraged. Several even appeared to be frightened by what they saw before them, and Bolan saw more than one man make the sign of the cross over his heart.

The officer on the other side of the window kept the shotgun trained on Bolan with one hand. With the other he used the Desert Eagle to indicate that the Executioner should turn around. Bolan began to turn as the man stuck his head through the window. His first sight of the scene brought an audible gasp.

Two men in uniform stepped forward as Bolan came to a halt, his hands held up at shoulder level. The first, a tall wiry man of obvious Indian heritage, shoved the barrel of a 9 mm Walther MPK submachine gun into his face. The second, shorter and heavier and wearing sergeant's stripes, stood back slightly, holding a Mekanika Uru subgun of the same caliber. He moved the barrel up and down as he shouted.

Bolan caught the idea, if not the words themselves. He raised his hands higher.

The sergeant's voice barked again and a third officer, looking to be barely in his twenties, holstered his 9 mm Taurus pistol and stepped forward cautiously. Starting at the Executioner's upraised arms, he began patting him down. His eyes grew wide as he reached Bolan's waist, then lifted Bolan's shirt to pull the Beretta and the Rad from their respective holster and sheath.

A collective intake of air came from the other cops as the Rad appeared in the young officer's hand. When he stepped back and flipped it open, other exclamations issued forth.

The sergeant looked at the weapon, then let his eyes circle the room again, stopping on the body in the chair. With a disgusted snort of fury, he stepped forward and brought the barrel of his subgun down on top of the Executioner's head.

The blow dropped Bolan to his knees. He felt the familiar wet sticky feeling as blood began to leak from the abrasion beneath his hair and drip down his face. The officer who had searched him now moved to his rear and snapped handcuffs around his wrists before using the chain between them to jerk him to his feet.

The sergeant snarled another question his way. Bolan didn't understand and shook his head. "I don't speak Portuguese."

The portly sergeant switched languages. "Who are you?" he demanded in English.

"A customer," the Executioner said. "I had come to check on—"

The answer bought him another blow with the barrel of the subgun, this time to the side of the face. The strike failed to break the skin, but Bolan felt his face begin to swell almost immediately. He fell backward against the seated body of Wayne Axe, then slid off the tortured man to sprawl over the desk.

"Customers do not come to such establishments armed as if they were leading a revolution!" the sergeant screamed. The officers who understood English nodded their agreement. "You have murdered these people in cold blood!" the man went on. "And you will die for it!" He paused, catching his breath as his flabby chest heaved with anger.

Both his head and face throbbed painfully as the Executioner half-sat half-lay over the desk. But as his brain tried to clear, he felt something amid the papers strewed across the desktop. His cuffed hands moved slightly beneath his back, and his fingers probed for the thin piece of wire they had brushed as he fell. A paper clip. If he could work it off the stack of pages it held together...

Switching back to Portuguese, the sergeant gave more orders to his men. Bolan felt rough hands grab both of his shoulders. They wrenched him from the desk just as the paper clip came off the stack of papers. He held it precariously between his second and third fingers as he was pushed and dragged to the door. Silently, he prayed that this small ticket to freedom wouldn't slip from his precarious grip, and that none of the officers would notice it. As they reached the door, the men suddenly halted to reposition their grips before leading him down the hall. The short pause gave the Executioner the opportunity to slide the paper clip deeper into the webbing between his fingers.

Had they been paying close attention, the Rio de Janeiro cops would have seen a slight smile cross the Executioner's lips.

A few moments later they were on the street. Several patrol cars, their lights flashing, were parked behind the vehicles in the spaces along the curb. As the dozen or so other cops walked toward them, Bolan was thrown into the back seat of the nearest black-and-white. The sergeant slid into the shotgun seat in the front. Another man got behind the wheel. The sergeant now carried the Beretta 93-R and Desert Eagle. As the Executioner watched him drop them on the seat between him and the driver, the back door opposite him opened and the young cop who had searched him slid in at his side. The young man still held the Rad in his hand.

Bolan went to work almost immediately behind his back, bending the paper clip into a makeshift handcuff key. Fortune had been with him, and in all of the confusion the officer who had cuffed him hadn't double-locked the cuffs. Snapping the lock was simple, but the time wasn't right. He would have to wait—and watch—until he saw his opportunity. He kept his hands, and the cuffs, concealed behind his back.

The young officer directed a question at the front seat as

the patrol car pulled away from the scene. The sergeant turned, his eyes falling on the Rad. The Executioner couldn't understand the Portuguese, but the gist of the conversation was obvious. The young cop wanted to know what to do with the knife. The sergeant flicked his head at Bolan, indicating the man should get the sheath from Bolan's belt. Bolan chose that moment to lean forward at the waist, feigning a confused desire to be cooperative. The young cop leaned toward him and spoke in Portuguese.

"I don't understand," the Executioner said again.

The sergeant spoke once more in English. "Lean back!" he ordered. "Lean back so he can get your sheath or I will order him to use the knife to cut your throat!"

Now pretending sudden understanding, the Executioner leaned backward. The movement gave him the opportunity to raise his right hand—the handcuffs still dangling from the wrist—and snake it down into the back of his pants. It came out holding the Spyderco Cricket.

As the young cop raised the Executioner's shirt and reached for the Rad's sheath, Bolan slipped his left arm around the man's neck in a headlock. At the same time, his other hand thumbed open the Cricket, and he brought the serrated blade up and hooked the tip into the young man's throat.

Both the young cop and the fat sergeant froze in place. The driver, his eyes busy on the road, continued to guide the patrol car through the busy traffic.

With the speed of light, Bolan released his grip around the man's neck long enough to take the Rad out of his hand. He resumed the headlock and brought the Rad into position on the other side of the man's throat. Pressing the dagger tip against one side of the young officer's neck, with the curved tip of the Cricket still hooked into the other, Bolan said, "Very carefully, Sergeant. I want you to hand me my guns."

The sergeant shook his head, his flabby jowls quivering. "No," he said flatly. "That, I cannot do."

The soldier pressed both knives harder into the young cop's throat. Two separate trickles of blood, small but unmistakable, began to drip down the man's neck. "Then say goodbye to our young friend, and what would probably have been a very promising law-enforcement career in the service of your city," he said, shaking his head sadly. His eyes drilled into those of the man in the front seat.

The sergeant took a deep breath. Then slowly the Desert Eagle came over the seat.

Bolan left the Rad in place, taking the Cricket away from the young man's throat long enough to grab the Desert Eagle. With the big .44 now in his hand, he let the small folding knife fall from his fingers to the floor of the patrol car and turned the Eagle toward the front seat. "Now the Beretta," he demanded.

The 93-R was extended, grip first. "Just drop it," Bolan ordered. The machine pistol glanced off the Executioner's knee on its way to the floor next to the Cricket.

By now the driver had seen what was happening. He kept nervously looking from the road, to the rearview mirror, to the sergeant and back to the road. He started to pull over toward the curb. Bolan swung the Desert Eagle toward the back of his head and said, "You do that, and you'll find your face all over the windshield."

The man's native tongue may have been Portuguese. But he seemed to understand English. In any case, he drove on, his knuckles white on the steering wheel.

"Now I'll need *your* guns," Bolan said to the sergeant.

"You will never get away with this," the sergeant said. "Before this is over, I will have your *cojones*."

"Colorful threat," Bolan said. "But not very effective. Pass your guns over the seat butt first and drop them on the floor. Or the bullet looking at you through this barrel is going to get a closer look."

His face a mixture of anger and despair, the sergeant dropped his Taurus to the floor of the back seat. A moment later he had unholstered the driver's weapon and done the same with it. "And now, *patron*," the overweight man said sarcastically, "of what other service to you may we be?"

Bolan swung his head around quickly, noting that two of the other patrol cars were behind them. They had turned off the flashing red-and-blue lights but kept close to the vehicle carrying the prisoner. "Get on the radio and tell those two cars to circle around you. Tell them you think I have friends who may try to free me. Tell them you're going to take another route to jail and you want them to act as a decoy."

A broad grin spread across the fat face in the front seat. "I will have to give such orders in Portuguese," the sergeant said. "Or they will become suspicious. And it appears you don't speak that language. You will not know what I tell them."

"Yes," Bolan said. "That's already crossed my mind. That's why I've decided to shoot you first if anything goes wrong." He nodded toward the driver. "You see, at this point you're dispensable, Sergeant. I can shoot you and still have a driver."

The cop looked as if he might want to shoot *himself* for so foolishly playing his hand. But he nodded, then turned to jerk the microphone from the radio. A brief conversation in Portuguese took place, then the two black-and-whites following them turned on their lights to clear traffic, pulled into the left-hand lane and passed them.

"Excellent," Bolan said. "You get to live. At least a little longer."

Sweat had broken out on the fat man's face. The young cop, still gripped in the headlock, coughed. Bolan took the Rad away from his throat and pressed the Desert Eagle into his temple. Sheathing the folding dagger, he jerked the young man's own pistol from the holster and dropped it next to the others on the floor. With a violent shove, he threw the man back across the seat against the opposite window and grabbed the Beretta off the floor.

With one gun on the young cop, the other trained at the front seat, Bolan spoke to the driver. "Take the next left."

The driver slowed, then turned onto a less traveled street. They passed a busy commercial area, then entered a neighborhood of multifamily apartment complexes. Bolan ordered the driver into a parking lot.

The man complied, shifting the transmission into park at the Executioner's next order.

"Now, if the three of you want to keep on living," he said, "you'll do exactly what I say. One by one you're going to get out of the car and walk over there." Bolan indicated a chain-link fence to their side that separated the parking lot of the apartments they were in front of from a similar complex adjacent to it. "While you walk, you keep your hands stretched out to the side. When you get to the fence, you're going to stick your fingers through the holes and face the other way." He paused for a moment, then continued. "I didn't have a chance to search any of you thoroughly. And we've all just seen what can be done with hidden backup weapons, haven't we?" His tone of voice made the words a statement rather than a question. "So if any of you so much as twitches in a way which doesn't please me...*bang*." He paused again, searching the faces to make sure they understood. He still wasn't sure how much English the young cop and driver spoke. But they nodded. And they'd get the idea from the sergeant.

"You first, Sarge," the Executioner said.

Keeping his hands in full view, the greasy commanding officer opened his door and waddled over to the fence.

"Now you," Bolan told the driver. "Don't turn off the engine. Leave the keys in the ignition."

The driver followed the sergeant's example perfectly.

"Time to say goodbye to you, too," the Executioner finally told the frightened young man next to him in the back seat. "Get out."

A moment later all three Rio cops had their fingers through the fence.

Bolan kept the Desert Eagle aimed their way as he got out of the back and circled the car. The handcuffs still dangled from one wrist. But that was a minor problem that could be taken care of later, when he had more time. As he walked, he could see the three men whispering among themselves. He opened the driver's door and called out "Silence!"

The men quieted immediately.

As soon as he'd slipped behind the wheel, one of the sergeant's hands shifted from the fence. He leaned forward and reached for his boot.

Aiming at the grass on the other side of the chain-link fence, Bolan squeezed the trigger. The big Desert Eagle roared and a .44 Magnum round whizzed an inch to the side of the man's boot. The semijacketed hollowpoint round cut through one of the steel fence lengths, severing it with a loud ring, then drilled on through the grass and into the dirt below.

The sergeant jerked back up to a standing position, and jammed his fingers back into the fence. His legs froze in place. But the flabby rolls pressing against his tight uniform blouse danced in fright.

The fence was still singing as the Executioner drove away.

THE SQUAD CAR had to be ditched fast.

Over the Rio police radio, the Executioner had heard voices calling out for the sergeant's car. The words had been in Portuguese, but the gradually increasing panic when the transmissions weren't answered left little doubt in Bolan's mind that a search for the missing officers was about to be launched. If he wasn't already, every cop in Rio would be soon be searching frantically for his lost brethren and the man believed to have committed the mass murder at Wayne Axe Imports.

Pulling out of the residential neighborhood, Bolan drove a fast two miles, then turned onto another side street. Four blocks later he pulled down an alley, killed the engine and vaulted over the seat into the back. Grabbing the Cricket from the floor, he exited through the back door and took off at a jog until he reached the corner.

A few cars drove past the houses and apartments as he slowed to a walk. But as in any big city, the residents of this middle-income area paid little attention to anything that didn't directly and immediately pertain to them. Bolan strolled to a

year-old Saturn parked in a driveway, found the driver's door
unlocked and slid behind the wheel. Ten seconds later he had
cracked the steering column with the butt of the Desert Eagle,
started the vehicle and was backing out of the driveway.

The Executioner drove back toward Vargas Avenue, slump-
ing low behind the wheel. A blue baseball cap, the letters on
the crown advertising a Rio trucking business, had been rest-
ing on the passenger seat of the Saturn. It now sat atop his
head. His mind raced as he drove the new vehicle. By now
the sergeant and his two men would have made contact with
the other officers. And the Rio police would have a good description of him to go on.

That was something else which needed to be taken care of
quickly.

Spotting a strip mall in the distance, Bolan changed lanes
and pulled the Saturn into the parking lot. A large discount
store was the shopping center's main attraction, and stood in
the middle of several smaller specialty shops. Parking the Saturn two rows from the front door, the Executioner got out and
walked quickly toward the store. He had just tripped the electric eye that swung the entrance door back when he saw the
blue-uniformed police officer standing guard in the foyer. Bolan's eyes fell to the man's waist. The gun, extra magazines,
nightstick and pepper spray were all of the usual weapons on
an officer's belt. But the weapons were not what worried the
soldier. At this point the walkie-talkie in the black leather case
was far more dangerous to him. It squawked with radio traffic
as he entered the building and passed the man.

The cop ignored Bolan as the soldier walked by.

The big man breathed a silent sigh of relief. The officer's
lack of interest meant that word of his escape, and his description, had not yet gone out over the airwaves. But that could
change any second, too. He had to get into the store, buy a
change of clothes and get out again as quickly as possible.

Bolan hurried past the checkout stands toward the men's
clothing department. With little regard to anything but size, he
grabbed a blue chambray work shirt off a hanger, a pair of

jeans from the many stacks on the display tables, and then hurried toward the shoe department. The first shelves he came to held rows of yellow leather steel-toed work boots. The boots had no boxes, and each pair was tied together with the laces. The Executioner grabbed a pair in his size, and with a quick about-face, hurried back up the aisle to a checkout stand. He took a place at the end of the shortest line.

From where he stood, the soldier could see the cop through the glass wall between the store and the entrance foyer. The man was all smiles, having struck up a conversation with an attractive young woman.

The line moved with the pace of a medicated snail as the soldier waited his turn, keeping one eye on the foyer. Several times the cop looked down and his hand moved to his walkie-talkie. Whether he was receiving calls, about to make a routine check in or the movements were simply the seminervous gestures of a male on the prowl, Bolan couldn't tell. But, at least for the moment, the officer was obviously more interested in the attractive young woman than he was in police work.

The Executioner's eyes had already scoured the store for another exit—there were none open to the customers. The only other way out of the building was through the gray metal doors at the rear of the store, and entering such an obvious employees-only area would draw unwanted attention. No, unless the cop finally lifted the radio out of its carrier, and it became evident that he had just gotten the call about an American escapee, strolling casually out the front of the store again was still his best bet.

Finally, an old man in front of the soldier hobbled away from the checkout stand. Bolan set his purchases on the counter. As the woman ran the bar code on each item past the scanner, his eyes flickered again to the foyer. The good-looking young woman was writing something on a scrap of paper. The Executioner paid for the clothes, then waited while the checkout girl stuffed them into a plastic sack and stapled the receipt to the bag. He watched the young woman hand the

scrap of paper to the cop. They exchanged smiles of a promised future meeting, then she walked on into the store.

The Rio officer turned to watch her, grinning like some
carnivorous predator who was about to make his kill.

Bolan kept his pace casual as he walked back toward the
same door where he'd entered. He stared straight ahead,
watching the cop in his peripheral vision. He had just reached
the electric door to the foyer when the man finally lifted the
radio from his belt.

The cop looked up almost immediately as Bolan walked
toward him. He dropped the radio and his hand fumbled for
the Taurus in his holster.

Bolan reached into his sack, grabbed the laces tying the
work boots together, and jerked them out. Dropping the sack
with the rest of his clothes, the Executioner used his free hand
to clamp down over the police officer's fingers and trap the
Taurus in its holster. He swung the boots by the laces, bringing
the steel toe of one of them down across the bridge of the
cop's nose. The man screamed in both surprise and pain, and
took a staggering step backward. The Executioner continued
swinging the boots, bringing them around in a figure-eight and
back across the officer's chin. The second blow hit the button
on the man's chin.

The Rio cop closed his eyes and he went down.

Only a few people had witnessed the fast-moving event, and
they froze in place. Bolan grabbed the sack off the floor and
stuffed the boots back inside as he walked briskly on through
the doors. As soon as he reached the parking lot, he broke
into a casual jog. The man and women he passed on his way
to the Saturn glanced his way—he was just another busy man
a little late for his next appointment. By the time he reached
the vehicle, no one paid him any attention. He slid behind the
wheel and a second later pulled out of the lot once more.

Five miles later, in the opposite direction from Vargas Avenue, the Executioner pulled into a service station. In the
men's room, he donned the jeans and boots, securing both
inside-the-waistband holsters to his belt and leaving the tail of

the chambray shirt out to conceal his weapons. Exiting the rest room, he took time to fill the Saturn's gas tank, paid with cash, then turned the vehicle back toward Axe Imports.

The black-and-white Rio police cars that had been at the scene had now been replaced by the unmarked cars of investigators. Although he couldn't read the lettering on the vehicle, what was obviously a crime-scene van was also parked along the street. Bolan drove past the building, then ditched the Saturn two blocks farther down the street. With the bill of the trucking firm cap low over his forehead, he walked back to the parking lot where he'd left the rented Chevy. The attendant was obviously interested in what was going on across the street. But he showed no signs of connecting Bolan to the excitement as the soldier handed him the ticket stub.

Bolan pulled the Chevy to the edge of the lot. He stopped to wait for traffic, and was just in time to see yet another unmarked car arrive at the scene. As he watched, the fat sergeant he had last seen with his fingers through the chain-link fence exited the vehicle. The man's fear had been replaced with rage, and his face was bright red with anger. The young cop whom Bolan had held at knife point was the chauffeur this time. He got out of the other side of the car. The two men gave Bolan and the Chevy only a passing glance as the Executioner turned onto the street.

They had turned their attention back to Axe Imports and were hurrying toward the glass doors as Bolan drove past.

SHE HAD A COUPLE more years on her face than he remembered. But she was still one of the most beautiful women he had ever met. She was also one of the most intelligent—a scholar in many areas, and a medical doctor. She was a complex woman, and years before she had won Olympic gold in both the hundred-meter dash and the women's low hurdles. She had made the Soviet Union proud in many areas. Not the least of which was as a spy.

Bolan's eyes were drawn to her table the moment he stepped into the Blue Mongoose Café.

Rogue Target

Marynka Platinov seemed to sense his presence, and looked up from the menu in her hands. She recognized him, too, recognized him in that process of general to specific in which people often remember old acquaintances they haven't seen for some time. The Executioner stood in front of the maître d' watching her go though this series of identification levels, and reading each one in the changing expressions on her face. She began with a general acknowledgment that he was someone she had met, then she realized it had been more than a passing acquaintance. The process ended with her face softening sensuously as she recalled the depth at which they had known each other, and what they had shared during that time.

Platinov's eyes locked with the Executioner's. She wore a bright red cocktail dress, with a single string of pearls around her neck. Bolan, now dressed in a dark gray suit to fit the atmosphere of the Blue Mongoose, knew there was no sense in ignoring her or pretending he was someone else.

Mack Bolan and Marynka Platinov knew each other. Far too well to pretend that they didn't.

The maître d', wearing a black tuxedo, arrived to end the drama. "Party of one?" he asked the soldier.

Bolan shook his head. "I'm meeting the lady." He nodded toward the table where Platinov sat.

"Ah, yes," the man in the tuxedo said. He led the way across the room.

The maître d' and the soldier passed the other tables between Platinov and the door where Blue Mongoose patrons sat sipping cocktails. Platinov smiled as the tuxedoed man pulled out the chair across from her. "Darling," she said in her Russian accent. "I thought you'd *never* get here."

Bolan smiled as he sat down. The maître d' was replaced by a waiter who asked if he'd like a drink. He ordered a beer.

"It has been a long time," Platinov said as soon as the man was gone with the order.

The soldier nodded.

"I think of you often."

Bolan nodded again but didn't reply.

"This does, however," she went on, "present us with a bit of a problem."

For the third time, Bolan remained silent. She was right. It did present a problem. There could be only one reason for Marynka Platinov's presence in Rio de Janeiro. She had come for the same reason he had come—to find Hugh Pollard. But the Executioner was looking for Pollard in order to take him back to the U.S. Platinov, who had been a KGB officer the last time they had met, now worked for Russian Intelligence. She would have been sent to snatch Pollard up and take him back to Moscow for interrogation.

"Is it a problem we can work around?" Platinov asked when she got no response.

"I don't know," Bolan said honestly.

The waiter brought Bolan's beer and another menu, and set them both on the table in front of him.

"As I see it," Platinov said, "our goals are the same. We both want to find the man."

"Yes." Bolan lifted the beer glass and took a sip. "But there will come a time when our goals diverge."

Platinov had what looked like an untouched martini sitting in front of her. "But the first order of business is to find him," she said.

Bolan leaned in and crossed his arms on the table. "Agreed," he said. "But then?"

Marynka Platinov stared into the soldier's eyes, and Bolan knew instinctively that she had undoubtedly used those eyes to manipulate many men during her years as a clandestine agent. But he saw no such attempt now. Platinov knew him too well to think that angle would work. What Bolan saw now was complete and total honesty. "You could use me to your advantage," the Russian agent said. "You have already created quite a stir, and are known to police." She lifted the martini glass but set it back down without drinking. "I wondered if it might be you earlier when I heard about the *Americano grande* and his daring escape from the local police."

Bolan didn't bother asking where she had heard the news.

It had come either from the radio, TV or secondhand from her Russian controllers.

"My face can be seen places where yours no longer can," Platinov continued simply. "I suggest we join forces. We have worked together well in the past." Her tone of voice suddenly changed, giving her next words a double meaning. "We always seemed...compatible."

Bolan took a moment to answer, then said, "I can't argue with that. But you still haven't answered my question. What do we do *after* we find him?"

Platinov shrugged her shoulders. "We will cross that river when we come to it," she said.

Bolan smiled, remembering the woman's penchant for American slang and how she frequently misquoted the expressions. "Do you mean we will cross that *bridge* when we come to it?"

Platinov returned the smile. "What I mean is that once we have located your Mr. Pollard, we will then deal with the problem," she said. "Perhaps by that time some sort of compromise will have presented itself."

"Compromise has never been my strong suit."

"Ah, yes." Platinov smiled. "If I interpret that correctly, and don't confuse it as I did the river and the bridge, it means you don't like to compromise."

"It does," Bolan agreed.

Platinov nodded, her face taking on a momentary sadness. "Neither do I," she said. "I think it is more likely that another of your colorful American expressions better expresses the position in which we will find ourselves then."

"And that is...?" Bolan asked as he lifted his glass once more.

"All bets will be off," Platinov said.

The waiter returned to the side of the table. "You have had time to look at the menu?" he asked.

"We have," Platinov said. But while they had indeed had time to look at the menu, fate decreed that they would never order.

Three dark-skinned men, dressed in equally dark suits, suddenly entered the Blue Mongoose dining room. The Executioner didn't recognize any of them, but he recognized their type. And he recognized the look that fell over Platinov's face. The three men began scanning the tables. "You know them?" he asked, ignoring the waiter.

"Only one," Platinov answered. "But one is enough."

The waiter stood waiting with practiced patience.

"The one in the middle," she said.

Bolan focused his gaze on a man who appeared slightly overweight in his ill-fitting suit. The Executioner's practiced eye noted that there was at least as much muscle as fat beneath the fabric. Except for a thick, carefully trimmed mustache, the dark-skinned man was clean shaved. Heavy facial stubble, however, had doomed him to a permanent five-o'clock shadow for as long as he lived. He was flanked by two more men who, although of slighter build, exhibited similar ethnic heritage.

"Iran?" Bolan whispered across the table.

"Iraq," Platinov said.

The heavy man's gaze suddenly fell on Bolan and Platinov's table. His face went through a process of recognition similar to the one Platinov had undergone when she first saw Bolan. But unlike Platinov, the dark eyes grew harder rather than softer as he identified the Russian woman in his memory.

The Iraqi turned to the side and the three men began to whisper among themselves.

"He knows you, too," the Executioner surmised.

"Oh, yes," Platinov said. "Indeed he does."

The waiter forced a smile. "Please," he said. "May I take your orders now?"

The Iraqi in the middle of the trio turned back to stare straight at them. Then, slowly, his hand moved inside his jacket.

"You could take our order," Bolan said, "but I think it would be wiser for you to wait."

"Excuse me?" the waiter said. "I don't understand."

"Right now," the soldier said, "I suggest you hit the floor and roll under a table."

An expression of confusion spread across the waiter's face. Behind him the Iraqi's hand came out of his jacket holding a 7.65 mm Turkish Kirrikale pistol. Bolan rose from his chair, grabbed the waiter and threw him across the room, into another table.

The first round from the Iraqi's weapon boomed from the Turkish side arm and shattered the martini glass on the table in front of Platinov. But the beautiful Russian woman had already rolled from her seat to the floor. The Executioner jerked the Desert Eagle from under his jacket as a second round skimmed across the table to his side. A middle-aged woman with gray streaks in her hair shrieked at the top of her lungs. The man with her gasped, freezing with his wineglass halfway to his lips.

Bolan hit the ground on his knees just to the woman's side. Using both hands simultaneously, he swept both her and the man from their seats and sent them sprawling out of the way. Using the table for both cover and a shooting rest, he extended the big .44 Magnum and rested his elbows on the tablecloth. A series of rounds blew from the Eagle and found their mark in the stocky Iraqi's chest. The man folded almost in half before toppling forward onto his face.

Screams of surprise and terror rose from the other patrons of the Blue Mongoose. The two Iraqis still standing had drawn identical Turkish pistols, and were now shooting indiscriminately at the tables behind which both he and Platinov had taken cover. "Everybody down!" Bolan ordered. A few men and women joined the others on the floor. But others sat frozen like stone statues in their seats.

Bolan heard the boom of 9 mm fire, and in the corner of his eye saw Marynka Platinov. In her hands he saw what looked to be the same Heckler & Koch 9 mm P-7M13 he remembered her favoring. Where she had concealed it in the tight-fitting red cocktail dress, he couldn't begin to imagine. But now, as she knelt behind the table at which they had sat, the hem of the dress hiked over her knees to reveal the straps of a white garter belt, the H&K recoiled in her hands and sent a deadly spray of lead at the Iraqis.

The remaining two Iraqis had taken different approaches to the battle. One, his coarse hair falling slightly over his ears, had ducked behind the cash register stand near the front door. The brown booth appeared to be made of wood but the cosmetic veneer must have been backed by steel. Something was causing Platinov's 9 mm rounds to ricochet, leaving only splintered holes in the wooden surface.

The second Iraqi decided discretion was the better part of valor. He turned and ducked out of the front door.

Bolan leaned slightly forward and lined up the Desert Eagle's sights on the cash register booth. Aiming at the top, he was about to squeeze the trigger when a flash of red caught his eyes. He relaxed his finger as Platinov sprinted through his sight pattern and out the door after the escaping man.

Bolan focused back on his sights. Starting at the top of the booth, he worked his way down to the floor, emptying the entire magazine of .44 Magnums in a straight line that split the booth in half. The two parts fell to the sides as the Executioner's left hand curled under his arm and drew the Beretta 93-R from shoulder leather. With no time to reload the Desert Eagle, he jammed it back into his holster and stood.

There was little doubt that the Iraqi on the floor behind the booth was dead as Bolan raced toward the door. The man's body was filled with holes, shards of sharp steel and splinters of the wood which had covered the booth's exterior.

Bolan hit the street, Beretta in hand, just in time to see Platinov round the corner at the end of the block. She held the long red dress in both hands, pulled up to her waist as her muscular sprinter's legs pumped furiously inside the nylons and garter belt. Bolan turned after her, racing past first one, then a second discarded high-heeled shoe. He turned the corner behind her just in time to see the flashing naked legs duck out of sight again—this time down an alley.

As he neared the mouth of the alley, Bolan heard a car

engine roar. He slowed at the corner, dropping into a combat crouch as he rounded the stone wall. Down the long narrow cobblestoned path, he saw Platinov's silhouette framed in the headlights of a vehicle speeding toward her. Between her and the headlights, the Iraqi raced frantically for the car.

The Executioner ran forward once more. He started to yell, "Don't kill him!" then realized there was no need. Platinov was a professional. She knew the importance of taking the man alive for questioning as well as he did.

But it wasn't to be. Platinov was less than four paces behind the man when the dark vehicle screeched to a halt. Knowing she would reach him before he could enter the escape car, the Iraq turned, his gun coming up. Platinov had no choice but to drop the hem of her dress and fire as her momentum carried her on. She had pumped three rounds into the Iraqi's chest by the time her body crashed into his and sent them both sprawling away from the car.

Seeing the uselessness of waiting now, the driver stomped the accelerator. The dark car barreled forward again, straight for the Executioner. Bolan ground to a halt, raised the 9 mm, thumbed the selector switch to burst mode and sent a trio of 9 mm hollowpoint slugs into the right front tire.

The tire blew far louder than the sound-suppressed rounds from the 93-R. The Executioner swung his weapon toward the left tire but had no time to pull the trigger. By the time he found his target, the vehicle was ten feet in front of him and still hurtling forward at fifty miles per hour. Bolan bent his knees, then vaulted as high as he could straight up into the air.

The top of the windshield and roof caught him at the ankles, flipping him twice in the air as the car raced past. He struck the hard ground on his side, the jolt sending shock waves coursing through his body and almost knocking the Beretta from his grasp. Rolling painfully onto his stomach, he brought the Beretta up in both hands as the three-tired car fishtailed down the narrow alley. Before he could fire again, the vehicle struck a wall, skidded along the stone, then jerked to a halt.

The Executioner leaped to his feet and sprinted toward the stalled car. Behind him, he heard running footsteps and glanced over his shoulder to see Platinov hurrying his way. He turned back, reached the driver's side of the car and saw a fourth dark-skinned man behind the wheel. The Iraqi's head had struck the steering wheel during the crash, and blood poured from a deep gash just above the eyebrows.

Bolan reached in, jamming a finger into the man's carotid artery as he heard sirens suddenly wail in the distance. The man had a faint pulse. As the sirens grew louder, he opened the car door, reached in and grabbed the Iraqi by the jacket, hauling him out.

Platinov came to a halt next to him. The feet of her hose had shredded against the concrete sidewalk and now the nylon curled up around her calves. The red cocktail dress was ripped down over one breast, revealing an off-white bra and the top of a half slip. Bolan looked up, wondering if the man she had shot was still alive.

Platinov knew the question without being asked. She shook her head. "Him?" she asked, looking down at the bleeding man on the ground.

"Alive," Bolan said. "Barely. Where are you parked?"

"Just around the corner." Platinov indicated the mouth of the alley.

The sirens were louder now as police cars raced to the scene. "Then you're closer," Bolan said. "Go get it started and back out. I'll carry him to the street."

Raising the long cocktail dress to her waist again, the Russian woman burst away with the same speed she had exhibited during her Olympic days. Bolan reached down, grabbing the Iraqi's arm, then lifted the man over his shoulder in a fireman's carry. By the time he reached the street, Platinov had backed a dull bronze Pontiac SSE to the mouth of the alley. She leaped out, opened the rear door, and Bolan tossed the Iraqi into the back seat, climbing in on top of him.

The sirens were almost deafening now. As Platinov pulled away, the flashing lights appeared at the other end of the block.

Bolan stayed low down, hidden below eye level in the back seat. The Iraqi was still unconscious but a passenger in the back with a woman driver—a woman in a ripped and torn cocktail dress who looked *nothing* like a Rio de Janeiro cabbie—would do nothing but draw suspicion.

Bolan looked at the gash on the Iraqi's head. "You have a medical bag in here somewhere?" he asked.

Platinov leaned forward and to the side as she drove, then handed a small black leather case over the seat. The soldier opened it and began applying a bandage to slow the Iraqi's blood loss.

Platinov drove straight for three blocks, then turned off the street, away from the sirens behind them. "You have set up a safehouse?" she asked over the seat.

Bolan shook his head. "Haven't had time. I just got here."

"It's no problem," Platinov said. "I have a place to take him." There was a long pause, then the woman continued. "I have thought of another of your American expressions which I believe now fits us."

Bolan waited.

"It is good to be working with you again," Platinov said. "I believe you Americans would say 'we are back in the sagebrush again.' It is a thing cowboys say, no?"

"It's a cowboy expression, yes," he said. "But it's 'back in the *saddle* again.' It's a line from an old Western song."

"Ah, yes," Platinov said. "I knew it had something to do with American cowboys. Back in the *saddle* again." She paused, then turned to glance at the Executioner as she drove down the busy road. A sly grin covered her face in the moonlight drifting into the Pontiac. "Perhaps," the beautiful Russian Intelligence officer said, "if things ever slow down, you can climb back in the saddle again yourself."

2

The ratchet sound echoed down the mountain as the ten-inch blade of the *navaja* clicked past the opening notches and locked into place. Ramone Lopez took a half step forward and brought the blade down across the one-inch sapling. For a moment frozen in time, the thin tree continued to stand motionless, and anyone watching might well have guessed that the target had been missed.

Lopez knew better. He had felt the slight resistance as the razor edge slid through the green wood. And when the top half of the sapling toppled to the ground a moment later, it brought a smile that curled the ends of his bushy mustache.

Lopez raised the tail of the bright red sash tied around his waist. He wiped the sticky resin from the *navaja's* wide clip-point blade, then began an attack to the head of an imaginary opponent. But rather than follow through with the slash, he stopped midway into it and tossed the giant Spanish folding knife through the air to his other hand. The feint had been high but now the actual attack with his left hand came back, from the opposite direction, low. His people called the technique a *cambio,* and had he been facing a real rather than imagined opponent, the *navaja's* edge would have sliced through the man's intestines, disemboweling him.

Lopez paused, mentally critiquing the *cambio.* He had caught the curved handle a little lower than he liked. The move hadn't been perfect. But then, true knife combat rarely was. What was important wasn't perfection but effectiveness. He had retained a firm grip on the knife, the advanced foist—a dangerous move for all but the most capable *navajero*—would have worked, and that was all that counted. Let others waste their time in the other Spanish knife fighting styles if they liked. He would stick with the practical and effective techniques of his people—the *Gitano,* or Gypsies.

Inserting his finger into the ring at the bolster, Lopez released the lock and closed the big blade. He looked down, studying the elegantly curved handle, the steel that ran along the spine above the dark wood, the perfect set of the pins that held that steel in place. Even after all the years he had carried this knife, its beauty never ceased to fascinate him. It had been hand crafted for his great-grandfather over a hundred years earlier by one of Seville's most renowned blade smiths. Passed down from father to son, it was now his.

Lopez returned the knife to the left side of his sash, folded width-wise to create a large "pocket" which ran around his waist. He didn't need the sash—it was merely to remind him of his heritage. Below it he wore a sturdy leather gun belt threaded through the loops of his faded jeans. A space-age-looking black polymer-framed 9 mm Vektor CP-1 semiautomatic pistol hung from its holster on his right-hand side.

The dark-skinned Spaniard grinned as a brisk breeze of air swept up through the valley below him. He liked the contrast the Vektor made with the *navaja.* Old and new. Traditional and state-of-the-art. The two weapons symbolized the way Ramone Lopez viewed himself. A man who valued his heritage but didn't cling to it.

Thing were about to heat up, and knowing he would have little time for rest or contemplation during the next few days or even weeks, Lopez paused, taking one last moment to look out over the early-morning Andes. Behind him, drifting from the small mountain cabin that had served as his home for the past year, he heard the eerie notes of flute music break the stillness of the thin air. As he listened, he stared down into the valley before him, taking in the trees, the rocks, the birds fluttering from limb to limb. A bush rustled as some small unseen animal scurried to new cover. He had, Lopez knew, the heart of a romantic. He not only saw the scenery, but he breathed it in until he felt the beauty flow through his very being. It energized him as if he had taken a draught from a tank of pure oxygen, or injected some adrenalin into his veins. Gypsies possessed a greater appreciation of beauty than the average man, and he wondered briefly if it might not be another gift Christ had given to them as He made His way to the crucifixion. Yes, he thought, the Gypsy gift from Christ. The thought broadened the smile on his lips as he lifted his line of sight to the snowcapped mountain peaks in the distance.

For Lopez, and many of his people, the gift had been the basis for their lifestyle for two thousand years. As the story went, Jesus had stumbled and fallen beneath the cross on His way to Calvary. Before the Roman soldiers could jerk Him back to His feet, a Gypsy woman among the onlookers had knelt and pressed a cup of water into His hands. In return, the Son of God had granted her, and all of her descendants, a special dispensation from the Eighth Commandment. From that point forward, Gypsies the world over had taken it for granted that they had a *right* to steal.

In the distance a covey of birds suddenly flew from a tree, frightened by a squirrel who darted toward them across a limb. Lopez's smile became a chuckle as the birds flew away. Gypsy birds, he thought. Robbing the squirrel of his food, and in flight before the furry little creature could exact his vengeance. And also like Gypsies, the birds had no permanent home. They flew from nest to nest, one step ahead of those from whom they had last stolen.

Lopez laughed again as the angry squirrel watched the Gypsy birds fly away. Peru, he knew, was no more than a temporary nest for him. Even after a year it didn't feel like home. But then no one place could ever feel like home to a Gypsy. Gypsies weren't born to homes but rather to lives of wandering, short stays in a succession of places, where their petty crimes were punctuated by an occasional bigger score.

Glancing down to his waist, Lopez's eyes moved from the *navaja* on one side to the Vector on the other. Yes, he was a

Gypsy, but he was also a man of the modern age. And what differentiated him from many of his kinsmen was the degree of his ambitions. To most of his people, a big score meant enough to subsist on while they ran from one theft or con game to the next. He, on the other hand, was about to score at a level that would enable him to retire in luxury for the rest of his life.

Lopez turned away from the valley. He had work to do, and although his vagabond heart rebelled at the thought of toil of any kind, it was sometimes necessary. He started back to the cabin. If he handled the next few days properly, he could retire and roam in Spain's Andalusian region, never working again.

As he neared the compound, Lopez heard the almost un-earthly flute music grow louder. Through the window he saw Juan Ortega seated cross-legged on the floor. Ortega wore a rag tied around his long gray hair and the baggy pants and shirt of the Peruvian peasant. Lopez watched the man's fingers work the holes in the flute. Ortega's eyes were closed in concentration, and the instrument seemed grafted to his cracked and wrinkled lips.

The Gypsy shook his head in dismay as he continued on to the door. Half of Ortega's brain had been destroyed over the years through heavy drug-and-alcohol use. But that made no difference to Lopez. The old man had possessed enough presence of mind to make introductions between his old friends and Ramone Lopez. And for the Gypsy's purposes, that was as straight as Ortega needed to be.

Lopez opened the door and stepped inside. Ortega finished the final notes of his mysterious song and looked up, a moronic grin on his face. "Good morning," he said in Quechua, the ancient tongue of his Inca ancestors.

Lopez, who had a proficiency for language, had picked up Quechua quickly. "Good morning," he answered in the same tongue. "Please, continue your playing. It relaxes me."

"Then I shall be delighted to do so," Ortega said. He turned toward the window and continued his music.

The Gypsy watched him for a moment in amazement. Could

this be the same man who, twenty years earlier, had once been one of the top leaders of the Shining Path? The most feared terrorist organization in South America? It didn't seem possible. But, Lopez reminded himself, twenty years of marijuana, alcohol, cocaine and every other substance the old man could lay his hands on, was bound to take its toll. He was just glad he had found Ortega when he did. In another year, the old man might well have been beyond coherence and unable to help him gain the trust of the Shining Path's current luminaries.

Lopez moved along the wall behind Ortega as the old man continued to play. Reflected in the window pane, he could see the old man's craggy face. Again Ortega had closed his eyes as his lips and fingers manipulated the flute. That was good. It would make what Lopez was about to do just that much easier.

On the unlikely chance that Ortega might open his eyes and see him in the glass, the Gypsy turned his back to the window. Carefully drawing the *navaja* from his sash, he held it under his armpit to muffle the ratchet noise as he moved the blade slowly past the opening notches. He glanced back over his shoulder to make sure Ortega hadn't heard the sounds.

The old man's eyes were still closed as the mysterious notes floated from his instrument.

Lopez watched him in the window as he stepped quickly forward. Juan Ortega had served his purpose. From here on the drunken, drug-addicted old man would be nothing but excess baggage.

With his left hand the Gypsy grasped a handful of gray hair above the bandanna. His right arm moved around Ortega's wrinkled neck, and then the razor-honed edge of the *navaja* swept back cleanly across the wrinkled throat.

The old man's eyes never even opened as he fell forward onto his face.

Lopez leaned down, jerked the bandanna from Ortega's head and wiped the knife blade clean. He looked down at the body on the floor as the last of the old Inca's lifeblood flowed onto the dirty wooden floor. For a moment the Gypsy wondered at the fact that he felt no remorse, but his curiosity passed quickly. While he had been gifted with a great appreciation for beauty, it had always seemed that he had been born without any capacity for remorse. Which, he supposed, was a gift in and of itself. He had never particularly enjoyed killing other men, but neither had it ever bothered him. He viewed it very much like some mildly irritating chore such as emptying the garbage—when it needed to be done, you did it without much thought and then went on with your life.

Lopez smiled with confidence as he finished wiping the big blade and tossed the bloody rag on top of Ortega's body. He was on his way now to the biggest score of his life. His final score. And while he knew more people—perhaps thousands or even millions, he supposed—were very likely to die at his hand, he felt no regret for them, either. Such was the Gypsy way.

At least *his* Gypsy way.

THE EXECUTIONER TURNED to study the Iraqi who was sprawled on the seat next to him. The bleeding had slowed beneath his hastily applied bandage, but the gash was deep, the white skull plainly visible beneath the blood. Bolan took a pulse once more and found there had been little change. It was still faint.

Bolan used a thumb to pry open one of the man's eyelids. A dark brown orb stared unseeingly back at him. Concussion. No doubt about it. For all he knew, the man might not only be unconscious, but he could also have slipped into a coma. When a light slap across the Iraqi's face brought no response, he pinched down hard on one of the heavily stubbled cheeks with a thumb and forefinger. Still, the Iraqi didn't stir.

A quick glance behind them insured Bolan there was still no pursuit. He turned to the front seat. "The wrong person's driving," he told Platinov.

The Russian agent misinterpreted the statement, and snorted

in a most unladylike manner. "Oh," she said. "You don't think I can drive well if we are pursued?"

"You're driving is fine," the soldier said. "But you're also the doctor and you can take care of this guy better than me." He paused to let it sink in. "If we're going to keep him alive long enough to find out what he knows, we've got to trade places."

"Oh. Sorry." Platinov leaned back from the wheel. "Should I pull over?"

Bolan glanced behind him again. Traffic was thick, but he could see no Rio squad cars or any other sign of a tail. "Yeah," he said.

Platinov deftly cut the Pontiac across two lanes and onto the shoulder. She left the engine running as she exited the vehicle, using the release button beside the seat to pop the trunk. Bolan got out of the back seat and circled behind the car. The Russian pulled another, larger black leather medical case out of the trunk as he passed. A moment later Bolan slid behind the steering wheel.

Which was the exact moment the black-and-white patrol car pulled off the street and rolled to a stop behind them.

There was no sense in cursing bad fortune, Bolan knew. It came and went just like its good twin sister, Lady Luck. He paused, looking back at the lone cop who sat behind the wheel. Through the windshield Bolan tried to get a read on the man's face. The Rio officer didn't appear disturbed, and the radio mike wasn't even in his hand.

Had he not yet gotten the word about the incident at the Blue Mongoose? Or had he simply not yet made the connection between it and the Pontiac? In either case, the officer was bound to have been briefed about the mass murder at Wayne Axe Imports earlier in the day, and the fact that a man matching Bolan's description had escaped custody. But as he started to open the door to his patrol car, he didn't look like a man who was getting too excited about anything. He looked more like just a friendly cop who had stopped to see if they needed help.

Glancing behind him, Bolan saw that Platinov had seen the car, too. She looked up at him from the back seat, then began digging through both of her medical bags and pulling out disinfectants, bandages, adhesive tape and other gear. She paused long enough to roll down the back window next to her so she could listen but it was obvious she planned to let him to handle the cop.

The officer approached, walking leisurely toward the Pontiac. His hands were empty, his Taurus holstered and still snapped down on the Sam Browne belt around his skinny hips. He spoke first in Portuguese, and Bolan forced an embarrassed smile across his face and said, "*No comprendo, amigo. ¿Español?*"

The man nodded and switched to Spanish. "*Sí,*" he said. "*¿Pero usted es noretamericano?*"

Bolan nodded. "*Sí,*" he said. "*Norteamericano.*"

A proud smile spread across the cop's face. "I spend four years in the New York City," he said in a Brazilian accent tinted with Brooklynese. "My *Inglés* pretty good."

Bolan smiled back good-naturedly. "Yes, I can see that," he said. "Then we'll speak English."

"You are having trouble?" the cop asked.

The soldier swung his head toward the back seat again. "My friend has fallen on the pavement and struck his head," he said. "My other friend is a doctor. We are trying to get him to the hospital."

The cop leaned through the window then turned back. His face still smiled, but a trace of suspicion had entered his eyes. "It's a very bad blow he has taken," he said. "But it doesn't look as if it was caused by a sidewalk."

The Executioner's mind raced for a better explanation. "I misstated myself," he said. "He did indeed slip and fall on the pavement. But, as bad luck would have it, this took place at the construction site where he was working. His head struck a stack of iron support beams. The edge of one of those beams is what caused the damage."

The cop looked back into the car. Bolan noticed that Platinov had tucked her legs up under her to hide her torn nylons. But there was no disguising the fact that her dress was torn at the bust line. "The *señorita* is hurt, as well?" the officer asked suspiciously.

Bolan shook his head. "Her dress caught on the corner of one of the beams as she rose from trying to help him at the site," he said. "She's okay."

The cop turned back to stare Bolan in the eye. Slowly, the suspicion faded from his face. Each rapid-fire explanation the soldier had been forced to come up with for the discrepancies in his story made sense on its own. But lumped together, they stretched credibility. Yet one of the many things Bolan had learned over the years was that while it was true that cops had heard every lie on the books, they had also *seen* every possible coincidence imaginable. Sometimes police officers were more willing to believe an incredible story than the average person on the streets.

Luckily, this was one of those times. "You are going the wrong way to the nearest hospital," the cop said. "Follow me." He turned quickly and hurried back to his car.

A moment later, both the lights and siren came on and the police car pulled back onto the busy street. Bolan pulled in behind. The cop took the next exit ramp off the thoroughfare.

Bolan didn't.

Instead, the soldier leaned on the accelerator and shot the Pontiac forward along the highway. He would race to the next exit, then get off. The cop would either think he had innocently missed the turn or would suddenly understand he'd been tricked. But either way—whether the officer's motive was to assist an injured man whose driver had gone astray, or apprehend and interrogate the driver who had lied to him—he would get on the radio and broadcast a description of the Pontiac and the people inside it.

In the rearview mirror, Bolan saw that Platinov had applied a fresh bandage to the Iraqi's forehead. "He is bad," she said simply.

"Coma?" Bolan asked.

He saw Platinov nod in the rearview mirror. "Probably. It's impossible to be sure without other equipment, but I believe so." Just then, as if to defy her, the man's eyes opened. He looked up, said several words in Arabic, then closed his eyes again.

"It means little," Platinov said before Bolan asked. "My Arabic isn't perfect. He said something about his mother."

The next exit ramp appeared on his right and Bolan slowed, guiding the Pontiac down the slope toward a stop sign. "Which way?" he asked over his shoulder.

Platinov glanced up quickly. "Turn left," she said, then went back to her patient.

In the rearview mirror, Bolan saw the Russian pull a syringe and a thick vial from her bag. She stuck the needle into the vial, then drew back the plunger to fill the syringe. As the soldier hit the brakes at the stop sign, she stuck the needle into the Iraqi's arm. When she finished, she rolled the used syringe up in the vial, and dropped it back into the larger of her medical bags. "It will eventually kill him," she said without emotion. "But before it does that, it will bring him to full consciousness for an hour or so." She glanced at her wristwatch. "He will be alert in perhaps fifteen minutes. By then, we should be at the safehouse." With a shrug also devoid of emotion, she added, "And he would probably have died anyway."

Bolan glanced at her in the rearview mirror. The woman was tough. Hard. But a pragmatist. Such was her job.

As was his.

The soldier wheeled the Pontiac left, staying in the fast lane, weaving in and out of traffic. Platinov kept one eye on her patient, the other on the road, guiding him through a series of turns. Things went well—almost too well. An uneasy feeling of impending fate began to creep up the back of the soldier's neck.

The catalyst for the feeling soon revealed itself.

As they made a right-hand turn, Bolan watched yet another black-and-white Rio police car pull out of a fast-food restaurant and fall in behind them. His eyes fell to the speedometer. He dropped their pace to just under the posted limit. Speeding would get them stopped, but any slower pace might bring questions of sobriety, or other crimes in progress, to the two uniformed men he now saw behind him.

As he had done earlier, Platinov now dropped out of sight in the back seat. Keeping the cops in view, Bolan drove on. He took the next right—onto another busy street—and the patrol car turned with them. Chance or design? There was no way to know. Not yet.

But the question was answered a moment later when a radio mike appeared at the lips of the officer in the driver's seat.

Bolan knew what was happening. The Pontiac's tag was being run. The cops in the car behind them had recognized the car's description from the helpful officer who had wanted to escort them to the hospital. Whether they thought the Pontiac had simply gotten lost or believed some mischief was afoot, it didn't matter. Within minutes—probably more like seconds—the red lights would come on.

Another quickly concocted story about losing their police escort in traffic might see them on their way again. Then again, it might not. Besides, now that Platinov had given the Iraqi the injection, there was no time for such delays.

The Executioner waited until the flashing red appeared in the mirror, then stomped the accelerator. The Pontiac had good pickup, and he gained a good ten lengths on the squad car before the driver behind him could respond. Then the screech of the siren broke the night sounds of Rio, and the black-and-white shot forward behind them.

Horns blasted, and angry faces in the vehicles he cut off shouted soundless words behind the glass as the Executioner cut in and out of traffic Upraised fists and middle fingers flashed by in his peripheral vision. The Pontiac left the long string of shopping malls and fast-food outlets and entered one of Rio's many nightlife areas. Bright neon winked to their right and left, and the strange combination of Portuguese guitar and Spanish flamenco, mixed with Andes flute and American rock and roll, created a cacophony of hybrid music in their ears. Ahead, a drunken man in blue jeans and a khaki vest staggered out into the street. Bolan swerved just as the man turned his frightened face toward the on-racing Pontiac. Luckily, the drunk dived the other way and fell to the street. The cameras and other equipment hanging from his shoulders twirled through the air on their straps, twisting into knots around his throat as he hit the pavement.

The Pontiac had speed. But the Rio squad car had more. Bolan could see the police were gaining, slowing the gap inch by inch, and foot by foot. In addition, the Executioner knew that the pursuit car had radioed in. Even now, other Rio cops would be dropping ticket books, coffee cups and half-eaten pastries and converging to block their escape path.

"We've got to stop these guys, then change vehicles," the Executioner said over the seat.

"We can't," Platinov said. "All of my equipment is in the trunk."

"New equipment I can get you," Bolan said. "A new life I can't."

"You don't understand," the woman said. "In addition to my equipment, my papers are back there. My *real* papers."

Bolan swore. Platinov was a good agent—one of the best he'd ever known. But she wasn't perfect, and this time she had screwed up royally. As quickly as such thoughts entered his mind, the Executioner pushed them away. The Russian woman knew her mistake as well as he did, and a lecture on professional trade craft now would be superfluous.

Nor would it change the reality of their present situation. And that reality was what he had to deal with at the moment.

It had become obvious that they couldn't outrun the police car behind them, and if he waited much longer they'd be cut off somewhere ahead by other cars and officers. So speed couldn't be the basis for their escape. Nor could firepower—not only would they be vastly outnumbered once the other squad cars arrived, but also the Executioner still had no intention of shooting innocent cops.

That left only one possible option for escape: deception.

By now they had left the nightclub district and entered a commercial area. The closed doors of auto-body shops and supply stores were spotted with twenty-four-hour convenience stores and gas stations. It was the latter that suddenly caught the Executioner's interest. At first, the plan that suddenly formulated in his mind seemed insane—the desperate act of a desperate man. But, Bolan reasoned, that was exactly what he was at the moment. Desperate. Not for himself, but for his mission. For his country. The situation, as it stood, was that he would not kill cops; that was a given. But if they took him into custody, one of the other countries now searching for Hugh Pollard might find the former CIA director while he whiled away his time behind bars. If that happened, America would be jeopardized. And a jeopardized America meant a jeopardized world.

The squad car, lights and siren still going strong, was now less than twenty yards behind the Pontiac. It had been blocked by two other cars, driving side by side in the lanes, when Bolan suddenly cut the wheel of the vehicle. The tires squealed in agony and the smell of rubber filled his nostrils as he cut through the front parking lot of a transmission shop and jumped the curb to an adjacent shopping center. Circling behind the row of stores and shops, he cut down the alley behind the connected buildings to the loading areas. The Pontiac flashed past brick walls and locked steel doors on one side, large white trash bins on the other.

The soldier looked up into the mirror once more as he neared the end of the alley. If the squad car had followed close enough to see his next move, the entire plan would fall apart. He breathed a silent sigh of relief to see nothing but the faint glow of the night lights over the rear business doors behind him.

Reaching the end of the alley, Bolan shot on out into the street amid more angry horns and screeching tires. Ignoring them, he crossed four lanes of traffic, narrowly missing several vehicles, then took a quick jog into the parking lot of a service

station. Racing past the pumps, he leaned to one side and dug
into his pants pocket as he neared an automatic car wash.

By the time he reached the entrance to the car wash he held
a handful of coins. A silent prayer of thanks escaped his lips
when he saw that the single stall was empty. Pulling to a halt
next to the automated pay booth, he jammed the coins into the
slot, punched the button for wash and wax, then cast a quick
look back to the mouth of the alley as he waited for the light
to turn green, signaling that he could enter. The light took
only a few seconds to change from red to green. Those few
seconds felt like a millennium.

Red-and-blue lights were already dancing down the alley by
the time Bolan pulled the Pontiac out of sight between the
concrete-block walls. He had forgone the initial underwash
option in order to get directly inside the building, and now
water cascaded down around the body of the Pontiac. Tidal
waves of soapy spray blocked his view of the street. And, he
hoped, also blocked the view of the car the officers would
have when they drove past.

The soldier turned and rested an arm over the seat. "How's
our patient?" he asked.

"Alive," Platinov said. She glanced at a gold wristwatch
on her arm. "But if we are to find out what he knows, we
must hurry."

Bolan heard the siren and turned back to the windshield.
Through the steady streams of water and soap suds, he saw
blurs of blue and red streak by. Behind him, he heard Platinov
say, "But it isn't this patient who concerns me."

The soldier turned back around. "Yes?" he said.

"It is you who has me worried," Platinov said. "I have
been in many car chases in which I have been the one pursued." She shook her head in disbelief, then her face changed
to a wry grin. "But this is the first time I have ever stopped
to wash the car."

Bolan smiled and turned back. The water stopped and mammoth red-and-brown brushes began to roll across the Pontiac's
hood, up the windshield and over the roof. But the squad car

had gone on, and he saw no signs of other cops in the area. At least for the moment, they were safe.

The chase had negated his following the woman's directions, and he now worried about the distance to the safehouse. The clock was ticking on the Iraqi. And the more driving they did, the stronger the likelihood became that they'd be spotted by the cops again. Glancing up at the mirror once more, he said, "How far?"

"Less than a mile."

By now the brushes had stopped, the car had been rinsed and the waxing light had come on. A watery, greasy-looking film began to shoot over the vehicle. Platinov leaned forward over the seat between them and pointed through the windshield. "If you will take that side street, we should be there in a few minutes."

Bolan pulled the Pontiac out of the car wash, his eyes scanning both ways. Clear. Cutting across the lanes—slower and more carefully this time—he turned onto the street where Platinov had pointed and entered a residential area.

THE PEAKS, VALLEYS and hills that made up the landscape of Rio de Janeiro were covered with three kinds of houses. The homes of the very poor were constructed of bamboo, scraps of tin and plywood and held together by mud. They seemed to be plastered to the sides of the mountains with that same mud. Such houses bespoke the poverty, misery and disease of those unfortunate enough to inhabit them.

The wealthy tended to locate their homes on hills and cliffs, as well. But these were constructed of wood, brick, exotic stone and mortar, and were, of course, far larger—so large in some cases that they reeked of exhibitionism. The blueprints used to build such houses had been drawn up with this unique mountainous landscape in mind, inserting homes into the terrain. It wasn't unusual to see a dwelling that rose three, or even four, stories into the air at the front but only one in the rear, where it butted up against a mountain. More often than not, flamboyant gardens of tropical fruits and plants accompanied such homes.

Other houses, less pretentious—on the outside at least—had been built down into the ground. Virtually large elaborate storm shelters, they were entered by doors in the roof and remained mostly hidden from view. It was as if their inhabitants had chosen to hide their wealth from the poor rather than rub their noses in it.

But regardless of the size or decor of the houses of Rio, they were all united by the odor that hung over the city. The abundance of dense vegetation combined with the salt sea to create its own distinct aroma. It wasn't bad, but it wasn't good, either. It created a unique atmosphere in Rio de Janeiro that could be found nowhere else in the world.

In another aspect, however, Rio differed not the least from any other large city. Somewhere between the very rich and the very poor was the middle class. Made up of small businessmen, midlevel bureaucrats, skilled proletarians and the same other people who make up middle classes the world over, they lived in comfortable but unostentatious houses. All looked similar, and all were laid out in neat little rows. The inhabitants of such houses worked long hours for the money they brought home. This meant they had very little time to pay attention to their neighbors.

Which is why shadow warriors the world over chose middle-class dwellings as safehouses almost exclusively.

Bolan pulled the Pontiac into the driveway of the nondescript house as Platinov leaned over the seat and punched the button on the remote-control garage-door opener. The door began to rise as the Pontiac rolled slowly on. Inside the garage, a low-profile five-year-old Nissan became visible. Decorating the walls was lawn-care equipment, tools and other garage items. Just enough to make the house appear lived in.

Platinov hit the remote again, and the door rolled down behind them. Together, they dragged the Iraqi out of the back seat, across the garage and through a door into the utility room. Bolan lifted the man over his shoulder as Platinov led the way past a washer and dryer, then opened another door into a short hallway. Directly across the hall from the utility room, the soldier saw the kitchen. But he followed Platinov to the left through the dining room. As he carried the Iraqi past the large wooden dining table, Bolan saw a lap-top computer, portable fax, a Polaroid camera and other equipment. Finally in the living room, he lowered the man onto the couch in a sitting position, then scanned the rest of the room. The nondescript modern home could have been found in any medium to large city in the world. Off-white, orange-peel-textured walls were trimmed with dark maple. The carpet was stain-resistant tan. Several armchairs and an antique rocking chair accompanied the couch, and well-stocked magazine racks, a coffee table littered with other magazines and books, and a bookshelf that featured not only books but standing framed photographs of Platinov with a man and children completed the picture.

The soldier nodded silently to himself. The proof of any good safehouse was in the details. And the Russian had done her job well. Should enemy agents break in to look around, it appeared that real people lived here. Hearing no other sounds from within the house, Bolan turned to Platinov. "You're working alone?" he said.

The woman nodded. "I always have. Except with you." She paused, and a quick smile flickered across her face. "You're an exception." Another pause brought a serious look to her face as she stared up into the soldier's eyes. "In more ways than one."

Bolan didn't answer, but he knew exactly what she meant and what message she was conveying. She didn't want him to think that she had the same relationship she'd had with him with every man she worked with.

The soldier turned his attention back to the Iraqi on the couch. The man's dark eyes opened momentarily, stared straight ahead, then closed again. A few seconds later they opened once more. This time he glanced around the room in confusion before his eyelids fell again.

"He's coming around," Platinov observed.

Bolan frowned. "What did you give him?"

"Actually, I don't know the name of the drug in English, and I doubt you would recognize it if I did." She reached out and grasped the Iraqi by both shoulders, shaking him lightly as he began to come around. "But it is no secret—both of our countries have it. It stimulates the nervous system and brings on coherency for one last brief time. But the effect is almost always fatal. I am not sure how it works, but it seems to use up the very end of the body's reserves. When it works."

Bolan felt himself frown as Platinov continued to shake the man. "It doesn't always work?"

"Nothing always works," Platinov said.

This time the drug appeared to be effective. Platinov slapped the Iraqi lightly across the face, and this time the man's eyes stayed open. The Russian agent glanced down at her wrist. "We'll have roughly fifteen minutes," she reminded Bolan.

The Executioner nodded. Leaning over the Iraqi, he said, "What's your name?"

The man stared ahead from beneath the bandage.

"English?" Bolan asked.

The Iraqi recognized the word but shook his head.

"I speak Arabic," Platinov said. "At least some." She looked at the man and began asking questions.

In addition to bringing him back to consciousness, whatever it was Platinov had given the man seemed to have driven all resistance from the man, as well. "My name is Iraj," he said. "Iraj Hussein."

Platinov frowned and spoke again. Bolan couldn't understand the words. But considering that the man was Iraqi, the question was obvious. The man on the couch shook his head.

"No relation," Platinov said, glancing to Bolan.

The Executioner hadn't expected it. Hussein was a common enough name.

As the Russian continued the interrogation, Bolan began searching the Iraqi. The man offered no protest. He had taken on the characteristics of a waxy schizophrenic, leaving his arms and the rest of his body in whatever position the soldier bent them into in order to reach his pockets.

In the front breast pocket, Bolan found a billfold and passport. Neither was under the name Iraj Hussein. He dropped them on the couch next to the man. Folding money and pocket change came out of the right front pocket, and a cheap Pakistani folding knife from the left. From the man's belt, he also removed a German-made flex knife. Curved to conform to the waistband in its Kydex sheath, it sprang straight as he jerked it out and tossed it over his shoulder behind him.

It was from the pocket of the Iraqi's jacket that the soldier found the only possible item of value—a crumpled cocktail napkin on which an address had been written—24 Ortez. The ink was smeared, but the numbers and letters were still legible. As he folded the napkin and stuck it into his own pocket, the Iraqi suddenly began to jerk spasmodically. Then, just as suddenly, he went limp. The dark brown orbs in his face now stared blindly into space.

"You get anything?" Bolan asked, turning to Platinov.

The woman shook her head. "Nothing we didn't already know. He and his team were sent to find Pollard. And they have a safehouse somewhere in the Rio area." She glanced to Bolan's pocket where the napkin had disappeared.

"An address," the soldier said. "It's in Copacabana." He moved quickly into the dining room, grabbed the Polaroid off the table, and looked down to insure it was loaded.

Platinov shrugged as he reentered the room. "The address cannot be of importance. Not even an Iraqi agent would be so careless."

Bolan thought of the fact that Platinov had left her real identification papers in the trunk of the Pontiac but decided not to mention it. "Maybe," he said. "Maybe not."

"So, what is the best it could be?" Platinov asked. "Their Rio de Janeiro headquarters? Their own safehouse?" She shook her head. "We are not looking for more Iraqi agents. We are looking for Hugh Pollard."

Bolan aimed the camera at the dead man on the couch.

"Correct," he said as he snapped the shutter. "But we haven't found him." The picture came sliding out of the camera and began to develop as it hit the air.

"The Iraqis don't know any more than we do," Platinov said impatiently. "Or they wouldn't have been playing these games with us."

Bolan shrugged as he started toward the door to the garage. "No, they don't know any more than we do. But what they know might be different than what we know. And if you add that to what we already know…" He let his words trail off; Platinov had gotten his point. He reached the door, then twisted the knob. "Of course, if you have a better idea at this point I'd be happy to listen to it."

"No." Platinov said, shaking her head. "It is not the best lead I have ever pursued, but at least it is a lead. And doing something is always better than doing nothing."

"Then let's go do something," the Executioner said as he opened the door to the garage.

WITH ITS THREE AND A HALF miles of beach bordered by the sea on one side and mammoth skyscrapers on the other, Copacabana was almost a city within a city. Unlike the rest of Rio de Janeiro—spread out around the Bay of Guanabara on the other side of Sugar Loaf and Morro de Leme peaks—the world-famous nightlife area was situated on the Atlantic Ocean itself.

The Pontiac had been "made" and could get them stopped by police at any moment. So they had left it hidden in the safehouse garage. Bolan now drove the Nissan through one of the three tunnels that linked Copacabana and Rio proper. They emerged first into the Leme area, one of Rio's most fashionable shopping districts. Mixed between the exclusive clothing emporiums, specialty outlets and exotic import stores were fashionable sidewalk bistros. Even with the windows rolled up and the air conditioner on, they could hear the music drifting into the streets. They passed some of the world's most famous hotels, then drove along a beach that accommodated over a hundred thousand sun worshipers during the day. Night had fallen now, but the sands were still crowded with men and women walking arm in arm, and groups seated around small fires on the sand.

They had stopped at a convenience store long enough to purchase a city map, and now Platinov unfolded it in her lap next to him. "If I am reading this correctly," she said, "Ortez Street is well past Lake Rodrigo de Freitas. In Old Brasil. Keep going straight."

Bolan nodded silently as he drove on past Leblon and Ipanema beaches. In the corner of his eye, he could see Platinov. The agent had changed into jeans and an orange tube top that left her rippling abdominal muscles bare. She had thrown a loose-fighting chambray shirt around her shoulders. The powder-blue shirt served a dual purpose. Its similarity to Bolan's added to the illusion that they were a couple. It also concealed her H&K. What it didn't, and couldn't, do was hide the raw animal sensuality that exuded from her every pore.

The Nissan came to a series of pedestrian-only side streets, and Bolan pulled into a parking lot. He unrolled the window long enough to take the ticket from the attendant, then followed the man's wave into an empty space. A few seconds later, he and Platinov were walking down the street, arm in arm, like any other two people in love in Rio.

Platinov looked like a honeymooning wife as she folded the map into her shirt pocket. They entered the area of town known as Old Brasil, and saw open shops selling jewelry, gem stones, silverware and every other item native to the ancient and mysterious land. Bordered by the stalls on both sides of the narrow walking street, they dodged the other men, women and children crowding the area. There was a feeling of life in the air, with lovers holding hands and families of tourists from all parts of the world laughing and speaking a variety of languages as they bargained for the best prices on souvenirs.

Bolan and Platinov stopped briefly at a sidewalk café and bought a bottle of water. The Russian studied the map. "This is confusing," she said. "There is no—how is it you say in

America?—no rhyme or reason to these streets." She looked up and smiled. "Rhyme or reason. I got that one right?"

"You got that one right," he said. He uncapped the bottle and traded it to her for the map. Studying the illogical maze of streets, which had stood for hundreds of years with little change, he finally located Ortez. They took off walking again, Platinov at his side.

The soldier followed the map down a street away from the shops. They entered a residential area made up of old Portuguese-style houses. Children now made up ninety percent of the people they saw, playing impromptu games of street jai alai, and often doing nothing more than chasing each other with the wild glee of youth. Many short side streets jutted off, some ending in the bay, others in clusters of small huts and one terminating at what looked to have once been a palace of some sort. Right in front of the stately structure ran another busier street with cars racing past.

Bolan stopped once more to peer at the map under a street light. Ortez looked to be two blocks farther down. They found it a few minutes later and turned, searching the houses of the short street for numbers. A "20" and then a "22" appeared on houses, but at what would have been 24 Ortez, they came to a huge boulder.

"I told you this could be nothing," Platinov said.

Bolan frowned, squinting down at the map, satisfying himself that they were at the right spot. Then, pulling the cocktail napkin out of his shirt pocket where it rode next to the Polaroid shot of Iraj Hussein, he focused his eyes on the smeared writing once more. The soldier nodded silently to himself.

"What is it?" Platinov demanded.

"It's not Ortez," Bolan said. "It's Ortiz. An *i* instead of an *e*."

Platinov moved in next to him. Her shoulder rubbed against his as she peered down at the crumpled napkin. "We passed it a few moments ago," she said. "The street that had the castle or whatever it was at the end."

Quickly, Bolan and Platinov retraced their steps to Ortiz.

They turned onto the street and started toward the busier intersection. On the other side of the speeding cars, they saw the palace with a large parking lot next to it. A trio of men had just parked a vehicle and were walking toward the front entrance. Bolan studied the numbers on the map once more. Number 24 was not only on this street with the palace, but it was also the palace.

Another open-air café was situated across the street from where they stopped. Jogging through the traffic, the soldier led the way to a table on the sidewalk. A waiter immediately appeared and they each ordered a cup of coffee. The man brought their cups a few seconds later, and they inconspicuously watched the palace as they drank. More cars appeared in the parking lot as they waited, their inhabitants exiting and walking toward the palace's front entrance. Other vehicles departed the lot. Traffic in and out of the palace wasn't heavy, but it was steady. It consisted of what appeared to be both foreign tourists and locals. Regardless of the birthplaces or nationalities, they all had one thing in common. They were all *male*.

"It is a whorehouse," Platinov said.

Bolan took a sip from his cup. "That would be my guess," he said.

Platinov sighed. "I told you this was a waste of time," she said indignantly.

"Maybe," the soldier said with a shrug. "Maybe not."

Platinov shook her head in disgust. "The reason this address is on the napkin is simple," she said. "The Iraqi was sent to this country to find Pollard. He wanted a woman while he was here. He learned of this place and either came here or was planning to come here as soon as he had time. The man was horny. So what?"

"So if he knew about this place," Bolan said, "chances are good that other Iraqi agents knew about it, too."

Platinov quieted as the soldier's logic became clear.

"You wait here," Bolan said. "I'll go in like a customer and—"

"Like hell I will wait here," the Russian woman said. "You could learn where Pollard is and sneak out another door."

"Want my word of honor?"

Platinov stood. "Under these circumstances, honor doesn't apply," she said.

"You don't think you'll be a little out of place?" the soldier asked as he rose to his feet.

Platinov snorted. "Don't be naive," she said. "I wouldn't be the first kinky housewife to accompany her husband to a place like this." She took his arm once more. "We will be married people whose bedroom has become stale. We're looking for a little variety. Something new."

Bolan took her arm as she extended it. She was right—they wouldn't be the average customers, but neither would this be the first time such an establishment had welcomed a couple through its door. Arm in arm, they crossed the street to the front gate of the palace. A nervous-looking American man clad in khaki shorts and a golf shirt had exited a car in the parking lot and was a few steps ahead of them. They waited while he entered the front door, then followed.

A foyer stood just inside the door and a hostess stand—not unlike one that might be found in a high-priced restaurant—stood at the opening to a hallway. A beautiful young woman with pale skin, wearing green panties, a matching bra, a black garter belt attached to green fishnet stockings stepped out from behind the stand. The tourist ahead of them glanced anxiously over his shoulder, then whispered something in her ear. She smiled, nodded, then looked past him to Bolan and Platinov. Taking them for Americans, she smiled even wider and said in perfect English, "Another hostess will be with you in a moment." She took the nervous man by the hand, and her high heels clattered off out of sight down the hallway. A second later the clicking heels halted. Muffled voices drifted out into the foyer. Then another set of heels clicked toward them.

A few seconds later, a darker-skinned woman appeared from the same hallway. She was tall and lithe, and although still attractive as she neared thirty, she had nevertheless seen better days. In addition to her spiked high heels, she had chosen white panties and a low-cut bra to contrast with the olive skin. Her smile was forced as she glanced from Bolan to Platinov and back. "My name is Marina," she said in heavily accented English. "You are looking for something a little...different?"

Platinov didn't waste time. "Yes," she said. "And you will do fine."

The Russian woman's firm, direct words cast a cloud of suspicion over the prostitute's eyes. She studied them both, frowning as she tried to find the correct words to express her thoughts. "Very well," she finally said. "But no...rough stuff."

"We wouldn't even think of it," said Platinov. "Both my husband and I are fiercely pacifistic."

The soldier suppressed a smile as he followed the two women down the ancient palace hallway, up a set of stairs and into a small room. The only furniture was a chair, the bed, and a nightstand that held a lamp and an old-fashioned black rotary telephone. The building appeared to have first been constructed in the seventeenth century, but renovations had taken place over the years. In addition to the phone lines, electricity had been added, and from somewhere down the hall a game show, the contestants speaking Portuguese, could be heard on television.

As Marina closed the door behind them, she said, "I must charge more for two. You wish to pay in American dollars or—"

Bolan cut her off as she turned back around. "American dollars," he said, extending a hundred-dollar bill.

The woman glanced down at the money but didn't reach for it. "I have no change," she said.

"I don't want any," Bolan replied.

Now, the suspicion in the prostitute's eyes turned to fear. Within Marina's frame of reference, the offer of such a vast amount of money could mean only one thing: pain.

Bolan understood the look on her face. "Relax, Marina
he said. "We're not going to hurt you. In fact, we aren't ev
going to touch you. What we want is information."

Platinov was growing impatient. She grabbed the hundre
dollar bill out of the soldier's hand, stuffed it into the oth
woman's bra between her breasts and pointed to a chair ne
to the bed. "Sit," she ordered.

The prostitute glanced at Bolan. She appeared to no long
fear him, but she was growing even more apprehensive abo
the demanding Russian woman. In short, Marynka Platine
scared the hell out of her. She followed the order and s
down.

Bolan and Platinov took seats on the bed facing Marin
The soldier pulled the Polaroid photo from his shirt and he
it up in front of him. "Do you know this man?" he asked.

Marina's eyes widened and her lips parted slightly. Sh
could tell the man in the picture was dead.

"Well, do you or don't you?" Platinov snapped.

Marina visibly recoiled from the words. "I don't kno
him," she said, speaking to Bolan. "But I have seen him. F
has been here."

The Executioner nodded. "Was he alone or with oth
men?"

"With other men," the prostitute said. "Other men...lil
him."

As Marina grew ever more frightened of Platinov, the Ru
sian grew more impatient with the prostitute. "Did you scre
him or did someone else?" the woman demanded.

Marina kept looking at Bolan as she said, "Someone else.

There was a pause, then Platinov spit out, "Well, who w
it, dammit!"

Bolan placed a hand on Platinov's knee to quiet her. "Wh
Marina?" he asked softly. "Who was this man with?"

"Susan."

"Is Susan here today?" Bolan asked.

The woman in the white bra and panties nodded.

Bolan smiled compassionately at her. "Marina, I need

talk to Susan." He glanced to the phone. "Tell her there's money in it for her, too."

Marina nodded, lifted the telephone receiver and punched one button. She spoke briefly in Portuguese, then hung up. "She is coming," the prostitute said to Bolan. She studiously ignored Platinov now, and it was obvious she wished the tough Russian woman would disappear into thin air. "You are...police?" she asked the Executioner.

"Of sorts," Bolan said.

A minute later the door opened and a frail woman with short blond hair entered the room. She wore a short transparent nightgown that did nothing to cover a smoothly shaved crotch. With her flat chest and skinny frame, she looked more like a ten-year-old than the middle-aged whore her wrinkled face betrayed. Bolan also noted the needle tracks on her arms.

Platinov stood and motioned the woman to take her place. "Sit by him," she said. "Your kind seems to take to him."

Bolan ignored Platinov's sarcasm. He wasn't sure what had spawned the Russian woman's sudden belligerence but it had turned the situation into an impromptu game of good-cop-bad-cop. And it was working. So he saw no reason to change tactics now. Smiling kindly, he said, "Susan, do you speak English?"

"I *am* English," she said in a Cockney accent.

"I'm going to show you a picture, and I want you to tell me all you can about the man," the soldier said. He removed the Polaroid from his pocket again.

"Marina mentioned money."

Bolan handed her another hundred as he held up the picture in his other hand.

The fact that the man in the picture was dead didn't have the same effect on Susan that it had on Marina. She simply nodded. "Yeah, I knew the bloody bastard," she said in the strong Cockney inflection "He liked to bite."

"What else can you tell me about him?" Bolan asked, dropping the photo back into his shirt.

"He was a pincher, too," Susan said.

"I'm not interested in the man's sexual habits. What el[se] do you know about him?"

"Arab of some sort," Susan answered. "Came here seve[ral] times. Always wanted me after the first time, and my tits a[nd] arse were always black and blue from the bites and pinches[."]

"Was he alone?" Bolan asked.

"No, never alone," Susan said, shaking her head. "Who[le] herd of the bloody wogs. Five, six, sometimes more."

The Executioner paused. There had been only three of the[m] at the Blue Mongoose. That meant more of the Iraqis were [on] the ground in Rio. "When was the last time you saw any [of] them?"

Susan glanced at the gold watch on her bony track-ridd[en] arm. "Five minutes ago, I'd say," she said. "Left him snori[ng] just down the hall."

The Executioner stood quickly. "Was he alone?"

Susan shook her head. "No, one of the others was wi[th] him. Just the two this time."

The Executioner pulled two more hundred-dollar bills fro[m] his pocket and handed one to each of the prostitutes. "Ta[ke] us there," he said.

Marina was still frightened and didn't move from the cha[ir]. But Susan was an old hand, and simply shrugged as s[he] opened the door and led the way down the hall. The Exec[u]tioner's hand moved under his shirt to the Desert Eagle. Sus[an] caught the move, and was street savvy enough to know wh[at] it meant. "Shoot him if you like," she said, nodding. "[He] didn't bite and pinch this time, but he did other weird things[."]

Bolan caught her arm at the door, moving her to the sid[e]. Drawing the big .44 Magnum, he twisted the knob and bur[st] into the room.

The bed, and a chair similar to the one in Marina's roo[m], was empty, but a cigarette still smoldered in the ashtray ne[xt] to the phone.

"He just left," Bolan said to Platinov. "Let's go."

Without another word, they raced down the steps and ba[ck] to the street.

TWO DARK CURLY HEADS could be seen inside a Hyundai as Bolan and Platinov burst back onto the street. Hiding his gun under his shirt once more, the Executioner watched it drive slowly away. He glanced toward the street they'd taken to the brothel. The Nissan was too far away. They needed other wheels.

For once, luck favored the Executioner. An early-'80s Chevy load of Brazilian teenage boys, laughing and drinking beer, pulled into the parking lot next to the palace brothel. They got out, whooping with drunken excitement. Bolan strode to the driver's side as a swarthy teenager emerged still holding the car keys.

"Park?" the Executioner asked.

The boy was forty sheets into the wind. He grinned lopsidedly and handed Bolan the key ring.

The soldier slid behind the wheel as Platinov moved through several wolf whistles to the opposite door. A second later, they were shooting out of the parking lot onto the street after the Hyundai. In the rearview mirror, the Executioner saw the boys slapping each other on the back as they entered the palace, too drunk to even know their car had been stolen.

Ahead, Bolan saw the Hyundai make a left off the street onto another of the busy modern avenues. The Chevy had been souped to the gills, the young owner obviously taking as much interest in the car as he did beer and women. It took only seconds for the Executioner to draw within a few lengths of the slow-moving Hyundai.

3

The Chevy followed the Hyundai through several turns, then passed Maracana Stadium. The soccer game in progress had drawn a full house under the overhead lights, and the cheers of the fans rose from the seats with the passion of ancient Romans at a gladiator duel.

Bolan walked the fine line between drifting so far behind the Iraqis that he lost them, and getting so close the hotrod became detectable. But still, the men in the car ahead appeared not to have spotted the tail; their silhouettes chatted away animatedly in the front seat.

Platinov put the Executioner's thoughts into words. "These two were at the whorehouse when we killed their comrades. They don't know about it yet."

"They're working a different shift," he said. "Probably just woke up a little while ago, and planning to take over for Ira and the others soon."

The Hyundai continued along the thoroughfares, turning occasionally and sometimes even doubling back on itself. It became obvious that the Iraqis were taking a long, circuitous route to wherever they were headed. They were still riding the high from visiting the whorehouse to pay close attention behind them. They were simply going through the motions and counting on the twists and turns in their path to lose any followers. Bolan shook his head. It was bad tradecraft.

The procession of two passed several more Rio landmarks, including the Museu Historico Nacional and the Museu do Indio as they made their way around the city. Then, finally they took a narrow winding road up one of the mountain foothills. Bolan glanced at the side of the hill just before turning onto the road. It butted against the taller Sugar Loaf Mountain, and culminated in a cliff overhead. The slope of the cliff was steep, rough and rugged, with jagged rocks, stumped trees and other dry-looking vegetation sprouting from the face.

The soldier turned to Platinov, who still had the map open in her lap. "You know where we are?" he asked.

The woman nodded, and anticipated his next question. "Yes. And this appears to be the only road leading up and down this hill."

Bolan was forced to fall farther back. Cars on the mountain road were few and far between, and the traffic could no longer be counted upon to camouflage them. He wound his way on up the foothill. High in the distance he could see an open-air trolley car—known as the *bonde*—making its way up the Moro Santo Antonio and then over the Colonial Aqueduct.

As they neared the top of the hill, Bolan slowed again. He had lost sight of the Hyundai around the twists and turns in the road, but that didn't worry him. If the map was right, and this was the only way up or down, the Iraqis would have to pass him again coming back. And that's exactly what they'd do if this was still part of their halfhearted tail-ditching scheme. Bolan didn't think it was. His gut-level hunch was that they were reaching the Hyundai's final destination.

At the top of the hill the road suddenly flattened, and the soldier saw a small residential community. The homes were built recently, but unlike the middle-income area where Platinov's safehouse was located, these structures were old-world in design. Primarily of wood and clapboard, they gave the area a holiday-like atmosphere. Bolan noticed a small real-estate sign—these were vacation homes. Rentals. Such an environment was as ideal for a safehouse as the neighborhood Platinov had chosen. People in a holiday cottage were accustomed to seeing strange faces come and go, and being strangers themselves who would soon be vacating the area, they paid little attention to what others did around them.

Bolan took a right, following a road that paralleled the perimeter of the cliff. Now he could see the drop-off from the top rather than the bottom. Looking down in the darkness, it appeared even more steep and foreboding.

Houses stood all over the flat area at the top of the foothill. Those set against Sugar Loaf Mountain had been built into the sides of the rock. The rest were freestanding. All of the vacation homes, however, had two things in common: they were of wood construction rather than brick or stone, and the porches weren't raised above the yards. The front doors were flat with the ground, and a plan of attack began to formulate in his mind.

The Hyundai had disappeared, but that didn't worry the Executioner. Space at the top of the hill was at a premium—the lots were small, and garages into which the car could disappear and hide were nonexistent. They would find the Hyundai again. The hill held less than a hundred houses, and it was simply a matter of driving the few streets until they saw it.

Bolan noticed a dark sedan as he made a right and continued along the perimeter road overlooking the city. A man wearing a light raincoat sat perfectly still behind the wheel as he passed. With the lights of Rio de Janeiro below, the soldier guided the Chevy around the cliff, glancing into the driveways that led to the homes with the view of the city.

Perhaps two hundred feet beyond the sedan, he spotted another vehicle—this time a Buick Le Sabre—parked in the street. Two men sat in the front this time. The driver wore a baseball cap. They turned slightly to look at the Chevy as it passed, and the Executioner got a quick flash of a well-trimmed mustache on the man in the hat. A slight nausea filled his stomach.

"Who are they?" Platinov wondered out loud.

"Can't be sure," Bolan said. "But my guess is M-I6."

The Russian woman chuckled softly. "Ah, yes," she said with a mildly condescending tone. "The British. America's little friend."

In a situation like this, there were no friends, Bolan thought.

Great Britain would be as happy to whisk Hugh Pollard away for intel purposes, then swear they had no idea what had happened to the former CIA director, as would North Korea, Cuba or Red China.

"Perhaps they have come to help you," Platinov said. Again there was a trace of sarcasm in her voice. "More than likely, they have come as they usually do to start trouble and then beg you Americans to get them out of it."

The soldier turned down one of the middle streets and spotted the Hyundai almost immediately. It had been parked behind a Honda in the driveway of one of the many nondescript houses. He drove on past, turned again and circled the street adjacent to the mountain. He and Platinov noted three more vehicles with men in them. Some of the men pretended to be looking at maps under the interior lights. One even tried to drop out of sight when the Chevy's headlights hit him.

Platinov shook her head in amazement. "Is it any wonder you Americans won your Revolutionary War?" she asked. It was a rhetorical question, and Bolan didn't bother responding.

"We're going to have to talk to them," he said as he guided the car back down the hill. Pulling into a scenic overview, he threw the Chevy into neutral and turned to the woman at his side. "They're stupid. Although they aren't as stupid as you think. They're watching the Iraqis and they saw us, too. They might not know exactly which country—" he paused "—or countries we're from, but they know we're here for the same reason they are."

Platinov agreed. "If we hit the house, they're likely to come in behind us and shoot us in the back."

Bolan nodded. "So let's go talk to them. You recognize any of the faces?"

"Maybe. It was too dark to be sure."

"Which one?"

"That master of disguise wearing a baseball cap," Platinov said. "Would anyone else—even an Englishman—except Sir Nigel Silversleeves be stupid enough to do that?"

"I thought I recognized him, too," Bolan said.

"He's not the brightest star in the sky," Platinov said. "Why would the Britons send *him* on something this important?"

The Executioner shook his head. "I don't know," he said. "He's some relation to the royal family, I understand. But you're right—he's no James Bond."

"Socialism, democracy, it makes no difference," Platinov said. "When it comes to bureaucracy, there's only one rule."

Bolan waited.

"Middle management will always find the absolute worst person for any specific job."

"Let's go talk to them," Bolan said. Killing the engine, he exited the Chevy. Platinov followed as he started back up the road on foot.

Keeping to the shadows at the side of the road, using the rocky terrain for cover, Bolan led the way to the first car he had seen upon reaching the top of the hill. The sedan hadn't moved, and the head above the wheel was still in place. Dropping to his belly, he crawled beneath the car's line of sight to the rear bumper. Behind him, he heard Platinov following. Scooting along the asphalt beneath the sedan's engine, he worked his way silently to a position just under the driver. Then, drawing the Beretta 93-R, he rolled out and up to his knees.

The sound suppressor threaded onto the Beretta's barrel shot through the window of the sedan, shattering the glass. A surprised face the Executioner didn't recognize turned to him, the lower lip falling open. Now that he was closer, Bolan could see the headset wrapped around the man's head and the tiny microphone extended in front of his face. He rested the sound suppressor on the bridge of the man's nose and held his left index finger to his lips. "You speak," he whispered, "and you die."

The man chose to simply nod his understanding.

The Executioner reached through the window and ripped the headset from the man's ears. Wrapping it around his own head, he heard an English-accented voice say, "What was that? It sounded like glass." There was a brief pause, then the same voice said, "Everyone, check in."

"G-7," came another English accent over the airwaves. It was followed by several more *G*'s with different numbers. Then the original voice said, "G-9? Are you there?"

"Good evening, Sir Nigel," Bolan said.

Silence filled the airwaves. Then, finally, the voice of Silversleeves said, "Who is this?"

"You still in the Buick?" Bolan asked.

"Yes," Silversleeves said. "Who are you?"

"You'll find out in a minute," the Executioner said. "We're coming up." He circled the car and got into the passenger seat while Platinov opened the door to the back.

The man behind the wheel continued to sit like a frozen statue.

"Well," Platinov finally said. "Drive."

NIGEL SILVERSLEEVES WAS holding a Walther PPK in his lap when Bolan walked up to the window. When he saw the Executioner, a wide smile curled his manicured mustache upward. "Ah, Mike Belasko, I believe," he said, using Bolan's alias before extending his hand through the opening. When Bolan ignored it and opened the door to the back seat, he withdrew the hand. "Good to see you again, old man," he blustered in embarrassment.

The Executioner took a seat in the back of the Buick as the two heads swiveled around to face him. He had nothing against Silversleeves. The fact was, the Briton was a nice guy, but he was incompetent at his work, and that could be nothing but a liability during this mission. The sooner Bolan could get rid of him, the better. Although that wasn't likely to happen before they took down the Iraqi safehouse. Silversleeves might be incompetent, he might even be stupid, but he was as loyal to the crown as an English bulldog to its master.

Platinov opened the other door and got in beside Bolan. Silversleeves raised his eyebrows in semirecognition as the Russian woman took a seat. Then full understanding set in.

"Ah, yes," he said. "And Dr. Platinov. The Soviet track star."

"Russian," Platinov corrected. "In case you hadn't heard, there is no more Soviet Union."

"Yes," Silversleeves said smugly. "Quite." His eyes moved back to Bolan. "The two of you are together, I take it?"

"Brilliant deductive reasoning, Sir Nigel," Platinov said. "You've obviously read your Sherlock Holmes."

"Yes, we're together," Bolan said. "Now, let's cut to the chase. What do you know about the Iraqis inside the house down the street?"

"Iraqis?" Silversleeves choked out. "No, no, dear fellow, we're just up here—"

"Cut the crap, Silversleeves," Platinov spit with undisguised venom. "Answer the man's question."

The Briton started to lie again, then a look of resignation fell over his face. "So it is," he said. "Very well. We know very little really. What we do know is that they're looking for Hugh Pollard. As you are."

"And as you are, too," Bolan added.

"Yes," Silversleeves said. "We were hoping they might lead us to him."

Bolan leaned back against the seat and stretched his back muscles. "Okay, Nigel. We're hoping the same thing. But we plan to work a little faster and more directly than you appear to be doing."

A look of horror came over the Briton's face. "My good man," he said. "You don't mean to say—"

"I don't mean to say anything," the Executioner said. "I am saying that we're about to hit the house." He paused to let it sink in. "You can come with us, you can follow us or you can stay out of the way. But don't get in the way."

Silversleeves reached into the pocket of his sport coat and pulled out a cellular phone. "I'll have to get clearance from London first," he said.

"You do that, Nigel," Bolan said. "In the meantime, we're

oing in. Remember not to get in our way. Our countries may
ave a special relationship, but on this one all bets are off.''

"And England and Russia have never liked each other,"
latinov added. "You would be wise to keep that in mind."

"My dear Dr. Platinov," Silversleeves said. His face re-
ected hurt, whether genuine or false, it was impossible to
ll. "Russia and Great Britain are now friends."

"Quite so," Platinov said in a sarcastic imitation of Silver-
leeves's accent. "Maybe you and I can play squash together
ometime, Nigel."

Silversleeves's face brightened for a moment. "You play?"
e asked. Then, suddenly realizing the Russian woman had
een making fun of him, he said, "Oh. Yes. So, will you
quire anything else from us?"

"Yes." The Executioner hooked a thumb over his shoulder.
You can take us back to our car."

The British agent hesitated, obviously wondering if such a
ove was beneath his station, but a quick glance back up into
e Executioner's eyes told him it would be a wise move to
llow the order regardless. He twisted the key in the ignition
nd started the engine.

Two minutes later Bolan and Platinov got out at the scenic
rnout again.

"If you can give me a few hours," Silversleeves said
rough the window, "I can get clearance. My men and I can
ack you up."

"We don't have a few hours, Nigel," Bolan said. "We'll
st have to do the best we can on our own."

"Well…" Silversleeves said. "Go ahead, then, I suppose."

Platinov shook her head in amazement once more as she
pened the door to the Chevy. "How does a nation like that
ven survive?" she asked.

"They aren't all like Nigel Silversleeves," he said. He
rew the car into drive and pulled back onto the road.

Her demeanor suddenly turned back to business. "You told
im you had a more direct approach to hitting the house. Don't

you think you should share it with me, Michael Belasko,"
she said, acknowledging his current alias.

"Sure," Bolan said. "I could tell you about it. But I thi
it would be more fun to just show you." He turned to her
they reached the top of the hill once more. "Fasten your s
belt, get your gun out and get ready. I'm sure you'll catch
as we go."

THE HOUSE where the Hyundai was parked was made prim
ily of wood just like the others on the hill. It had a loo
almost Caribbean look to it. Which meant that practically
entire front wall exploded as if it had been hit with a mor
round when the Executioner drove the Chevy through the fr
door.

Bolan and Platinov were out of the car before the fly
splinters of wood had even settled. In his right hand, the I
ecutioner gripped the big .44 Magnum Desert Eagle. In
left was the Beretta 93-R.

Platinov had drawn her H&K P-7M13. She gripped the
round 9 mm pistol in both hands.

Two Iraqi agents had been sitting on the couch in the liv
room when the vehicle burst in. Dressed in nothing but wh
T-shirts and underwear, they seemed frozen in place. Th
continued to stare straight ahead but now the Chevy block
their view of the television on the other side of the room. Th
black-bearded faces had gone white. As the shock began
wear off, they both lunged for a pistol which rested on
couch between them.

Both hands reached the gun at the same time, and the res
looked like something out of a Three Stooges episode. A
zarre tug-of-war ensued. It lasted less than a second.

Bolan ended the contest with a double-tap of .44 Magn
rounds into the chest of the man on the left end of the cou
Dead in his seat, he released his fingers from around the g
of the pistol and jerked spasmodically as his white shirt a
shorts soaked crimson.

The gun came free into the hand of the other Iraqi, but

fingers were clamped around the barrel, and as he now frantically tried to twirl the weapon around in his hand Bolan cut loose with a quick burst from the Beretta. The trio of subsonic hollowpoint slugs caught the man in his throat and pockmarked face. Tufts of singed chin hair floated up into the air in the wake of the 9 mm rounds. The tug-of-war ended with the Executioner as the only winner.

On the other side of the room, Bolan heard Platinov's H&K go to work. He twirled to see her depress the squeeze-cocking device on the front of the grip. The Chevy's front bumper had come to a halt in the area joining the living room with the kitchen, and now the Russian woman's steady stream of semiautomatic fire was directed past it. The Executioner's eyes followed her aim, and he saw one of the dark-skinned Iraqis they had followed from the palace whorehouse. The man's days of paying to bite and pinch prostitutes were in the process of ending. He performed a spasmodic dance of death on the linoleum floor as round after round flew from Platinov's H&K. The revolver he wore in a shoulder holster over his shirt never had time to come out.

Return fire did come, however. From the hallway to the side of the kitchen. The Executioner dropped prone on the ground behind the car, catching a glimpse as he fell of a figure holding an AK-74 in the hall. The car now blocked him from the rifleman's view. But Platinov, on the other side of the vehicle, was a clear target. Until she hit the carpet a second later and rolled beneath the Chevy's chassis.

Looking between the front tires, Bolan could see a pair of bare feet and hairy calves. They vibrated slightly as the men in the hallways continued to pour full-auto .223 rounds into the car's body. Extending the Desert Eagle across the floor, the Executioner sighted between the tires. His finger moved back on the trigger, and a massive 240-grain .44 Magnum slug rocketed from the barrel of the Desert Eagle. The big semijacketed hollowpoint bullet struck the shooter in the ankle, nearly severing his foot. The injured limb shot up out of Bo-

lan's sight above the bumper as the man began to hop up a
down on the other foot.

A hard smile at the slapstick quality of what was happeni
crossed the Executioner's face. As the hopping foot left t
ground, he lined up the Desert Eagle's sights on the spot wh
it would land again. When it did, he squeezed the trigger a
blew off the rifleman's big toe. Now the man's entire body
the ground.

The next round drilled through the Iraqi's heart.

Suddenly, all gunfire ceased. The television the men h
been watching was still on, and on the other side of the
Bolan heard a voice singing a Pepsi-Cola jingle in Portugue
He turned to look under the car at Platinov. "Be careful,"
whispered. "Let me go check it out first."

Platinov was wedged under the car. Getting out was goi
to be awkward—and therefore dangerous—no matter how s
tried it. She'd be an easy target for any Iraqis who might s
be alive and hiding in the house. The doctor was brave
she wasn't stupid. She didn't argue, but just nodded.

Slowly, Bolan rose to a kneeling position, keeping the e
gine block between him and the hallway. His ears pricked
the slightest sound, he peered over the hood of the car. T
house remained silent except for the Pepsi commercial. He s
nothing in the hall but the downed gunman. He had seen o
their dark shadows in the Hyundai as he and Platinov trail
the car, but unless he missed his guess, this was the other m
who had been at the palace. The AK-74 he had fired earl
had fallen on the carpet next to him.

Rising to his feet, the Executioner moved cautiously arou
the hood of the Chevy toward the hallway. The men in
living room were clearly dead, as was the man in the kitch
whom Platinov had shot. Behind Bolan, the Pepsi commerc
had become a Colombian situation comedy. With the big
Magnum held tight at his side, the Executioner edged do
the hallway.

It was a small house, and appeared to have only two be
rooms and one bath. Just before he reached the first door,

urned briefly back to the living room and whistled. As he
nched forward again, he heard the faint sounds of Platinov
olling out from under the car.

Bolan entered the first bedroom, dropped low for a split
econd to look under the bed, then rose and walked toward
he closet. The door was closed. Holstering the Beretta, he
tepped to the side. Keeping the Desert Eagle ready, he
eached around and swung the door back. When nothing hap-
ened, he dropped to one knee and peered around the corner.
Clothing hung from hangers on the rods. But only to waist
evel. There was no place to hide.

Soft footsteps in the hallway caused him to turn. First an
H&K P-7M13 and the hand holding it, then Platinov herself,
ppeared in the doorway. Without speaking, the Executioner
nodded toward the wall, indicating the bedroom on the other
ide of the one he was in. Platinov returned the nod, then
moved on down the hall out of sight.

Bolan left the bedroom and walked across the hall to the
athroom. The shower curtain was open. The bathroom was
s devoid of human life as was the rest of the house. He met
Platinov in the hallway as she came out of the second bedroom
haking her head. "Dammit," the Russian woman said as she
tuck her H&K back under her shirt. "We needed someone to
ive us some answers."

"We'll look around," Bolan said. "Maybe we'll find an-
wers some other way." He jammed the Desert Eagle into his
olster and retraced his steps back to the living room.

A split second later, the hand cannon was back in his hand
s a sudden barrage of bullets flew into the house through the
estroyed front wall.

THE EXECUTIONER HIT the ground behind the Chevy next to
he dead Iraqi in the hallway. Who was firing at them? More
f the Iraqis just coming back to the safehouse? Maybe, but
seemed unlikely. They had already encountered—and
illed—more agents from that country than he'd have ex-
ected to be in Rio. The Iraqi's were already pushing the limit

on how many operatives would have been assigned to sea
for Hugh Pollard.

Another string of fire peppered the living room and forc
Bolan farther down behind the car. Was it Silversleeves a
his British agents? That was unlikely, too. Great Britain's a
America's goals might not run parallel on this mission as th
so often did on the global scene, and Silversleeves might
be the sharpest knife in the drawer, but the Briton wasn't th
stupid. He would never endanger the special relationship b
tween their two countries with such an overt act of violenc

More fire—triggered from full-auto assault rifles—bl
through the space where the front wall had once been. Roun
struck the already well-dappled Chevy, turning the body i
a sieve. Furniture exploded in pieces, with chips of wood f
ing through the air like shrapnel. But now they didn't j
come from the open front of the room. More guns had join
the assault through the side windows. Bolan sent the remain
of Desert Eagle's magazine back out in return to let the ene
know he was there, then slammed the big .44 Magnum ba
into the waistband holster beneath the chambray shirt. Rea
ing across the dead Iraqi, he grabbed the AK-74. Quic
dropping the magazine, he saw a half load remaining in
steel box mag. His eyes returned to the dead man. Extend
from the rear pocket of the slacks the man had worn w
another magazine. Bolan rolled the body to its side and slipp
it out. A moment later the AK held a full load and the se
spent magazine was in the Executioner's own back pocket

Using the other side of the engine block for cover this tin
Bolan rose to one knee and sent a full-auto burst over the tru
of the car. He had aimed at muzzle-flashes that were near
the front porch, and his rounds found a home just behind the
Grunts, groans and screams issued forth as the firing abrup
halted and the flashes faded away. Several dark shadows
to the yard just outside the house. Others skirted to cover
the sides of the demolished front wall.

The Executioner whirled a fast three-sixty, scanning the a

for Platinov. But the beautiful Russian agent was nowhere to be seen.

Through the broken glass of one of the side windows, Bolan caught a tiny gleam of light. It was the glow often seen from a flash suppressor at close range, and he swung the AK-74 that way and held back the trigger. More slugs rocketed from the Soviet-made assault rifle, and the head and shoulders of a dark-skinned man fell through the window opening into the room.

Movement to his rear spun the Executioner back around. Now he saw Platinov crawling along the carpet toward him. She had found another of the AK-74 rifles somewhere, and it was now strapped across her back on a web sling. Her hands each held an extra magazine, and a third was clenched in her teeth. As soon as she caught Bolan's eye, she sent the mag in her right hand flipping end-over-end through the air.

The onslaught from outside the house continued as Bolan reached up, caught the magazine and stuffed it into the other back pocket of his jeans. He looked back to the man hanging halfway through the side window, and some small detail caught his attention. The battle raged on, and whatever detail he had noticed had no time to surface to his conscious mind.

Three men, all armed with military assault rifles, suddenly rushed the smashed front entrance to the house on the hill. Turning toward them, the Executioner cut loose with a full-auto figure-eight of fire. Two rounds struck the man on the far right in the face and chest as the AK's barrel dipped down and across the trio. The man in the middle was spared—for a moment—as the next three rounds took the rifleman on the left in the groin, abdomen and finally the head. But the last few slugs of the volley stitched back across the middle man, and he fell to the ground just in front of the Chevy with bullets through the nose and throat.

To his side, also using the engine block to shield her, Bolan heard Platinov cut loose with a steady string of semiauto fire from her own Soviet rifle. As the Executioner dropped the near empty magazine and jammed the one Platinov had thrown him into the receiver, he glanced up to see two more men fall to the ground not ten feet away. They were close now, and in the moonlight entering the house he suddenly understood the tiny detail which had tried to register earlier in his brain.

The new attackers were dark-skinned like the Iraqis. But they were not Iraqis. But the Executioner had little time to further contemplate the new recognition. He had no idea who the men were or what government they represented. All he knew was that they seemed to just keep coming. And if he didn't stop them, neither he nor Platinov would live to find out who they were.

Through the window opposite the hanging man on the side wall Bolan saw a dark figure approaching. With a full load in the AK-74 now, he opened up. Whoever it was fell below the window out of sight. He was replaced almost immediately by two running forms who neared the window at the same time. Another long burst knocked them both off their feet. The second and third bodies had to have fallen on top of the first because by the time Bolan downed a fourth attacker, the pile had grown over the bottom of the window. He could see the last dead man lying awkwardly on top of the heap, framed by the window as if he had just watched a gunfight on television.

Platinov's own AK-74 continued to jump steadily in her hands. Two more of the aggressors fell in death just in front of the Chevy's rear bumper.

Bolan ran his rifle dry again, then inserted the half-empty magazine he had originally taken out of the rifle. Mentally, he reminded himself that he had been forced to holster the Desert Eagle empty, and prepared himself to drop the AK and switch to the Beretta as soon as the rifle bolt froze open again. That didn't take long, as suddenly a stream of men came rushing forward from out of the darkness in a last-ditch frontal wave. Thumbing the rifle to semiauto to conserve his remaining rounds, the Executioner popped off several well-placed shots into faces and chests. To his side, he heard Platinov doing the same.

The last man was less than three feet in front of the Executioner when Bolan fired his last round. He had to angle the weapon upward, and the bullet caught the man just under the chin. It drilled through the soft palate, up into and through the brain and out the top of his skull, taking blood, bone and gray matter with it to coat what remained of the ceiling of the house.

The Executioner dropped the AK-74 and drew the Beretta. Setting it to fire 3-round bursts, he raised it to shoulder level and extended it in front of him.

Death, the Executioner knew, was only a heartbeat away, and he regretted it with all his heart. Not for himself—he had resigned himself to a fiery warrior's end long ago. But death meant the cessation of action, and if his actions ceased, here and now, it would be the world that paid. If any of the other countries of the world—even those supposedly friendly to the United States—got to former CIA director Hugh Pollard before he did, the future looked dim.

But as he prepared to fire his final rounds, Bolan suddenly heard several car engines start in the darkness. Tires screeched. The smell of burning rubber mixed with the cordite already filling his nostrils as the vehicles raced away. Bolan listened to the engine noise grow ever more quiet as the attackers fled. He had no idea how many of the hardmen were abandoning their cause. But he knew it was over.

At least for now.

The Executioner turned to Platinov, who had a look of awe mixed with concentration covering her beautiful face. "Who are these bastards?" she asked in a low husky voice.

Bolan shook his head. "I don't know," he said. "But we're going to find out."

In the distance—somewhere down the mountain—police sirens sounded.

"Come on," Bolan said. "We don't have much time."

"What do you want me to do?"

"Find some paper."

"Paper?" Platinov asked, incredulously.

"Don't argue. Just do it!" Bolan shouted.

Platinov was more accustomed to giving orders than taking them, but she did it.

The sirens were growing louder. Returning the Beretta to the shoulder rig beneath his blue chambray shirt, Bolan jammed a full magazine of .44 Magnums into the butt of the Desert Eagle, then holstered it at his side once more.

The living room was in shambles—both from the Chevy's crash through the front of the house and the ensuing firefights. Somewhere along the line, the television had finally gotten shot and was now silent. Bolan's eyes searched through the rubble on the floor until he found what he wanted. A ballpoint pen. Not far away from the pen, upside down, was a small ashtray. Reaching down, he whisked both items off the floor. As he unscrewed the pen, Platinov returned holding a white-paged legal pad. "Find some clean pages from the middle," Bolan said.

As the Russian flipped the pages, Bolan broke the ink cartridge from the ballpoint pen and let the ink drip out into the ashtray. As soon as a small pool had formed, he cast the empty plastic to the ground again and knelt next to the nearest dead man. Platinov caught on and knelt next to him. Quickly, Bolan jammed the fingers of both dead hands into the ink. Then, more carefully, he rolled them across the pad the woman extended to him.

The sirens grew louder with each passing moment as Bolan and Platinov moved from body to body, gathering fingerprints. They took those of both the Iraqis who had been in the house, and as many from the attackers as they could before red-and-blue police lights appeared down the street in the distance.

Several of the men still had not been printed when Bolan stood. "That's it," he said. "We've got to get out of here. The back."

Platinov nodded and followed as Bolan turned and raced to the back bedroom of the house. The window had been painted shut and wouldn't budge. Drawing the Desert Eagle, he gripped it by the barrel and smashed the glass. Platinov jerked the larger shards from the corners of the frame out as he holstered the weapon once more.

A moment later they were outside the house and sprinting away from the arriving police.

BOLAN LED THE WAY through the backyard of the house, crossed the gravel street leading to the next row of vacation homes, then cut between two of them. A step behind him, he heard the swift and practiced patter of Marynka Platinov's track-star feet. He leaped over a small white picket fence into another backyard, and heard Platinov do the same right behind him.

He didn't know if the beautiful Russian woman could still win the Olympic hundred-meter hurdles, but if she'd lost any of her speed over the years it hadn't been much.

The two of them crossed another street at full speed. They had barely ducked between two more houses when they saw the flash of red-and-blue lights behind them as a squad car turned the corner. Both Bolan and Platinov hit the ground, flattening against the grass as the lights raced by. As soon as the car was gone, they were on their feet again.

One more block of world-class sprinting on both of their parts got them to the side of the hill. The soldier slowed as he reached the cliff, coming to a stop at the edge. He looked down in the darkness. There was just enough moonlight to make out the rocks, roots and dwarf trees growing out of the side of the cliff. These, along with whatever fissures they encountered as they went, would have to serve as hand-and-footholds during their descent. Glancing to Platinov, who had now joined him, he said, "You ready?"

Platinov looked over the precipice into the darkness. "No," she said. In the moonlight, her face looked drained of blood.

Bolan turned to face her fully. "What?"

"I said no," the woman repeated. She paused, then said in a strange, insecure voice he had never heard from her before, "I suppose now is not a good time to bring it up—"

"You're afraid of heights?"

"Yes."

"You kidding?"

"No," Platinov said. Her shoulders shivered visibly.

The soldier laughed before he could stop himself. Such a fear was completely out of character for a woman who regularly faced death in a thousand other ways without so much as blinking.

"It's not funny," Platinov said, her voice angry now. "It's something I have never been able to overcome. Few people know it."

Bolan glanced back in the direction they had come. Several blocks over, he could see the flashing lights at the Iraqi safehouse. Other lights—some flashing red and blue, others white strobe searchlights—were now moving about the neighborhood. The police had reached the scene and quickly determined that whoever was responsible for the attack hadn't had time to get far away. It was only a matter of minutes before they would widen their search to include the spot where Bolan and Platinov now stood.

"Well, I won't tell anybody about your phobia," the soldier said. "But I'd say this was the perfect time to finally come to terms with it, wouldn't you?" He didn't wait for an answer. "I'll go first. Watch where I go, and you can use the same route."

"I thought you were never supposed to look down," Platinov said uncertainly.

"You're going to have a tough time in this case if you don't," Bolan responded. Then, without another word, he dropped to his knees and turned away from the cliff. Slowly, he began lowering himself over the side.

Bolan made his way slowly down the face of the hill, dropping from outcropping to outcropping, and making use of every available exception to the otherwise smooth surface his blind hands and feet encountered in the semidarkness. When he was fifteen feet below the perimeter road, he heard a resigned sigh from above. He looked up to see Marynka Platinov lower herself over the edge.

The soldier's eyes had adjusted to the darkness now, and he could see the potential footholds below him. But each new root, rock or crack in the foothill's surface had to be tested first to make sure it wasn't too loose to support his weight. When it was, pebbles and sticks went cascading down the hill and he was forced to search out a new path. The going was slow. Excruciatingly slow. And added to the stress was the fact that police lights could now be seen lapping over the cliff from along the perimeter road.

The soldier might not be having fun, but for an acrophobic like Platinov the descent had to be a living hell.

Bolan was roughly halfway down the cliff when he heard the car doors slam above him. He looked up to see the whirling red-and-blue lights coming from a stationary position. The car was parked perhaps a hundred feet to the right of where he and Platinov had begun their climb. Fifteen feet above him and just to his left, he could see the Russian woman half-squatting on a large tree root jutting from the side of the hill. "Flatten out!" he whispered upward.

Platinov didn't answer but she had heard him, and pressed herself so hard against the rock that she almost molded into it. Bolan did the same directly below her. With his face against the cool stone, he kept one eye on the flashing lights above.

A moment later the silhouette of a man wearing an octagonal police cap appeared against the moon at the edge of the road. Then the white light of a police flashlight joined the red-and-blue beams. The light shot straight downward over the cliff to the bottom, then began moving toward them as the officer walked along the road, checking the side of the hill.

Bolan held his breath as the light neared. If the beam struck either of them, they were sunk. They still had close to a hundred feet before they reached the ground—still too far to jump. Any type of fast escape was out of the question if they were discovered at this point. All the cops would have to do was leisurely drive down to the road below and wait on them with their guns drawn.

The flashlight moved steadily closer as Bolan waited. Twenty feet. Fifteen feet. Ten feet. Five feet.

A voice, speaking Portuguese, sounded above. The light disappeared as the officer holding it turned to answer. A brief conversation ensued. Then car doors opened and slammed shut again. A moment later the red-and-blue lights drove away.

The soldier began his descent once more. Fifteen minutes later he was hiding within the scrub bushes at the bottom of the cliff and waiting on Marynka Platinov.

The Russian might have suffered from an irrational fear of heights but she was a warrior through and through. She had learned long ago that courage wasn't the absence of fear; it was the ability to force one's self to continue *in spite* of fear. The total absence of fear, Bolan knew, had another name: stupidity.

Platinov was only ten feet above him when the thin branch growing from the hillside snapped. Bolan heard a rush of breath escape her lips as rocks and pebbles rained down over his head and shoulders and she came sliding down the steep slope. Reaching up, he extended his arms and the woman fell into them.

Bolan looked down into Platinov's terrified eyes. There was a tiny scratch on her face just above one eyebrow. Small as it was, it stood out in bold relief under the moonlight, and rather than distract from her beauty, the small flaw seemed to accent it. Platinov looked up at the soldier, and for a moment all the hardness, the toughness, the professionalism evaporated from her face. For a brief second she wasn't the top-notch spy and warrior he had known and worked with on this mission and in the past. For that moment she was a frightened little girl.

No, Bolan thought. A frightened little girl wasn't right, either. She might not be a woman capable of killing at the moment, but she was a woman. All woman. As much woman as he had ever known.

The moment vanished and Platinov became the professional espionage agent once more. She climbed down from his arms. "Thank you," she whispered, her voice holding a trace of embarrassment. "If you make even one comment, I swear I will shoot you."

He reached out and took her hand.

A moment later they were running toward the distant lights of Rio de Janeiro.

4

Ramone Lopez was just sitting down to breakfast when he heard the helicopter in the air outside. He rose from the table, walked to the door and stepped out.

The helicopter hovered momentarily above the mountain peaks in the background, then began to descend. As it neared the flat area a hundred feet from the cottage's front door, Lopez saw Boris sitting next to the pilot. He wondered momentarily what the Russian's real name was. Not that it mattered. He had dealt with the black-market man for over six years now, first running AK-47s and other weapons to the Basques in Spain and more recently to the Shining Path here in South America. Boris didn't care where the weapons went if he got his money.

The helicopter skids hit the ground, sending pebbles and other debris flying to the sides. Lopez waited for the men to get out. It had been almost a year now since he had stumbled onto, and befriended, Juan Ortega. A cantina in Seville had been the site of their meeting, and with Lopez buying the drinks the old Inca was more than happy to provide the entertainment, imparting to the younger man tale after tale of his former Shining Path glory. Lopez had recognized some of the stories as the wishful thinking of an old man now a hopeless drunk and drug addict. But he had also known some of it had to be based on fact. And on those facts, the Gypsy had begun to form his plan.

Ortega had come to Spain years earlier, one step ahead of the Peruvian police. He was homesick, and it hadn't taken

Lopez much effort to persuade him that sufficient time had elapsed for a safe return to his beloved Andes. As a Gypsy who had run small-time con games all his life, Lopez knew that all most people needed to believe what they wanted to believe was a gentle push. So he had pushed. And Ortega had believed.

With the heat in Spain being turned up on the Basques—and Lopez's name beginning to come to the attention of authorities as a gunrunner—the Gypsy had transferred his business with the Russian black market to South America. Ortega had provided his introduction to the Shining Path, and they had become his new customers. The logistics of brokering each deal between Boris and the South Americans had been a little more difficult at first simply because of the distance involved. And with no inside contacts he could pay off within the Peruvian Customs Department, a new challenge had been presented. But that had been solved with the recruitment of his American confederate. A CIA man, no less, with all of the CIA's contacts and influence at his disposal.

As Lopez watched, the helicopter pilot cut the engine and the rotor blades began to slow. He caught himself laughing softly. The thought of the CIA man and Boris, a former KGB officer, working together always struck him as ironic. But money—be it in dollars or rubles—always made for strange bedfellows. And while not every man was a Gypsy with the right to steal, it seemed that every man, given the opportunity, was just as much a thief at heart.

Boris lumbered down from the seat next to the pilot and walked forward, his shoulders instinctively lowered beneath the whirling blades above his head. Lopez could see that the Russian wore the same brown suit as always—a carry-over from his old KGB days when dark brown suits seemed to have been Soviet issue. Boris had gained weight in the two months since Lopez last saw him, and combined with his crimson complexion he looked like a heart attack waiting to happen. The Gypsy held no love for the man, but he hoped the Russian didn't die on him in the next few days. After that, whether or not Boris lived or died would make no more difference than what his real name might be. They'd both have enough money to go their separate ways and never see each other again or wonder about real names or anything else.

Two more Russians Lopez recognized as Boris's men dropped out of the helicopter. Both carried Russian-made PPS-43 submachine guns, the stocks folded over the tops of the weapons. And both, like Boris himself, appeared to be in their late fifties. They looked around nervously as they followed their leader.

The last man to leave the helicopter was dressed in an expensive gray pin-striped suit and a tie that looked to have cost more than all of the Russians' clothing put together. He stepped carefully down from the chopper, looking as if he was more worried about scuffing his Gucci loafers than being attacked by some unseen enemy. His hair was carefully coiffed, and sprayed so heavily that rather than blow beneath the wind from the chopper blades it swayed back and forth like a helmet.

Lopez studied the man. He had never met him but he knew who he had to be. The CIA man. The key to getting this final shipment into Peru.

Boris walked up but didn't extend his hand or waste time on other preliminaries. The helicopter blades had almost halted now, and with them their noise. So he didn't have to shout when he said, "Are you ready?"

Lopez nodded. "Shall we go inside?"

Boris turned to the two men behind him and waved them toward the open front door. They scurried forward with their subguns ready to insure there would be no surprises hidden in the cabin. Lopez forced a smile. "After all these years, my friend," he said, "you still don't trust me?"

The Russian shrugged. "We have done business many times," he admitted. "But pistols and hand grenades are one thing." He paused dramatically. "What we are about to bring you is another altogether."

"If anything, this would seem to be a situation in which we

could trust each other even more than usual," he said. "Everything up to this point has been easy. On this transaction there will be more than enough money to go around."

"Perhaps," Boris said, then glanced around, frowning. "Where is your pet dog?" he asked.

Lopez smiled. The Russian meant Ortega. "He met with an unfortunate accident," the Gypsy said. He nodded to the fresh pile of dirt fifty feet from the house.

Boris grinned and a lifetime of Soviet dental neglect was revealed. "How unfortunate," he said. "Heart attack, I suppose?"

Lopez didn't return the smile. It wouldn't hurt Boris to know that he was capable of murder. "No," he said. "But it was indeed a problem with his blood flow. It decided to quit circulating and run out his neck."

By then the American had arrived next to them. But again there were no handshakes, and Boris offered no introductions. The two men with the PPS-43s emerged from the cabin, nodded and then walked back toward the helicopter.

Lopez, Boris and the well-dressed American went inside.

"May I offer anyone a drink?" Lopez said as they took seats around the small wooden dining table.

Boris shook his head.

The CIA man looked at his watch. "A little early for me," he said.

Lopez sat down. "Then we shall get straight to business. There are several things we must discuss." He paused as the other two men nodded. "How soon will our delivery arrive?"

Boris reached up and rubbed a hand across his ruddy cheek. "The ship will be in port at Lima by tomorrow."

"An American ship?" Lopez asked, looking to the other man.

The man in the expensive suit nodded. "A multiple-cargo trading vessel," he said.

Lopez frowned. "You have hired the crew yourself?"

The American laughed. "Of course not," he said. "What we are bringing you doesn't take up that much space. It's hidden, and the crew knows nothing about it.'' He raised a hand, glanced at his carefully manicured nails, then set it on the table once more. ''I have two agents on board posing as crew members, keeping watch on things. They don't know what they're guarding, either.''

''How is the shipment concealed?'' Lopez asked.

A wry expression covered the American's face. ''All ten of them are already in backpacks,'' he said. ''Loaded in the middle of a carton containing twelve hundred other backpacks on their way to sporting-goods and camping stores all over Peru.''

Both the Russian and the Gypsy saw the irony, and joined in the laughter.

Lopez picked up a pencil and a pad of paper from the table in front of him and wrote on it. Tearing the page from the pad, he handed it to the Russian. ''Here are the coordinates of the camp,'' he said. ''You will bring the shipment the rest of the way in the helicopter?''

''Is there a place to land?''

''Yes, easily.''

''Then we can use the same helicopter.'' Boris nodded at the door. ''How soon will we get our money?''

The Gypsy shrugged. ''As soon as possible,'' he said. ''First we must convince the nations we are dealing with that what we say is true, and that we indeed have the capabilities of carrying out our threats if they don't cooperate.''

''Exactly how do you plan to do convince them of that?'' the CIA man asked.

Lopez looked the American in the eyes. ''However it becomes necessary. You are bringing us ten very special backpacks. If necessary, we will sacrifice one to prove what the other nine are capable of doing.''

The American's face went white for a moment, then the color returned. ''You do that and it's on your head,'' he said. ''I wash my hands of it.''

Lopez smiled. ''Just like Pilate,'' he said.

The American frowned, the Biblical allusion obviously not in his frame of reference. ''Whatever,'' he said in a threatening voice. "But I want to go on record as being against it. As far as I'm concerned, if they call your bluff, we call off the whole deal."

Boris shook his head in contempt. "How the Soviet Union fell and the United States lives on never ceases to perplex me," he said. Turning to face the CIA man, he said, "We have come too far and there is too much money involved to call this off. We will do what we must to convince the various governments that what we say is true."

The American stared at him. "If you do, you keep me out of it," he said. "It's not my fault. You understand that?"

Lopez forced himself to speak softly. "Should we assume then, that if we are forced to perform a demonstration of our capabilities, you will be so offended that you won't want your money?"

"I did my part," the CIA man said. "I'll take the money."

The Gypsy fought the urge to reach across the table and slap the hypocrite. "Perhaps it won't come to that," he forced himself to say calmly. "In any case, there are other things we must now discuss."

"Such as?" Boris asked.

"Hugh Pollard. And the fact that while he was hiding out in South America he learned of our plan."

The CIA man leaned forward across the table. "He'll be taken care of soon. I have men all over South America looking for him."

"So does every other country in the world," Lopez said. "But so far, none of them have found him. I set the Shining Path on his trail. They were killed in Rio de Janeiro. Apparently by an American. An American who was working with a Russian woman." He turned to face Boris. "A rather unusual arrangement, it appears. Do you know who they are?"

Boris's thick eyebrows lowered, and his red face scowled. "The American, no. The woman, yes. They are both potential problems. In any case, when we leave here I will solve that problem personally."

Lopez nodded. "Good. But back to Pollard. The problem,

as I see it, is that regardless of which country finds him first, they don't want to kill him." Turning to the CIA man, he went on. "Your country wants to take him back to stand trial and learn what information has been compromised. The other nations want to keep him alive in order to gain that information."

The CIA man shook his head. "I see where you're going," he said. "But it makes no difference. Everyone already believes he's a traitor. I saw to that. No one is going to believe what he has to say about us. Even if they did, it's too late. The Shining Path will have taken delivery and be set up all over the continent before the week is out." He chuckled softly. "Take it from me. Even if they found him yesterday, bureaucracy doesn't move that fast."

Boris nodded his head. "I must agree with our American friend," he said. "Pollard's story will sound like nothing more than false leads from a traitor attempting to divert attention from himself."

"I hope you are right," Lopez said. "There is one final thing we must work out."

Both the American and the Russian waited for him to continue.

Lopez leaned forward and folded his arms across the table. "The Shining Path have no experts in setting up devices such as the ones you will be bringing."

Boris waved a hand across his face. "They're ready to go. All that needs to be done is to enter a code into the digital timers."

"And what is the code?" Lopez asked.

Now it was the Russian's turn to pick up the pencil and write on the pad. When he was finished, he slid it across the table to Lopez. "But there is yet one more thing which should be made clear."

Lopez raised his eyebrows and waited.

"As you know, I'm still active with Russian Intelligence."

Lopez nodded. "The other transactions we have conducted

over the years wouldn't have been possible had you not been
with them," he agreed.

"And our new friend here has all of the resources of America's Central Intelligence Agency at his disposal," Boris
added.

"I am aware of that, as well," Lopez said. He frowned,
wondering where Boris was headed.

The CIA man flicked an imaginary speck of lint off the cuff
of his jacket. "What he's driving at, Mr. Lopez," he said, "is
that if you try to fuck us over on this deal—like maybe disappear after the money's been paid off, before we get ours—
you better have a place set up on the moon. There's no place
on this planet you'll be able to hide."

A quick surge of fear shot through Lopez's body. He had
lived outside the law, and in doing so dealt with deadly people
all his life, but what the American had just said reminded him
once again that he was playing in the big leagues now. As
quickly as it had come, however, the fear subsided. It was
unfounded. He had no intention of double-crossing the men
who sat across the table from him. "As I told Boris earlier,"
he said, "there will be more than enough money to go
around."

"Then you have nothing to worry about," said the CIA
man. But he didn't sound convinced.

Boris stood, preparing to leave. "My people will meet yours
in the jungle very soon," he said.

Lopez and the American rose from their chairs, as well.
"You won't be there yourself?" Lopez asked.

Boris shook his head. "There is no need. And I have other
work to take care of."

"The American and the Russian woman?" Lopez asked.

Boris didn't answer. He turned and walked out of the cabin.
The American followed.

BOLAN PULLED the Subaru into the driveway of the safehouse,
hit the remote control and the garage door opened. He pulled
in next to the Pontiac and killed the engine by reaching up

into the cracked steering column. The Subaru had been the first vehicle they had seen upon arriving at the bottom of the hill, and the Executioner had appropriated it for their return to Platinov's safehouse. The Chevy had been abandoned inside the Iraqis' safehouse.

Bolan and Platinov got out of the car as the garage door fell behind them. The Executioner glanced to the beautiful Russian woman as he followed her to the door. She had been uncharacteristically silent during the drive back, and he suspected he knew the reason.

Marynka Platinov was, quite simply, embarrassed. She was a pro through and through. And although even the best of professionals had weaknesses, they didn't enjoy having them exposed. And they particularly didn't like having them brandished in front of other pros.

In the dining room, Bolan wasted no time getting the portable fax machine up and running. A moment later the fingerprints he had taken at the house were on their way to Aaron Kurtzman at Stony Man Farm. The Advanced Fingerprint Identification System—better known simply as AFIS—was being improved all the time. In addition, Kurtzman, the computer wizard of Stony Man, had the ability to hack into the police files of nearly every country in the world. And if he ran across one he hadn't as yet been called upon to crack, it wouldn't take him long to figure a way in.

Platinov had headed for the kitchen as soon as they entered the house. Now, she appeared on the couch in the living room holding a bottle of Stolichnaya vodka and two glasses. She looked up at Bolan and raised one of the glasses.

The soldier shook his head.

She poured a finger and a half into a glass, downed it and then set the glasses and bottle on the coffee table.

Bolan joined her a moment later. "What made the cop at the top of the hill quit searching for us?" he asked. Platinov had been closer to the two men than he, and she also spoke Portuguese.

The woman's face flushed slightly as the vodka hit her system. She smiled. "It was his superior who arrived and distracted him," she said. "He told him to stop wasting time looking down the hill." She glanced at the bottle of Stolichnaya, but left it where it was. "He said no one in their right minds would try to descend the hill that way."

"He was probably right," he said.

"Of that, I am certain," Platinov said. She turned on the couch to face him, tucking her legs up under her. "So, what do we do now?" she asked.

"Wait," Bolan said. "The prints are on the way."

"On the way where?"

Bolan didn't answer.

"Ah, yes." The beautiful Russian woman nodded. "I understand."

The Executioner nodded. "It shouldn't take long. My man on the other end is as good as they come. My guess is we should get at least one or two hits."

A sly grin spread across the Russian woman's lips. "My computer will have a record of the fax," she said.

"Not by the time *our computer* is through dealing with it, it won't. The memory of the whole transaction will automatically be erased. Just disappear into thin cyberspace."

Her ordeal on the cliff had been harrowing, but now Platinov was beginning to relax again. "I suspected as much." She chuckled. "If I didn't, I wouldn't have mentioned it to you."

Bolan nodded, and reminded himself that while they might be working together, might even have developed a friendship, might even be feeling a little more for each other than friendship, their goals were not the same. He couldn't afford to let down his guard.

"The group that attacked after we got there," she said. "They weren't more Iraqis."

"No," Bolan said. "Hispanic of some sort? Indian? Shining Path?"

"I'm not sure."

Bolan glanced into the dining area where the fax machine waited on the table. "That's what we're hoping to find out."

"Where will it lead?" Platinov wondered out loud.

"To Hugh Pollard, I hope." The soldier stared at the coffee table in front of him.

Platinov cleared her throat softly, and he turned back to face her again.

"So," the Russian said. "Like you said, we have a short wait on our hands." Her smile had disappeared and her face had taken on a sultry look. "I wonder how we should spend that time?" She stared back into his eyes as she scooted closer to him on the couch. Bolan felt the heat rise in his chest. Platinov reached out, and suddenly they were locked in each other's arms, her lips pressing hard against his. She had just reached for his belt when the fax machine suddenly kicked on in the dining room.

Bolan's Russian was good—good enough that he had passed himself off as a Soviet several times in the past, but he didn't recognize the words that now came out of Platinov's mouth. He guessed by the tone and expression on her face, however, that what she had just said hadn't been learned in any Sunday school.

Rising, the soldier hurried into the dining room. Platinov followed. With the woman next to him, Bolan read the message as it rolled out of the machine. Two of the Iraqis were confirmed as members of an elite Iraqi intelligence branch of Saddam Hussein's Republican Guards. That hardly surprised him. The rest hadn't yet been identified but Kurtzman had added a note that he was still searching.

The Iraqis were not what interested Bolan, however. After the inserted note came a name corresponding to one of the sets of fingerprints he had taken from the dark-skinned men of the second attack. The soldier felt himself frowning. Only one had been positively identified so far, and there was a similar memorandum from Kurtzman that this search, too, was continuing. But the brief bio that accompanied the name held no hint whatsoever of any government connection. In fact, it appeared that the man—one Arturo Diaz—was a direct enemy of his native government in Uruguay. He had a lengthy criminal record ranging from petty theft as a juvenile all the way through armed robbery and murder, for which he had served time. Kurtzman had also found police intelligence reports linking Diaz to one of Uruguay's most notorious drug-manufacturing and smuggling organizations, the Rio de la Plata cartel.

"Looks like we are about to visit Montevideo," Platinov said as she read the fax while standing next to him. She reached for the phone. "I'll make the necessary airline reservations." Turning back to Bolan as she lifted the receiver, he saw the coy smile cover her face once more. "But then, we will undoubtedly have another forced waiting period before takeoff."

The soldier reached out, took the phone from her and set it back in the cradle. Not completely without personal regret, he said, "I've got my pilot standing by."

Platinov said the same words he had heard earlier. But this time she cursed with even more feeling than before.

A moment later they had thrown the fax, the laptop computer and various other gear into the Subaru and were headed for the airport.

THROUGH THE WINDSHIELD of the Learjet, Bolan could see a wide smile covering Jack Grimaldi's face as he led Platinov across the tarmac. Stony Man Farm's number-one pilot had flown the Executioner and the beautiful Russian agent around the world several years earlier, and it was clear he hadn't forgotten her. Of course, a face and body like Marynka Platinov's would be hard to forget—especially for a man as fond of women as Grimaldi.

Grimaldi reached across the front seat and opened the door. "So," he said in a comic-stern Russian accent. "Colonel Platinov. We meet again."

Platinov laughed and Bolan remembered that the two had hit it off well before. He helped her board the plane. "Jack, you sound like Boris Badenov from the *Rocky and Bullwinkle* cartoons," Platinov said.

Grimaldi's eyebrows lowered with feigned menace. "Moose and Squirrel must die," he growled.

Platinov laughed again and took the seat behind Grimaldi as Bolan strapped himself into the one next to the pilot. Grimaldi's mood changed immediately. Out of Platinov's sight, he shot an inquisitive look Bolan's way.

The soldier shrugged. "We've teamed up," he said simply.

"For how long?" Grimaldi whispered. He knew as well as Bolan did that sooner or later their missions would be in direct conflict.

"As long as it's practical," Bolan said.

Grimaldi shrugged. "You da man," he said as he turned to the controls in front of him. A moment later he had takeoff clearance, and the Lear taxied down the runway and rose into the air.

A quick glance behind him told Bolan that Platinov had taken the opportunity to catch some sleep. Maybe. Her eyes were closed and she was breathing regularly but she might just as easily have been faking it—hoping he and Grimaldi would relax and discuss something of interest to her as a Russian agent. That wasn't going to be the case. Grimaldi was far too seasoned to fall into a trap like that, and Bolan had no intention of talking, either. About anything. The soldier closed his eyes. Platinov could sleep or she could fake it—he didn't care. He intended to catch a few winks for real. There was no telling when he'd have another chance.

When Bolan next opened his eyes, the sun had risen and the plane was already descending. He looked down to see mile after mile of coastal beach, spotted here and there with vacation resorts. Turning slightly, he saw Platinov awake behind him. She had slept. Her eyes were slightly swollen, and were still in the process of opening as she sipped coffee from a paper cup. She caught Bolan's eye and raised the cup in the air, tapping it with a long slender index finger. "I just made it," she said. "Want some?"

"Thanks," the soldier said. As Platinov rose and walked to the rear of the plane, he reached inside his jacket and pulled out the fax Kurtzman had sent. Unfolding the pages, he located the description and criminal record of Arturo Diaz. The Stony Man computer wizard had included the man's last known address but there was an asterisk after the number and street, and at the bottom of the page Bolan read, "Address over six months old. Cannot be verified at this time."

The soldier put the papers back in his jacket as Platinov returned and handed him another paper cup. For a man like Diaz, an address six months old was like a ten-year-old address for a normal citizen. The odds that he'd still be there weren't good. But it was a place to start. And they had nothing better to go on.

The coffee was little more than lukewarm, and Bolan finished it in two swallows. Standing up, he looked down at Platinov, who had returned to her seat. "You bring any other clothes?" he asked. Like him, she was still dressed in the jeans and chambray shirt of the night before.

The woman smiled. "Do you think I never change clothes?" she asked. "Do you wonder if I bathe, as well? Of course I brought other clothes."

"We're going to look up a drug smuggler," he said. "So we're going to pose as drug smugglers. We should look the part." He moved past her to the end of the jet where a row of metal lockers had been bolted to the wall. Opening several, he looked through them, then pulled out a white linen suit, a black shirt and a pair of basket-woven shoes.

Platinov had followed him back to where she'd left her luggage. Next to the computer and fax cases, she opened a black leather suitcase and began digging through the clothes packed inside. She came out with a short black skirt, a peach-colored tube top and matching high heels. "These will do?" she asked.

"Perfect," he said, nodding.

"Then the difference between female drug smuggler and common whore is slight, if existent at all," said the Russian woman.

The soldier pulled the suit off its hanger. "You may have a little trouble concealing your weapons," he said.

Platinov shrugged. "That is what purses are for," she said. She stood, shrugged out of her shirt and unzipped her jeans.

Bolan turned his back. Behind him, he heard the sound of the Russian woman's jeans sliding down.

Platinov laughed. "What is wrong?" she asked. "You have suddenly become prudish on me?" She laughed again, then said, "You won't see anything you haven't seen before." When Bolan didn't answer, she added, "Or are you afraid things have begun to sag during the years since you last saw them?"

Bolan turned back. Marynka Platinov stood next to him, totally naked. Nothing was sagging.

Quickly, they changed and resumed their seats. They had barely sat again when the jet's wheels hit the runway. Grimaldi had radioed back to Stony Man during the flight, and Hal Brognola, the Farm's director of sensitive operations, had made a call to Montevideo. Customs was quick—and cursory. The hundred-dollar bill Bolan "accidentally" let fall out of his pocket was quickly swept up off the tarmac by a Uruguayan officer. He waved them through, their baggage unchecked.

Inside the terminal, Bolan rented a Saturn, picked up a map of the city and a few minutes later he and Platinov were driving through Uruguay's capital city. Even in the early morning, the smell of fresh beef hung in the air from Montevideo's many meat-packing plants. The city was divided into two major divisions—the Old City, or Ciudad Vieja, and the New City or Ciudad Nueva. With Platinov navigating as Bolan drove, it was the New City they crossed first. Montevideo had been founded in 1726 by Spanish settlers, but what Bolan and Platinov saw before them now reflected very little of that colonial past. High-rise office buildings and other modern architecture lined both sides of the street.

The Old City was their destination, and Bolan guided the Saturn out onto a small peninsula on Montevideo's west side.

Here the houses and buildings were older. But once again they reflected little of Uruguay's long history of struggle under Spanish rule. If they symbolized anything, it was poverty.

The house at the address Kurtzman had found for them was high-end for the neighborhood. Which was only to say it was the best home in a very bad neighborhood. Bolan parked the Saturn on the dirt road outside the house and he and Platinov walked to the front door. They had made a bad decision in changing clothes this early. They might look like well-to-do drug runners. But well dressed stood out in this poverty-stricken area.

Bolan rapped his knuckles on the splintery front door. What was a man like Arturo Diaz, who was connected to a wealthy drug cartel, doing living in indigence? Of course, it was an old address. Had his connection to the Rio de la Plata cartel come recently? It was possible. But something in the Executioner's gut told him that was stretching things a bit too far.

Bolan rapped again when he got no answer. Then a face appeared through the dirty glass in the top half of the door. Bolan saw a tired woman who looked fifty but was probably thirty. She wore a ragged man's sport shirt unbuttoned to the waist and no bra. A six-month-old infant had his lips glued to her right breast. Through the glass she looked from Bolan to Platinov and back again, and her face grew even more tired. But in the weary eyes, the soldier also saw a trace of anger.

Shifting the baby to one arm, she reached down and opened the door.

"El Guarani," the woman said.

Bolan frowned. "*¿Qué?*" he said.

"You seek El Guarani?" the woman said, switching to English.

Bolan's frown stayed on his face. The Guarani were an Indian tribe indigenous to nearby Paraguay. Perhaps Arturo Diaz was actually Paraguayan.

"We are looking for Arturo Diaz," Bolan said.

"Yes," the woman said impatiently. "El Guarani."

Platinov was growing impatient, too. "Yes," she said in her Russian accent. "Where is El Guarani?"

"El Guarani is no good," spit the breast-feeding woman. "He is a drug dealer." Her eyes dropped to survey Bolan and Platinov again, and although she didn't say it, her expression added, "Like you."

"Just tell us where he is," Bolan said. He reached into his pocket and pulled out a roll of American bills. Peeling off a twenty, he extended it.

The woman's hand was like lightning as she whisked the bill out of his fingers. "He no longer lives here. I don't know where he is."

Bolan felt sorry for her. But she had to know something of value. *"Señora,"* he said politely, "I just gave you twenty American dollars. I'm willing to give you twenty more." He paused, then added, "Or I'm willing to take the first twenty away from you again."

The woman stared at him and hugged the baby closer to her. "He has a sister who lives near here," she said, looking down at the money still in Bolan's hand. "She is no better than him. They are both criminals."

The soldier pulled another twenty off the roll but held it out of her reach. "Where?" he said.

The woman didn't know the address but she gave good directions.

Bolan gave her the other twenty and he and Platinov turned back toward the Saturn. They were halfway across the yard when a Toyota turned down the street. It slowed as it neared the house. Through the windshield, Bolan could see the driver and another man in the passenger seat. Behind them unclear shadows indicated two more men. The men in the front seat were clearly Caucasian, the one riding shotgun overweight with the bloated face of a heavy drinker. He looked as out of place in the Old City as Bolan and Platinov. Other drug dealers looking for Diaz? Somehow the Executioner didn't think so. And the look on Platinov's face beside him confirmed his hunch. She obviously knew them.

The soldier's hand disappeared under his jacket and came to rest on the Beretta. But he left it in its holster when Platinov made no move for the weapon in her purse. Yes, she knew the men. That was obvious.

The Toyota came to a halt in the street just on the other side of the parked Saturn. Now Bolan could see that the two men in the back seat were also Caucasian. The passenger window came rolling down.

"Marynka?" the man with the red bloated face said in a Russian accent. He was smiling, but the smile was mouth only and didn't reach his eyes.

The fact that both of his hands were out of sight beneath the window didn't escape the Executioner's attention, either.

Bolan kept his hand on the 93-R as Platinov said, "Hello, Fyodor." She was as tense as the man to whom she spoke.

"Who is your friend, Marynka?" the man called Fyodor asked.

"Just a friend," Platinov said. "We are currently working together."

The bloated man smiled at Bolan. "You are American, eh?" he asked.

Bolan nodded.

"Yes, I thought so," the red-faced man said, nodding. He glanced back and forth between the two of them, then said, "We have been hearing stories about your work together." The forced smile stayed on his face, but the eyes darkened even further. "This isn't good, Marynka," he said, turning back to Platinov. "We don't work with the Americans. At least not on this." Suddenly, his hand rose over the window, holding a Russian Makarov pistol.

Bolan jerked the Beretta free of shoulder leather. He fired a split second ahead of the red-faced Russian. A trio of 9 mm rounds struck the man high in the chest, but Fyodor triggered off a round from the Makarov nonetheless. The Executioner's hollowpoint rounds had thrown off his aim, however, and the bullet flew two inches to the side of Bolan's face.

Platinov seemed frozen in place, uncertain what to do.

The Executioner added another 3-round burst of sound-suppressed 9 mm slugs to Fyodor's chest, then turned the Beretta toward the back seat. Another trio of rounds took out the window and drilled on to hit at least one of the men in the back of the Toyota. Blood shot up and around the back seat, coating the rear windshield and what remained of the window. Taking a step forward, Bolan added another burst to each man. He was taking no chances.

The Beretta's slide locked back on the empty magazine, but the Executioner had already drawn the Desert Eagle. Platinov had finally decided to act, as well. She had located the H&K inside her purse, bent her knees to the level of the car window and pumped a quartet of her own 9 mm bullets past Fyodor, into the Toyota's driver. The transmission was still in drive, and as the man's dead foot slid from the brake the car rolled slowly forward into the curb next to them. Bouncing against the concrete, it stopped, its inhabitants all dead.

Bolan turned to Platinov as the roar of the gunfire died down in his ears. The Russian agent seemed frozen once more, the H&K held in a death grip and still aimed ahead of her into space. Her eyes appeared to have glazed over, and stared sightlessly into the same distance.

Marynka Platinov hadn't only known these men, but also they had been fellow Russians, and fellow agents. They had been her people. She had been forced to choose between them and Bolan; she had made her choice in a microsecond, and now the enormity of that decision was just sinking in. She was left speechless and paralyzed.

Bolan reached out and took her gently by the arm. "Get in the car," he said softly.

Platinov didn't move.

Bolan pushed gently, escorting her to the car and opening the door.

Marynka Platinov got into the Saturn on her own. But the woman sat silent as a mannequin as the Executioner drove away.

IT WAS ONLY a few blocks to the house of Diaz's sister. Which meant Bolan didn't have long to snap Platinov out of her semicatatonic reaction to the shooting. He turned a corner, then glanced to the beautiful and confused woman next to him. "Okay, let's have it," he said.

His words seemed to bring her back to reality. At least partially. Platinov turned in the seat and looked over her shoulder, as if trying to return to the scene to make sure she hadn't just imagined it. Then, slowly, she turned back and faced forward again. "It is fairly obvious. Fyodor was a fellow Russian agent. I have known him since the old KGB days." She paused and took a deep breath, then went on. "I was forced to make a decision. I did so. Now I am forced to live with that decision."

"Okay," Bolan said. "Fyodor was a fellow agent. How about the other men?"

Platinov shrugged. "I didn't recognize them, but that means nothing. I don't know everyone in Russian Intelligence."

"But you're assuming they were agents, too?"

Platinov turned to face him. "Of course. It is only logical."

Bolan shook his head as he continued to drive slowly. "Not necessarily," he said. "Something about the way that whole deal went down stinks to high heaven."

Slowly, little by little, Platinov was returning to the real world. "What do you mean?" she asked.

"Why would they try to kill us?" Bolan asked. "It doesn't make sense."

"They didn't try to kill us," Platinov said. "They tried to kill you."

"Fyodor aimed at me first. That doesn't mean his second bullet wouldn't have been aimed at you."

"Nor does it mean it would have," Platinov said. "He wanted to kill you because you would take Pollard back to America. Why in heaven's name do you think he would have killed me?"

"Call it a hunch," the soldier said. "But there was more

going on back there than Fyodor just wanting me out of th
way so he could get Pollard.''

Platinov shook her head angrily. ''You Americans and you
hunches,'' she said. ''American cowboys on television wer
always having hunches. Fyodor and the other men were Rus
sian agents sent here by the same Moscow that sent me. T
do the same job.'' She turned to Bolan. ''And I helped yo
kill them. Do you understand what that means? It means
have turned on my own people. I am a traitor.''

They were nearing the end of the directions they had bee
given. But the Soldier had no idea what they might face whe
they got to Diaz's sister's house. And if another firefight brok
out, the last thing he needed was a Platinov restricted by self
doubt. He pulled the Saturn to the side of the road in front o
a ramshackle old house. In the yard several young boys wer
kicking a half-deflated soccer ball back and forth. They gav
the Saturn curious looks but didn't stop the game.

Turning to face Platinov, Bolan stared into her tortured eyes
Behind them he saw a soul in chaos. The woman might b
one of the best no-nonsense professionals he had ever worke
with but she was only human. Right now, she needed reas
surance that she had done the right thing. She was far to
smart, however, to fall for some shallow song-and-dance num
ber. Nothing but the truth would satisfy her.

So it was the truth the Executioner presented to her. ''Let'
look at the facts,'' he said. ''We wouldn't have shot if the
hadn't. They forced you into what you did.''

''They didn't force me into anything,'' Platinov said. ''Yo
did.''

Bolan was slightly taken aback with the words. But not fo
long. While his conscious mind might not have been expectin
her to lay the blame at his feet, his heart had known all alon
why she had sided with him instead of her countrymen. Sh
wasn't trying to shift the blame; she, too, was simply speakin
the truth. She had been forced to choose between her fellow
agents and the man she knew as Mike Belasko. An American

And she had chosen him.

"You're blaming yourself for something over which you had no control," Bolan finally said. "Suppose the situation had been reversed."

"What?"

"I said, suppose things had been reversed. Suppose they'd driven up and it had been me who pulled the gun first. Suppose I decided to kill them just for being in competition with me for Pollard. Just because they were there."

Platinov hesitated before answering. "I would have killed you," she said. "Or at least died trying."

Bolan nodded. "So, don't you see? You are not a traitor to your country, Marynka. You work for Russia, not the men in that car. Your mission is to find Hugh Pollard by whatever means is necessary. You did what you had to do, and if things had been different, you'd have acted differently."

Platinov frowned slightly, letting his words sink in. She turned to face the windshield as the half-flat soccer ball suddenly struck the glass, then settled on the hood of the Saturn. "The situation isn't quite as cut-and-dried as you think."

A boy trying his best to grow a wispy mustache jerked the ball off the car.

"It never is," the soldier said as the boy muttered an apology as flat as the ball in his hands, then turned away. "There are no easy answers in our game. Things are rarely black-and-white. The decisions we make are never a hundred percent clear."

Platinov nodded silently, then shook her head as if disagreeing with herself. "I know that," she said. "What bothers me is that we never learn if the split-second decisions we made were the best ones or not."

"Like you said, you live with it." Bolan paused. "Sometimes there are no best decisions. Just decisions."

Other people—older men and women—were beginning to come out of the dilapidated houses to stare at the out-of-place Saturn. Bolan threw the transmission back into drive and pulled away from the house. "You ready to talk to Diaz's sister?" he asked.

Platinov nodded. "As ready as I will be," she said. "But I will always wonder. About both things."

Bolan frowned. "What both things?"

"Whether or not I did the right thing." Platinov paused, then added, "And whether I told you the truth."

The soldier turned to face her, his expression inquisitive.

"If the situation had been reversed," Platinov sighed. "I am not one hundred percent convinced I would have killed you. Perhaps I did the right thing back there. But perhaps I did it for the wrong reason."

Bolan turned the final corner and began searching for the house. He knew what she was inferring, and he had no reply.

But Platinov wasn't quite ready to let it drop. "Did I kill my fellow countrymen for my country?" she asked herself out loud, not expecting an answer from Bolan. "Or did I kill them because of how I feel about you?"

THE HOUSE to which they had been directed fit in well in the run-down Old City barrio. A one-story frame dwelling, it had needed paint for perhaps twenty years. The gray-brown color of rotting, termite-infested wood was far more prevalent than the white spots of paint that remained. A broken washer-dryer stood on the front porch, just past the rusting pickup that rested on concrete blocks in the front yard. What had once been a garage attached to the house had been converted into a room. A carport had been added above the short length of mud and gravel passing itself off as a driveway. One of the support columns was missing, and the carport roof sloped toward the street at a forty-five-degree angle.

Bolan parked the Saturn and he and Platinov circled the pickup to the front door. From the open windows—those not broken and repaired with cardboard or scraps of plywood—came the steady beat of samba music. As they neared the porch, the music ended and a disc jockey began to speak rapidly in Spanish.

The Executioner adjusted the Desert Eagle and Beretta, then reached out and rapped on the splintered wood of the door.

Behind it, a male voice slurred words in Spanish. Then feet shuffled toward them.

The door swung open to expose a tall barefoot Latino man wearing stained brown slacks and a ribbed undershirt that might well have lost its white at the same time as the house in which he lived. Oily black hair fell past his shoulders, finally coming to rest in snakelike coils atop overdeveloped pectoral muscles. In contrast, his heavily tattooed arms—lions, tigers, bears and a faded picture of Popeye the Sailor—seemed to have been ignored by the barbells. They hung like limp sticks at his sides. The fingers of one of his hands curled around a can of beer.

"Who the fuck are you?" the man belched in Spanish.

Before replying, Bolan studied him for a moment, trying to get a read on the man. Which would work better? Money or force? Deciding to try the easy route first, the Executioner reached into his pocket and pulled out his roll of bills.

The man had lifted the beer can halfway to his lips when the money appeared. His hand froze as he stared hungrily at the bills.

"We're looking for Arturo Diaz," Bolan said, peeling off the top two bills and extending them.

The man had reached for the money the moment Bolan's hand moved forward. But at the sound of Diaz's name, his skinny arm jerked back. His eyes lifted from the money to the Executioner's face. But in them, Bolan didn't see the fear of reprisal for selling out a friend. Instead, he saw loyalty.

. "I know no one of that name," the man said.

From behind him came a voice. "Benito, who is here?"

The man turned halfway around from the door. "Shut up!" he screamed.

"Is that Arturo's sister?" the Executioner demanded.

Before Benito could answer, a frail woman wearing ragged cutoff jeans and a soiled T-shirt appeared at his side in the doorway. Bolan still had the money in his hand, and now she stared at it. Greed filled her eyes. Or perhaps it was merely survival. The soldier couldn't tell which. But it mattered little. She wanted the money even more than the man had.

"I am the sister of Arturo Diaz," she said. "What can I—"

Benito, who was either her husband or a live-in lover, back-handed her across the mouth and sent her sprawling out of sight behind the door. "I said shut up!" he screamed.

The woman was back in a heartbeat, obviously not unaccustomed to the back of her husband's hand. "You are a fool!" she screamed at the man in the doorway. "Arturo will never keep his promise to include you! Take the money and tell these people what they want to know!"

Her words earned her another backhand. But this one didn't knock her out of sight—just dropped her to one knee, where her lip began to bleed.

Benito took a swig of beer. "Go away," he said, and started to close the door.

The Executioner felt the heat rise in his chest as he stepped forward and stuck a foot in the doorway. He didn't like wife-beaters any more than any of the other wolves of the world who took advantage of the weaker sheep. Jamming the money into his pocket with his left hand, he reached out with his right and grabbed a handful of Benito's throat. The man with the skinny arms and big chest reacted predictably, trying to pull away. Rather than fight him, Bolan allowed the move to pull him on into the house. He heard Platinov follow.

Inside the door, Bolan saw piles of dirty clothes and old newspapers. The stench of urine, feces, mold and stale beer assaulted his nostrils and filled him with disgust. But he turned his attention back to the man in his hand, his fingers tightening around Benito's throat. "My monetary offer has now been withdrawn," he said in a low voice. "Where's Arturo?" One eye stayed on the man while the other scanned an opening that led into the living area. Somewhere within the rest of the squalid house, he knew Arturo Diaz might be lurking.

Benito's frail arms had risen to his throat. Now they tried vainly to pry the Executioner's hand away. When he realized this was futile, he tried a kick. Bolan easily sidestepped the movement and bore down harder on the man's windpipe. "Where's Arturo?" he demanded again.

The woman had risen to her feet again and now she reached out with both hands, also trying to get Bolan's hands off her husband. "Please!" she screamed. "Please! Don't kill him."

"It would be the best thing that ever happened to you," Platinov said to the Executioner's side. She reached up and pulled the other woman's hands from Bolan's forearm.

"I...can...not...speak...." Benito choked out hoarsely.

Bolan let up the pressure but kept his hand around the other man's throat.

"Tell him where Arturo is!" Diaz's sister screamed. "He is using you for a fool! My brother will never include you in his plans!"

Benito was trying to rub his throat, but Bolan's hand was still in the way. "I do not—"

Bolan squeezed down again before he could add the word know.

"*Madre de Dios!*" screamed the woman. "Then I will tell you!"

The soldier turned to look at her.

"Please, let him go first. I promise I will tell you all I know."

Bolan dropped his arm. No sooner was it down than Benito slapped his wife again. The Executioner reached for him, but Platinov stepped between them. "That is enough!" she said. Grabbing Benito by the groin and the back of the hair, she pulled one way on his testicles and the other on his hair. The man shot to the crumbling wooden floor with a crack. Platinov leaned over him and jammed a forearm into the same throat Bolan had nearly ripped out a moment before. His cries of pain were quickly choked off. A moment later his eyes closed.

"Please! Do not kill him!" the woman pleaded again.,

Platinov rose to her feet. "I haven't killed him," she assured the woman. "But it is time he took a nap." She shook her head, then added, "Although like I said, it would benefit you if we did kill him."

"He is all I have."

"Then you have less than nothing," Platinov said, looking down at the unconscious man.

Bolan directed the conversation back to business. "I withdrew the offer of money from him," he said. "Not you." Pulling the bills out once more, he placed four of them in the surprised woman's palm and curled her limp fingers around them. "Where is your brother?" he asked gently.

The woman glanced down in fear, assured herself that her husband could not see or hear, then stuffed the money into her bra. "I don't know much. But I will tell you what I do."

Ranking as an equal with any Asian or Middle Eastern country, Peru offered the wonders of the past to both archaeologists and tourists. Indeed, the nation seemed to be one gigantic, mysterious and ongoing discovery. New evidence of ancient civilizations were uncovered almost daily, and these new discoveries answered many questions about mankind's past. For each question such discoveries answered, however, they seemed to ask ten more.

But it wasn't as tourists or archaeologists that Mack Bolan and Marynka Platinov had come to Lima. And the only mystery that interested them was the one concerning the whereabouts of former CIA Director Hugh Pollard.

Bolan lifted the cup of strong Brazilian coffee to his lips as he watched Platinov press the receiver from the black pay phone in the corner against her ear. He sat at a corner table in the airport restaurant, glancing around the room as he waited, more from habit than from necessity. He had learned many things in regard to combat and survival over the years. Those lessons had been ingrained into his soul, and were now as much a part of him as eating, sleeping or breathing. One of them was that whenever he entered a new building, a new room or a new area of any kind, he looked for escape paths. He had done this so many times he no longer realized it on a conscious level. Now, as his eyes scanned the restaurant, he saw it was little different than that of any other airport eating establishment at any major terminal the world over. Several doors led into the glass walls that separated the room from the concourses. Along one wall was a cafeteria-style food line, with bottles of beer and soft drinks jammed into a tub of ice next to the cash register. The tables were of aluminum and simulated leather, and the waitresses wore conservative blue skirt-suits not unlike the female flight attendants who passed outside on their way to or from their flights.

The soldier nodded unconsciously. Exit could be made through any of the entrances. The only other way out was behind him, unseen, through the swinging steel doors he had to assume led to the kitchen.

Bolan watched Platinov tap the buttons on the phone as he took another sip of the strong coffee. He had offered to let her use the phone aboard the Grimaldi-flown jet that had brought them to Lima, but she had politely declined. He hadn't had to ask why. The Russian agent had a snitch in Lima. She had called him Carlos—which meant his real name would be anything except Carlos. She knew any call made from American-owned equipment in the possession of the soldier could likely be traced at a later date. And regardless of how she felt about Bolan personally, she had no intention of sharing her sources with a country that was a friend one day but an enemy the next. He couldn't blame her. He would have done the same.

As he waited, Bolan watched people of all nationalities enter and leave the restaurant. A Muslim woman wearing a veil entered behind her husband. An obviously American family, wearing Bermuda shorts and T-shirts, paraded to the cafeteria line. A short stocky Asian man in a conservative business suit and black horn-rimmed glasses stopped in the doorway. He surveyed the room, didn't see the person he was looking for, glanced at his watch and left.

Setting the coffee back down on the table, Bolan watched Platinov cup a hand around the mouthpiece. She had taken a small notebook and pen from her purse, and now jotted something down. He could guess what it was—another phone number. If the snitch was as good as she claimed, he'd have several levels of security built up around him.

If he didn't, he wouldn't last long in this game.

Platinov hung up the phone, and dialed the new number. Bolan saw her eyes flicker to the pay phone number printed on the instrument. A second later she tapped the number into the phone and hung up again. She waited against the wall, and thirty seconds later the phone rang. Her hips bobbed provocatively in her tight blue jeans as she reached for the receiver.

Bolan nodded silently to himself. It was a common enough system. The snitch had one number, which he gave her. She called it and got another number to call. Then she entered the number from which she was calling, he received the information at yet a third phone, double-checked to insure she hadn't called from an office with equipment where his call could be pinned down, then called her back.

Or so he thought. Bolan watched Platinov turn her back to him and the rest of the customers in the restaurant as she grabbed the receiver on the second ring. He also saw a slight movement of her elbow, which brought a smile to his face.

The soldier waited, glancing to the side wall as a party of men and women wearing tour-group name tags, and clucking away excitedly in French, began at the salad line. Two more Asians carrying briefcases followed them silently. He looked back to Platinov.

Turning sideways now, Platinov began to speak. Gradually, Bolan saw her face grow angry until she practically spit words into the receiver. The conversation lasted less than a minute, during which she gripped the notepad and pen in fingers that threatened to crush them. Finally, she slammed the receiver back into the cradle. The soldier saw another subtle movement of her elbow as she turned her back once more—the kind of movement one might make to pull something off the receiver. Something that had been planted on it when she first answered the phone.

And that something now dropped just as subtly into her purse as she turned back and started across the room to the table.

By now the French tourists and Asian businessmen had

found tables and were eating. As Platinov crossed the room, the short stocky Asian man who had surveyed the restaurant earlier returned in the company of three more countrymen in business suits. He pointed to the table where the other Asians sat, said something to his friends in what sounded like Korean and the quartet hurried to its table.

Platinov sat next to Bolan, her face seething with controlled rage. She lifted the cup waiting on the table in front of her to her lips and made another angry face, which told the soldier her coffee had grown cold, then she set it back down. A little too hard. Brown fluid spilled up and over the sides onto the table.

"I take it things didn't go quite the way you'd hoped."

"Very observant," Platinov said. She mopped up the coffee with her napkin.

"What happened?"

"He knows why I am here, and he knows how important it is. And unless he is lying, he knows where Pollard is."

"So he's holding out for big bucks?"

"Not only that. He is planning a bidding war." Platinov started to lift her cup, remembered the temperature of the coffee and set it back down. "He is a mercenary little bastard," she said. "He plans to sell to the highest bidder."

Bolan nodded. It wasn't unusual in the world of shadow warriors and their informants. Snitches rarely had loyalties to anyone but themselves. And in this case, it was a seller's market. With a lot of buyers eager to purchase the whereabouts of Hugh Pollard.

"Did you arrange to meet him?" Bolan asked.

Platinov laughed. "He isn't going to tell me where he is under these conditions," she said. "He knows he has made me angry enough to get the information from him for free."

"So why don't we?" Bolan asked. He finished his coffee and set the empty cup back down.

Platinov frowned. "Why don't we what?"

"Get the information for free."

"And how do you propose we locate him?"

"I'd propose we take that little tracking device you just dropped into your purse and go find a place to send the number it traced to your people. They'll locate the phone, and we'll be on our way." He paused, then added, "Of course, Carlos might not still be there, but it's a start."

Platinov started to protest, but Bolan interrupted her. "If you'd rather send the info to my people, we can do that, too. My computer man might not have the exact frequencies you used, but it won't take him two minutes to figure them out."

There could be only one reason Platinov had tried to hide the tracker from Bolan—she planned to pass the information on to other Russian agents without his knowledge, let them pick Pollard up and cut Bolan out of the deal. For that reason he expected an increase in the anger and frustration Platinov had already exhibited, and was surprised when she suddenly laughed.

"We can do that here," she said. Reaching into her purse, she pulled the tiny tracker out. Bolan studied it briefly. No bigger than the smallest TV remote control, it had a window through which he could see a digital readout of a phone number. But at the same time he read the number, he felt a cold chill crawl up the back of his spine.

The Korean businessmen at the table across the room had spoken softly as they ate—too softly to be clearly heard from where Bolan and Platinov sat. Now they suddenly stopped talking. The Executioner realized suddenly that while he hadn't heard their words, he had picked up enough of their conversation to realize they were North Korean, not South Korean.

Before he could say anything, Platinov rose, returned to the pay phone and tapped in more numbers. Bolan kept one eye on her, the other on the Koreans, as he watched her read the number from the tracker into the receiver. The Koreans returned to their conversation, acting as if they had noticed nothing. Bolan knew why.

They were good, and they had done it inconspicuously. But just as he had done, they had watched Platinov attach the

Rogue Target

device to the phone. Now, again as he was doing, they were waiting for the Russian to get her information back from Moscow. They wouldn't make their move until she returned. But as soon as she had what they wanted, all hell was likely to break loose.

Slowly, casually, the Executioner reached under the table and drew the Desert Eagle. He kept it hidden as he pretended to drink more coffee from his empty cup.

Two minutes later Platinov was back. "I have an address," she said.

"Good," Bolan said. "But we've got something that needs taking care of first."

Platinov frowned. "What?" she said.

"A gunfight," the Executioner said.

He rose from his chair as the North Korean agents suddenly stood and drew weapons.

MARYNKA PLATINOV KNEW she was in trouble the moment she decided to hide the tracking device. Not physical trouble— that wouldn't come until after they had found Hugh Pollard and she tried to steal him away from the big man sitting across the room at the table. Belasko wouldn't try to hurt her until that time came. In fact, she had sensed in him—both in the past and in the present—a basic goodness that meant he wouldn't even hurt her then if he could possibly keep from it. Which was one of the things that was causing her to fall in love with him.

And that, Platinov knew, was indeed the source of her trouble. It was emotional, not physical.

Platinov felt a flush flow to her face as she shielded the small tracking device from view with her body. She shifted her weight casually from one leg to the other, knowing it would make her ass wiggle provocatively in the tight jeans. The movement was designed to distract his eye while she attached the device to the phone, much like the sleight-of-hand techniques employed by a magician. Or was it? she wondered as she pressed the tracker's suction cup to the receiver. What was her real motive? Had she wiggled her hips to distract or entice him? She was no longer sure. But of one thing she was certain. She knew Belasko well enough to know that nothing she could do sexually would deter him from his mission. Oh, he was attracted to her. Of that she had no doubt. He was, after all, only a man. And he had proved he was attracted to her in the past—proved it, in fact, better than any man she had ever known.

A smile crossed Platinov's face at the memory, then faded into a frown. She tapped the number into the phone. As she waited for the call to go through, she again questioned her motives. Was she hiding the tracker from him in order to cut him out and pass Carlos's location on to other Russian agents as she had originally told herself? Or was she just looking for an easy way out of the inevitable dilemma they were about to face? Was she looking for a way in which they might avoid the upcoming conflict and perhaps have a life together?

And was she, Marynka Platinov, a former KGB officer and now a Russian Intelligence colonel, really thinking like this?

Platinov kept the phone blocked from view as she continued to wait for it to be answered. Carlos finally answered, and told her of his plans to sell Pollard to the highest bidder. She was angry at herself already, and the snitch's smug confidence increased that anger to rage. She glanced to the tracker, keeping the informant on the line as the digits of the number from which he was calling appeared, one by one, in the window.

It took all the self-discipline she possessed to keep from screaming. Instead, she said simply, "I'll check with Moscow, Carlos. I'll find out what they're willing to pay, and get back to you."

"Use the same number," Carlos said insolently.

Platinov hung up and returned to the table to find her ruse hadn't worked. He knew she had tracked Carlos's number. She was surprised that this didn't anger her further, and even more surprised when she found herself laughing that he had caught her. She supposed it amused her because he had proved, once again, that he was the best at this game.

The Russian woman returned to the phone, dialed Moscow gave them the number and waited as they traced the infor mation through the Peruvian telephone system. When she had obtained the address that corresponded to the number, she re turned to the table. "I have an address," she announced.

"Good," the soldier said. "But we've got something tha needs taking care of first."

Platinov felt herself frown, wondering what could be more important than finding Carlos before the agents from othe countries whisked him away from under their noses. "What?" she asked.

"A gunfight."

Suddenly, he was standing before her with the big Deser Eagle in his hand. With the other hand, he leaned across the table and knocked her off her feet.

Platinov fell to the floor as explosions sounded in her ea and bullets whisked over her head. She rolled to her side jamming a hand into her purse for the Heckler & Koch Around her she could hear the screams of the men, women and children who had found themselves in the wrong airpor restaurant at the wrong time. The sounds of terror were drowned out periodically by roaring gunfire. Beneath the table Platinov could see several sets of legs in dark slacks. From the way they stood and moved, it was obvious these men were the ones firing. Lining up the three-dot sights of her H&K she depressed the squeeze-cocker on the front of the grip and sent a 115-grain semijacketed hollowpoint round into the groin of the nearest man. His howls rose over the gunfire as he fell to the floor, grasping his crotch with both hands. A Korean Type 68 pistol, a much modified version of her country's own Russian Tokarev, fell next to him. The weapon—and the Asian face grimacing in both pain and horror—told her all she needed to know.

The men were North Korean agents. They had followed their own set of leads to Lima, spotted her from intelligence photos and hung around the restaurant to find out what she knew.

The big .44 Magnum continued to blare above her as Platinov switched her sights to another set of legs. Her next round caught a man in the upper thigh. A geyser of blood shot forth as if driven from a fire hose as the 9 mm slug clipped his femoral artery in half. He fell next to his partner on the floor.

The Russian agent rose to one knee, cautiously bringing her eyes above the table. In her peripheral vision, she saw her partner in a combat crouch, firing the Desert Eagle with his right hand as his left hooked under his arm and found the Beretta. The Desert Eagle's slide locked back empty. Then, almost faster than her eye could follow, he jammed it into his waistband and began firing the sound-suppressed machine pistol. Softly coughing trios of 9 mm rounds now replaced the .44 Magnum explosions.

Turning her own weapon toward one of the two remaining men, Platinov took up the slack in the trigger. But before she could fire, a near silent 3-round burst sheared off the top of the man's head. She swung the H&K to the last Korean, who was bolting toward one of the doors in the glass wall. Beyond the wall, in the corridor outside, she could see people frozen in their tracks, their mouths gaping open in awe. She pulled the trigger but her 9 mm hollow point round was a split second behind the three from Belasko's Beretta. All four rounds met in the middle of the Korean's back and sent him flying forward. He crashed headfirst into the transparent wall next to the door, shattering the glass into thousands of tiny shards.

Down the corridor, whistles sounded. Platinov took a step forward and saw men in brown police uniforms running toward the restaurant.

"Let's go," the big American ordered. He pulled her past the cafeteria line and through a set of gray steel doors she hadn't noticed before. They sprinted past cooks and other employees who were crouching behind stoves, tables and chairs, and out another door to the outside of the building. A black-and-white Peruvian police car had been sent to cover the back, and it screeched to a halt just as they emerged into the sunlight.

Before the driver could get out or draw a weapon, Belasko leaped forward. With his left hand, he grabbed the driver's collar and jerked the man's head through the open window. Platinov watched him send a dynamite-filled right cross straight into the officer's nose. Blood spurted forth as Belasko released the man's collar and a set of gold lieutenant's bars that had been ripped from the uniform blouse fell to the ground outside the car.

Platinov sprinted to the front of the vehicle and aimed the H&K through the windshield at the other cop in the passenger seat. She nodded her head sideways, and yelled, "Get out!" The other officer—wearing sergeant's stripes—got out of the car with his hands in the air. Platinov stepped forward and brought the H&K down on top of his head. He sprawled on the pavement.

"Get his hat," her partner told her. She looked up to see he had pulled the driver from the car and dropped him on the ground. He already wore the man's eight-point cap.

The Russian immediately understood why. She leaned down, grabbing the other hat from the ground where it had fallen. Tucking her hair up beneath the crown, she slid into the passenger side of the vehicle.

Belasko slumped in the seat, keeping the fact that the hat was the only part of the uniform he wore out of sight beneath the window. Platinov did the same. "Keep your face hidden, too," he ordered as he backed the car around and started back in the direction from which the officers had come. "They don't have women officers down here. And you don't look like a man."

Platinov dropped her face to the floor of the car as they drove past two other police cars speeding toward the back of the restaurant. "I'm delighted you noticed," she said under her breath.

The American didn't reply.

A MILE FROM THE AIRPORT, Bolan pulled the police car into an alley in a residential neighborhood. They left the hats on

he seat, and walked quickly past the trash cans, chain-link
nd wooden fences and other debris that decorated the packed-
dirt pathway. On the other side of the block, the first vehicle
hey came to was a ten-year-old Chevy Blazer.

"I will keep watch while you hot-wire it," Platinov said.

Bolan glanced through the driver's window. "No need," he
aid. "The keys are inside." A moment later they were driving
way.

The address Platinov had obtained took them to an upper-
middle-class house that would have been right at home in a
similar neighborhood in the United States. Bolan frowned at
he brick home as he drove slowly past. The curtains on the
front windows were closed. There was a basketball net in the
driveway, and an assortment of yard ornaments decorating the
well-kept grass. "You must pay him well," he said.

"Too well. But that is about to stop."

Parking the Blazer two houses down, Bolan and Platinov
got out and walked to the door.

Carlos had not expected to be found. He had counted on
he system of calls and return calls to keep him secluded from
Platinov and the other clandestine operatives he was trying to
play against each other. He sat alone, on a threadbare couch
n the living room, engrossed in an Argentinean sex magazine.
A rerun of *Happy Days* was playing on the television when
he Executioner kicked in his front door.

Carlos looked up in surprise as Bolan burst into the room,
he Desert Eagle leading the way. Platinov wasn't far behind
with her H&K trained on the man's head. She wasted no time,
striding across the room and stopping two paces in front of
he man on the couch. She glanced down at his lap, then back
up into the frightened eyes. "Zip up your pants, you disgusting
little worm," she barked.

His face turning purple, Carlos covered himself with the
magazine as he complied. Behind Bolan, on TV, dubbed-in
Spanish voices spoke for Richie Cunningham and Arthur
Fonzerelli.

Transferring the H&K to her left hand, Platinov slapped the

magazine away from Carlos's trembling fingers and sent i
flying across the room. She brought a backhand across hi
face, which sent him rollicking to his side on the couch
Reaching down, she grabbed a handful of his thinning hai
and jerked him back to a sitting position, then doubled-up he
fist and knocked him to his other side with a right hook. "Si
up, you little rat bastard!" she ordered.

A trickle of blood ran from Carlos's lip down his chin a
he returned to a sitting position. He stared at the Russia
woman towering over him. His face was a mask of both terro
and awe.

Bolan studied the man. No, his name wasn't likely to b
Carlos. He was clearly not Hispanic, looking more to be o
northern European descent with his thinning blond hair an
light skin. Probably a descendent of the many Germans wh
had immigrated to South America after World War II. Whe
they'd entered the house, he had been wearing rimless spec
tacles, but now they lay on the hardwood floor to the side o
the couch. Miraculously, they hadn't broken.

Platinov hit the man again. His head rocked back, and h
coughed out a white tooth gleaming with red. Bolan stoo
back and watched. Carlos was Platinov's informant and ha
tried to double-cross her, and Bolan saw no reason to interfer
with her tactics. Besides, the Russian hadn't been performin
up to her usual standard of proficiency recently. He suspecte
he knew why, and that situation would eventually have to b
dealt with. But right now she needed to prove to herself sh
could still execute her duties and regain her self-confidence.

"Stand up, you slime bag," Platinov ordered, and took
short step back to give him room.

As soon as he was on his feet, Platinov raised the H&K an
pressed the barrel against his forehead. A metallic click echoe
through the room as she depressed the squeeze-cocker. "So,'
she said in a low, menacing whisper, "you would play game
with me, Carlos? You snotty little bastard. You have been wel
paid by me and my people for years. This is how you woul
repay us?"

"Marynka—" Carlos started to plead, but the H&K acros

his face cut off the words and knocked him back to the couch once more. Platinov stepped forward as blood began to gush from the man's cheek where the squeeze-cocker's front sight had ripped through the flesh. This time she stuck the pistol barrel inside his mouth. The little man began to sniffle. Tears poured from his eyes to mix with the blood on his face.

"You are going to take us to Pollard. Now." Platinov said. "Am I correct?"

The H&K bobbed up and down in time with Carlos's nodding head.

"Stand up!" Platinov shouted. She pulled the gun from his mouth.

Carlos rose slowly and warily to his feet, thoroughly cowered. "My face...." he whined.

Platinov snatched up the skin magazine, rolled it into a small paper club and smacked him across the mouth with it. "Your face will be no uglier than before," she snapped. Grabbing a throw pillow from the couch, she jammed it into his hand. "Press it against the skin to stop the bleeding. It is not deep." She glowered at the little man with the contempt one might have for maggots eating rotten flesh.

Carlos took the pillow and started to press it against his face. Then, suddenly, he bolted past the woman standing before him toward the door. Bolan took a step to the side and reached out, grabbing him by the shirt collar. The soldier shifted his weight and, using the little man's own forward momentum, spun him and sent him flying back to the couch.

Carlos's head struck the wall just above the back rest, adding a new injury to those Platinov had already given him. He twisted back around, the red lump on his forehead already the size of an egg.

Platinov looked down at him with an almost pitying expression on her face. "Carlos, Carlos, Carlos," she said, shaking her head. Then, reaching down, she grabbed one of his ears and began dragging him toward the door. Tiny whelps escaped his split lips behind the pillow. Bolan turned and led the way back out the door.

When they reached the Blazer, Carlos dropped the pillow from his blood-and-tear-streaked face long enough to whimper, "Marynka...will I get paid for this?"

Platinov's eyes shot to Bolan's. They held a look of awe. She shook her head again in amazement, then opened the rear door and pushed Carlos inside. Taking the passenger seat as Bolan slid behind the wheel, she finally answered the question. Her voice was vaguely weary as she said, "Yes, you will be paid." She turned in the seat and rested an arm over the back as Bolan pulled away from the curb. "Carlos, do you have any family?" she asked.

The question sounded strange under the circumstances. But from behind the pillow Carlos said, "Yes...a sister in Heidelberg."

Platinov nodded, then turned back to face the front. "Good," she said. "Please make sure I get her address." After a brief pause, she continued. "I haven't decided exactly what to do with you after we find Pollard," she added. "But if I kill you, I'll send your money to your sister."

ANCON, A SEASIDE resort town roughly twenty-five miles north of Lima, was a haven for sunbathers, patrons of all water sports and expatriates the world over. Many were American. Which made it the perfect place for a man like Hugh Pollard to hide in plain sight.

The cottage Carlos pointed out stood just far enough from the sea to be out of reach of the incoming tide. It looked little different from dozens of others that scattered the beach. Bolan guided the Blazer along the asphalt road that followed the curvature of the beach, fifty yards inland. As they passed the cottage, the soldier saw a shadow pass by one of the windows facing the road. Someone was home. Pollard? Bolan felt his teeth tighten against his jaw. After all they had been through, it suddenly seemed just a little too easy.

Pulling off the road a quarter mile past the cottage, the soldier threw the transmission into park and turned to the back seat. "Carlos," he said. "Are you sure that's where he is?"

Carlos nodded. "I have been out here before. To see him for myself—right after I first heard the rumor that he was in Ancon." The blood-soaked throw pillow sat on the back seat next to the informant, and he turned to glance at it now. "I wouldn't pass on information like this without being certain."

"Unless you thought you could make a dime at it," Platinov, who had turned in her seat next to Bolan, said sarcastically.

Carlos's hand rose to his face and gently tapped the bandage on his cheek. Bolan had found a basic first-aid kit in the glove compartment of the Blazer, and Platinov had—somewhat reluctantly—dressed her informant's wounds. His face was now spotted with white gauze and adhesive tape, with antibiotic cream squeezing out around the edges of the bandages. "I am telling the truth," he said.

"You're sure?" Bolan repeated.

"I am certain," Carlos said. "I wouldn't lie to you." He tapped his face lightly again. "Especially not after this."

"You'd better not," Platinov said. "I'm the nice one. If I find out you have been playing more games, I will let my partner have his turn."

The soldier weighed the facts in his mind. He didn't doubt that Carlos believed Pollard was in the house. The beating Platinov had given the little snitch would keep him honest—at least for a while. But he could simply be wrong.

Swiveling her head to Bolan, Platinov suddenly switched languages. "What do you think?" she asked in Russian.

"He doesn't speak Russian?" the Executioner asked, glancing to Carlos's blank face.

Platinov shook her head. "Only a—how do you say in English?—smattering. If we speak reasonably fast, he will pick up nothing."

Bolan glanced again to Carlos. If the man understood their words, he wasn't acting like it.

"What do you think?" Platinov asked again.

"I think this is suddenly far too easy," the Executioner replied. His eyes rose above the skinny shoulder of the man in the back seat to stare at the cottage through the Blazer's back windshield. "There are things that simply don't add up. If it's really Pollard we just saw through the window, he was already as safe here as he was going to get. Unless—"

Platinov read his mind, turned back to Carlos and returned to speaking Spanish. "When did you learn he was here?" she demanded.

"Just the day before yesterday," the little German said. "I came out here to make sure yesterday."

Bolan nodded to himself. It was as he'd guessed. "No one knew Pollard was even in South America until he showed up in Rio at Axe Imports," he said in Russian. "That's when the whole world started looking for him. Word leaked out and found its way back to Carlos—not the other way around. That's when Carlos began focusing on exactly where in South America Pollard might be."

Platinov squinted in concentration. "Which means the big question is why did Pollard decide to go to Axe in the first place? We have assumed so far that he wanted Axe's aid in helping him hide."

Bolan nodded. "But like I just said, he was already as well hidden as he was going to get. He took a chance going to Rio—a chance he didn't have to take."

Platinov's frown deepened. "Perhaps word of his presence here leaked out before? Perhaps someone found out he was here? Maybe someone we don't know about?"

"That's a lot of perhaps and maybes," Bolan said. "And if that was the case, why did he come back here after Rio?"

"Perhaps he had no other place to go," Platinov offered. "With Axe dead."

"It's possible, but it's thin. It looks to me like Hugh Pollard was doing just fine right here, masquerading as a retired American businessman or college professor or whatever cover story he came up with. Keep in mind that Pollard wasn't the usual political appointee who lands the spot of CIA director. He worked his way up in rank all the way from field op. He knew his business, and his cover would have been good."

Platinov nodded. "Yes, we have that information, of course."

Russian Intelligence wouldn't be much of an outfit if it hadn't. "There's got to be another explanation as to why he went to Rio to see Wayne Axe," Bolan said.

"Yes," Platinov said. "I agree that is more likely. But what is it?"

The Executioner shook his head. "I don't know. But I think it's about time we found out." He reached for the door handle. "You see anyone else around the house? Any signs that anyone else might be inside?" He twisted to stare back at the cottage again. An old Ford pickup sat in the gravel driveway. Broken seashells formed a lawn of sorts between the house and the asphalt road. Looking past the house to the sandy beach, Bolan could see a few men and women in bathing suits walking along the shoreline or seated on towels and in reclining chairs. A group of teenagers played a rag-tag game of volleyball using a rope with torn remnants of netting hanging down. None were within two hundred feet of the house. And there was no visible sign that they, or anyone else except whoever drove the pickup, had any connection to it.

Opening the door, Bolan got out. Platinov joined him on his side of the Blazer and they took each other's hands without thinking—just another happy couple taking a few minutes out of their day to enjoy the ocean. But Bolan felt a jolt of electricity go through him as his fingers wrapped around those of the woman. Platinov jerked slightly, and he knew she'd felt it, too.

The Executioner forced the sudden emotion away from his heart and brain. This was no time for distractions.

With her other hand, Platinov reached back and opened the door to the backseat.

"I can wait here," Carlos said, his voice holding a trace of hope.

"And I can grab your ear again if you don't get out." Platinov said sternly.

Carlos joined them.

"Here is the story," Platinov told him. "We are a couple. You are our friend. And I use the term *friend* loosely."

"When we get up to the door, we're lost and stopping to ask directions," the soldier added. "You just let me do the talking until we're sure it's him. All you have to do, Carlos, is keep your mouth shut."

"I can do that," Carlos said, nodding anxiously. He fell in at Bolan's side as the soldier and Platinov began strolling down the asphalt, still holding hands, toward the cottage.

As they neared the small house, Bolan could see movement once more through the screen that covered the open window. As they drew even closer, he could make out a face seated at a wooden table inside a kitchen. The man wasn't Hispanic. But that didn't mean he was Hugh Pollard. Bolan watched out of the corner of his eye as they passed the window. The man at the kitchen table was eating a bowl of cereal. His hair had been buzzed into a short stubby cut, and he sported a beard and mustache. He didn't look like the pictures Bolan had seen of the clean-shaved former director. On the other hand, a change in looks could only be expected under the circumstances.

Whoever he might be, the man in the kitchen was observant. His head shot up from his cereal bowl to the window as they passed.

Platinov had to have seen him look at them, too. "Honey," she drawled loudly in an accent that made her sound as if she'd graduated from the University of Alabama, "I told you to look at the cotton-picking map. If you'd listen to me once in a while, we might actually get where we want to go."

Stepping up onto the porch, Bolan slipped one hand under his shirt to the Beretta. With the other he rapped on the door. Platinov rambled on, complaining to her "husband," her voice continuing to sound as if she should be sitting in a porch swing sipping a mint julep. But one of her hands was out of sight in her purse.

Footsteps crossed the house behind the door. Bolan heard the knob being twisted. He reminded himself that Hugh Pollard was a highly skilled clandestine operative and combatant. The Executioner tightened his grip on the 93-R. If a fight broke out, he'd do his best to take Pollard alive. But if a choice had to be made, dead ex-CIA director was preferable to one in the hands of another country.

A moment later the door swung open. The man with the beard and short hair wore a white T-shirt, gray work pants, and appeared unarmed. He looked up at the Executioner with an uncertain face.

It was Pollard, all right. In spite of the short hair and beard, Bolan could see it now in the undecided eyes. With his right hand still on the gun beneath his shirt, Bolan reached for the man's neck with his left. Strangely, the movement seemed to calm rather than frighten the man.

"Wait," Pollard said. "Let me—"

Ignoring the man's protest, the Executioner grabbed a handful of Hugh Pollard's neck. His right hand came away from the Beretta, cocking behind his shoulder in preparation to punch. He was about to deliver a knock-out right cross when Pollard's voice rose in both pitch and volume. "Wait!" he said again, then went limp in the Executioner's grasp.

Bolan held the man up by the neck and stopped the right cross halfway to Pollard's jaw.

Pollard stared at the big fist almost in his face, and a nervous smile played at his lips. "We need to talk," he coughed around the Executioner's fingers. "Please. Won't you come in?"

6

Slowly, the Executioner let his fist fall to his side. The fac[e] above his other hand, beneath the buzz cut and stubby bear[d] began to relax. The strength appeared to return to Hugh Pol[l]lard's legs, and Bolan released the man's throat and let hi[m] stand on his own.

Pollard's face took on a weary smile as he turned to loo[k] at Platinov, then gave Carlos a cursory glance. Turning bac[k] to the beautiful Russian woman, he said, "Marynka Platinov[,] I should have known Russia would send their best." His ches[t] jiggled in a nervous chuckle that looked more forced tha[n] natural; rather than amusement, it bespoke an edgy relief tha[t] he wasn't about to be shot. "Although your Southern accen[t] could use a little work."

Bolan kept a close eye on the man as a moment of uneas[y] silence fell over the people on the porch. He was getting th[e] feeling that there was far more to Pollard's situation than h[e] knew at this point. But he couldn't let himself forget that Pol[l]lard was a well-trained master of deception.

The man with the newly grown beard turned back to th[e] Executioner. "You're American?" he asked.

Bolan nodded.

Pollard returned the nod. "Not from my outfit, though," h[e] said, changing the nod to a shake of the head.

"No," the Executioner said.

Pollard stared up into Bolan's eyes. The Executioner coul[d] almost see the wheels turning. "I didn't think so," the forme[r]

CIA director said. He rubbed his neck where Bolan's fingers had left the skin red. "Military intelligence of some sort?"

Bolan shook his head.

Pollard answered with another nod. "I didn't figure that, either," he said. "You know, the CIA doesn't know everything that goes on in the world—not even everything in the intelligence community within our own country. But from time to time, there have been rumors about a...shall we just call it a special group that does work similar to ours?"

Bolan didn't respond.

"What should I call you?"

"Mike Belasko."

"Please. Come in. We need to talk."

Bolan reached out, grabbing the man's arm this time. "We don't need to talk," he said. "You're going back to the U.S. with me." Out of the corner of his eye, he watched Platinov for a reaction. There was none.

"Please," Pollard said. "We—all of us—have something we need to do here first. Give me five minutes. If I can't convince you, I'll go back with you willingly." He glanced to Platinov once again. "It would be preferable to going to Moscow, I'm sure. No offense, Colonel Platinov."

"None taken," Platinov said. "And from your point of view, you are correct."

Bolan hesitated. From the time the door had opened, he had gotten the gut feeling that there was something going on behind the scenes—some reason that Pollard had gone to see Wayne Axe that had nothing to do with Axe helping the former CIA man hide out. And Pollard hadn't attempted to either flee or fight when he saw Bolan. He had seemed relieved. It was almost as if he had hoped an American he could trust would find him.

The Executioner decided to play along with the man and see where it led. He raised his watch to his eyes. "Your five minutes start now," he said.

"Then please," Pollard said. "Come in." He turned back

into the house, slow enough to make sure the Executioner could tell it wasn't a trick.

Bolan's hand returned to the butt of the Beretta anyway.

TRAILING A STEP behind Pollard, his eyes glued to the man's hands, Bolan led Platinov and Carlos into the small living room. The curtains to the side of a sliding glass door led to a patio, and framed a peaceful view of the sea. The view it offered looked like some giant postcard or a travel poster that might read Come To Peru!.

Pollard stopped in the middle of the room and waved at the furniture. "Make yourselves comfortable," he said.

Bolan continued to keep his eyes on the man as he took a seat in a rocking chair next to a small coffee table. Through the glass door, he could see the whitecaps as the incoming waves hit the reef a hundred yards from the house, broke, then bubbled onto the sand. Platinov dropped into a recliner on the other side of the table but didn't recline, sitting instead on the edge of the seat and leaning forward, one hand still hidden inside her purse.

The living room and kitchen were actually one big open area, and now Pollard pulled a straight-backed aluminum chair away from the kitchen table. He started to sit, then suddenly stopped. A smile crossed his lips. "Let me get us something to drink," he said.

"Be very, very careful while you do," Bolan said. He glanced to his watch again. "And keep in mind your five minutes are rolling."

Pollard nodded and turned back to the refrigerator. Quickly, he opened the door, and pulled out a bottle of Cook's champagne. From a cabinet next to the refrigerator, he took down four champagne glasses, then returned to the living room. "A small celebration," he said, taking a seat on the kitchen chair. The glasses clinked together musically as he placed them on the coffee table between him and Bolan.

Platinov looked at the man as if he'd just grown a second head. "You want to celebrate the fact that you will soon be in an American prison?'' she asked, then glanced to Bolan. ''Or, perhaps, in Siberia?''

The fear seemed to have left the former CIA man altogether now. He laughed. ''No, Colonel Platinov,'' he said. ''I want to celebrate finally 'coming in the from the cold,' as they say in spy novels.'' His eyes fell to her hand inside the purse. ''You won't find any need for that,'' he smiled. ''The only weapons I have in the house are kitchen knives and a cheap folder I bought to take to Rio. But hang on to your gun if it makes you feel better.''

''I will,'' Platinov said.

Carlos stood awkwardly to Bolan's side, like all informants always the outsider when real operatives gathered. Pollard glanced at him. It was clear that the former CIA director knew what, if not precisely who, the man was. ''Does he speak English?'' he asked Bolan.

''Yes. And Spanish. But not Russian,'' Platinov answered.

Pollard nodded and immediately switched to Russian. ''And the fact that you answered me explains who he belongs to,'' he said. The cork popped from the bottle and he waited while a small amount of foam ran over the top, then settled. The former CIA director poured three glasses and handed them around. ''I'm not going to ask you anything about your...special group,'' he said, as he extended Bolan his.

''I couldn't answer you if you did,'' the soldier answered in Russian as he took the glass from the man's hand.

''Nor would I expect you to,'' Pollard came back. He continued to speak as he filled the last glass. ''But I must ask one question. I hate to be blunt but if you refuse to answer, I'll refuse to talk.'' He stopped pouring long enough to hold a hand up and halt any response. ''Yes, you could beat whatever information you want out of me. But it'll save time if I cooperate. And believe me, when I get finished, you'll realize we don't have that much time.''

''Ask your question and let's find out,'' Bolan said. He raised his wrist and looked at his watch once more. ''And I'd get started if I were you.''

Pollard squinted hard at the big fellow American, as if sizing him up. "My guess is you're a man of honor, so I think you'll answer me honestly. What is your mission in relationship to me?"

"To get you back to Washington to stand trial before some other country gets their hands on you," Bolan said simply.

Pollard nodded. He finished pouring the glass of champagne he had started but left it on the table. "And your mission would be to take me to Moscow for debriefing," he said to Platinov. Then, to both of them, "Hear my story. I think I can convince you of two things. First, I will go with one of you willingly. But second, we can't go yet." He raised the champagne glass, then set it down again. "I won't ask how the two of you came to be working together, either. In the world of clandestine operations, you never know who you'll end up in bed with." He expression didn't change but the double entendre was evident. "But have you decided how you're going to divide me now that you have me?"

Platinov looked at him coldly. "No," she said.

"But eventually, the fact that your missions conflict is going to make things extremely interesting for all three of us." Pollard finally lifted his glass. "But let's drink to what I'm about to share with you." He lifted the glass to his lips.

Bolan felt the impatience rise in his chest again. Pollard was indeed a seasoned operative. But he had also been the CIA director, which meant he had turned into a politician, as well, with all the pomp and ceremony that entailed. Bolan was a soldier, and he had no use or time for all the formalities. He took a quick sip of champagne, then set his glass back on the coffee table. "Okay," he said. "We've had more than enough preliminaries. You have two minutes left before I throw your butt in the car and take you back to Washington to stand trial."

Pollard nodded. After another glance away from Bolan to Platinov, he said, "It comes in two parts."

"Fine," Bolan said tersely. "Start with the first."

"About two years ago," Pollard said, "I began to suspect there was a traitor—a double agent—highly placed within the

CIA. Periodically, we got intelligence reports from the field concerning new, and highly sophisticated weaponry, showing up in the hands of other countries—China in particular. These new weapons were not exactly the same as ours, mind you, but they were close enough that they wouldn't have been possible without the same technology that had been exclusively ours only months before.''

Platinov snorted through her nose. ''You Americans never cease to amaze me,'' she said. ''You think you are the only people with brains? You find it impossible that other minds could have developed similar technology?''

Pollard smiled tolerantly. ''No,'' he said. ''I don't. But I think it's unlikely that so many of these developments could have happened so quickly. At least by coincidence.''

''Go on,'' Bolan said. As Pollard spoke, he listened carefully, constantly trying to balance two contrary possibilities in his mind. On the surface Pollard's story stank of the typical cover someone who had sold out his country would invent. On the other hand, there was always the chance the man was telling the truth. ''So you think it was a mole?'' he asked.

''At first I did,'' Pollard said, nodding. ''But a mole is an enemy agent who gets planted in the system and then works his way up, waiting and watching, for the right time to do the most damage. I conducted my own secret investigation—thoroughly checked out everyone who was in a position to access the knowledge that had been leaked. No one fit the bill of a potential mole.''

''Then what?'' Bolan asked.

Pollard shrugged. ''Just a good old-fashioned traitor,'' he said. ''Not an enemy agent—someone who started out on the right track, then for whatever reason turned against his country.''

''The damage is the same,'' the soldier said.

''Yes, it is,'' Pollard agreed. ''But the moral ramifications are more significant. At least in my opinion. Even if you're an enemy, working for your country against another country is one thing. But betraying your own country is quite another.''

"This good old-fashioned traitor," Bolan said, "sounds like exactly what the U.S. was about to charge you as being when you fled the country.''

A deep sadness crept through Pollard's eyes. Whether it was genuine or just good acting, the soldier couldn't tell. "Yes," the CIA man said. "That's true.''

"But now you're telling us it wasn't you. You were set up?"

"Yes. And the man who set me up did one hell of a fine job of it." Pollard finished his champagne and set the glass back down on the table.

Bolan rocked forward in his chair. "And next you're about to tell us who it was?" He still had no indication as to whether the man was lying through his teeth or telling the truth.

"I am," Pollard said. He took a deep breath. "Like I said, unsure who I could trust, I conducted my own personal investigation. I worked nights, weekends and told no one what I was doing.''

"How very convenient," Platinov said sarcastically. "Because you didn't know who you could trust, you told no one of your suspicions. So there is no one to back up your story. It sounds to me as if all this overtime was when you were actually accessing the secrets which you sold to the Chinese.''

Bolan watched Pollard's face closely. What Platinov had just said was a distinct possibility.

Pollard shrugged. "It looks that way only if you insist on looking at it that way," he said. "The truth is that I wanted, at first, to find the traitor who was betraying me, my agency and my country." He took another deep breath. "When I was accused I also wanted to clear my name. Then, I had to find the real traitor." There was a long pause. Then the former CIA director answered the question he could see on both faces. "Yes, I found him. There was only one other man who had access to all of the things which the Chinese came up with so suddenly. William Brookings.''

Platinov drained her champagne glass and set it down next to the others. Her voice still held all of the sarcasm she could muster. "Why did I know you were going to name him?" she asked.

Pollard turned to her, and the tolerance he had shown earlier was gone. In its place was a controlled rage. "You think I am accusing him because he testified against me," he said. "Or you think I'm jealous that he was appointed in my place, or that he was my most convenient scapegoat. And your contempt for me is both obvious and understandable. But it is also wrong. We do have a traitor in the CIA. Not me, but a traitor nonetheless. Brookings."

Marynka Platinov let a smile cover her face. "You've had more than one traitor over the years," she said.

Pollard's eyes narrowed. "Yes, Colonel Platinov, we have," he said. "But treason is not an exclusively American trait. I have made good use of hundreds of Russian Judases myself."

Platinov glared back at him but didn't respond.

It was time for Bolan to cool things down before the two of them went for each other's throats. "Do you have any way to prove your innocence?" he asked Pollard.

The former CIA man turned back to Bolan, and some of the color left his face. "I don't know," he said. "But I think so."

"Go on."

"Okay," Pollard said. "The part two I promised you." He sighed quietly. "Selling technology to the Chinese wasn't the only thing I came across during my investigation of Brookings. He's also involved in other things."

"Such as?" Bolan asked.

"I believe he has contacts to the Russian black market. And that he's assisting them in getting former Soviet weapons into the hands of terrorist groups." Pollard glanced to Platinov. "I don't wish to offend you, Colonel Platinov but there are also rumors that some of your own intelligence officers are involved. They're here, right now, in South America under the pretense of looking for me. They're actually setting up a deal—which I'll explain in a minute.''

Bolan watched two emotions race across the beautiful Russian woman's face in the time it took her heart to beat twice. First, Platinov was offended. Then a flicker of confusion softened her features as she remembered Fyodor and the other men. Bolan could tell she was wondering—hoping, in a way—that Pollard's words were true, and that Fyodor and his men had indeed been working against her country rather than for it.

None of this, however, did Platinov intend to share with Pollard. ''Whenever you Americans cannot find the true answer,'' she said, letting a trace of sarcasm creep back into her voice, ''you blame it on the Russian black market.''

''We do indeed over-blame the black market,'' Pollard said. ''But that doesn't mean it doesn't exist. Do you deny it?''

Platinov sat back in her seat and sighed. ''No. Go on,'' she said.

It was Bolan's turn to ask a question. ''The Russian black market has been getting weapons to terrorists ever since the Soviet Union fell,'' he said. ''Without Brookings. Why would they suddenly need his help? Why cut him in on the profits?''

Pollard shrugged. ''I'm not completely certain myself,'' he said. ''But as best I can put it together, there's a Spaniard who had Russian black-market connections in southern Europe and has come to Peru. He's brokering his weapons here. And in short, this is our hemisphere. Brookings—the CIA—we can get things done in South America that the Russian criminals don't have the connections to pull off. With Brookings on the payroll, they could more easily get their weapons shipments through customs. He'd know which palms to grease, and could use various U.S. cover companies to keep from drawing suspicion.''

Bolan sat silently. It made sense. On the other hand, it could still be nothing more than an elaborate cover story invented by Pollard to cover his ass. Bolan glanced at his watch. ''You've earned a couple of extra minutes. Keep going.''

"I'll summarize for now, and fill in the details later." He paused. "Does the name Juan Ortega mean anything to you?"

Bolan searched his memory. The name did ring a distant bell somewhere. "Vaguely," he said.

"Ortega was the second-in-command of the Shining Path. The planner. A genius when it came to strategy and design."

Bolan nodded. "I remember him now." He searched his brain for what he knew about the Shining Path in general. The terrorist organization had been founded by Ayacucho University philosophy professor Abimael Guzman, and it was still active in Peru.

"Ortega is an Inca Indian, like many of the Shining Path but he disappeared after the Path staged the prison riots of 1983. Rumor has always been that they got rid of him—hid him out somewhere—because he was developing drug-and-alcohol problems which compromised his usefulness."

"Is this going somewhere?" Platinov asked impatiently.

"Yes," Pollard said. "Since I've been here, I've continued my investigation trying to clear my name. One of the things I've stumbled onto is this connection between the Shining Path, the Russian black market and Brookings. And the Spaniard I mentioned—I don't know his name—is the link. He was evidently introduced to the Path by Ortega, who it turns out had been hiding out in Spain."

The Executioner shifted his weight. If this was true, it confirmed who the dark-skinned men who had attacked them at the Iraqi safehouse were: Shining Path. If Pollard knew about them and their arms shipments, chances were good they knew about him and they were trying to find the former CIA man just like the rest of the world. Their motive would be different. Rather than pump him for intel, they'd want him dead before he blew the whistle on the Russian connection.

Bolan studied Pollard's face. Again he had to remind himself Pollard was a master of deception. The feeling in his gut was that the man was telling the truth. Although was he? It all made sense. But there was no proof. "So this is why you

went to visit Wayne Axe?'' he asked. ''So he could get word
to the CIA about the arms shipments?''

Pollard nodded. ''I had to get word of the weapons coming
in to someone who could stop them. Even if it meant risking
my own safety.''

The statement made the soldier's mind up for him. He was
now ninety-nine percent certain Pollard was lying. The man
was trying to come off as the innocent victim of a frame job,
and he'd been doing a good job until now. But a few shipments of rifles and other small arms to the terrorists of South
America wouldn't make much difference one way or the other.
It wasn't enough for Pollard to risk the sweet deal he had here.

Bolan stood. ''I'm taking you back to the U.S., Pollard,''
he said. His hand disappeared under his shirt, and his fingers
curled around the butt of the Desert Eagle. He kept one eye
on Platinov as he said, ''We can do it the easy way or the
hard way.''

Pollard shook his head vigorously. ''Look,'' he said. ''Just
give me a chance to prove what I'd just told you is true. I can
take you to—''

''Stand up,'' the Executioner ordered. The Desert Eagle
came out from under his shirt. ''Call me crazy if you like, but
I don't believe you'd have risked your own safety to keep a
few AK-47s out of Peru.''

Pollard kept his seat. ''I wouldn't have,'' he said. ''If that
was all there was to it.'' He paused for a moment, then his
face took on a look of intensity. ''But we aren't talking about
AK-47s anymore. The stakes have been raised. The next shipment is nukes.'' He stopped abruptly to let it sink in, then
continued. ''The Shining Path has plans to blow the hell out
of all of Peru, and maybe the rest of South America, before
this is all over.''

Bolan sat back down. If that was true—and again, the operative word was *if*—Pollard's story did indeed make more
sense. But there were still some holes in the narrative. ''How
do you know all this?'' he demanded. ''You haven't been in
a position to utilize the CIA's resources for over a year.''

"The oldest, and still the best, intelligence resource known to man," the former director said. "Human intel. Informants." He glanced to Carlos briefly, then back to Bolan. "How do you think I got set up in this house? I've still got a few contacts down here. And one good one."

"How good?" Bolan asked.

"Good enough that he's a member of the Shining Path," Pollard said. He paused. "Plays both sides of the fence, of course."

"Then how do you know you can trust him?" Platinov broke in.

"I don't," he said. "Not any more than you trust *him*." He glanced to Carlos. "Sometimes they tell the truth, sometimes they lie. You have to separate the wheat from the chaff."

"That's exactly how I feel about you right now," Bolan said. He stood once more. "Maybe you're telling the truth, maybe you're lying, but it's worth checking out. Let's go."

"Where?" Pollard asked.

"I want to meet your Shining Path man. And for your sake, he'd better have something more concrete than you do."

Pollard and Platinov both stood at the same time. "He's been trying to find out where the nukes are going to be stored," Pollard said. "By now, he should know."

"Let's hope so," the Executioner said. He raised the Desert Eagle until the muzzle was looking Hugh Pollard in the eye. "Because if this turns out to be anything but *exactly* what you've said, I may just save the United States the cost of a trial."

BOLAN KEPT the Blazer just beneath the speed limit as he retraced the path back to Lima. Occasionally, he glanced into the rearview mirror. He had plastic wrist restraints with him but hadn't bound Pollard. The former CIA director knew Platinov's hand had never left her purse, and that she'd be only too happy to shoot him before she let him escape. Besides, the longer he knew Hugh Pollard, the more Bolan's gut-level reaction to the man was positive.

That didn't mean he didn't still want proof.

As they neared the outskirts of Lima, the Executione[r] glanced into the mirror once more. This time his eyes fell o[n] Carlos, at the other side of the back seat. Platinov's informan[t] had more or less outlived his usefulness. He was now a wil[d] card, and had already made it clear that he would sell out t[o] the highest bidder.

Dusk had fallen when they entered Lima. Bolan felt hi[s] eyebrows lower in thought. Carlos now knew that Bolan an[d] Platinov had Hugh Pollard. Agents around the world woul[d] pay big money for that information, just as they would hav[e] paid for Carlos to lead them to the house in Ancon. So, wha[t] to do with the informant? He couldn't just drop the man of[f] at the nearest corner; the little snitch would head for the near[-] est phone to sell this new intel. Kill him? No. Carlos couldn'[t] be trusted. But he didn't deserve death. Neither could Bola[n] take the man along to meet Pollard's connection. Carlos woul[d] be nothing more than deadweight, and it was never a goo[d] idea for informants to meet each other.

The main reason the Executioner needed to ditch the littl[e] informant was that he'd be yet another distraction. Even dur[-] ing the inevitable firefights they were sure to soon encounte[r] Bolan would have to watch him to make sure he didn't ge[t] away. He was already being forced to keep one eye on Pollar[d] in case the former CIA man was lying and tried to escape[.] And at the same time, the other eye would have to be o[n] Platinov to insure she didn't whisk the CIA man away from under his nose.

Bolan suddenly took an exit off the highway toward th[e] airport. There was only one good answer to Carlos. Grimaldi[,] Stony Man's ace pilot would have to baby-sit Carlos unti[l] what the snitch knew was no longer of any value and it wa[s] safe to let him go.

"Where are you going?" Pollard asked. "This isn't the way to—"

"Just keep quiet," Bolan said. "Sit back, close your eye[s]

and pray that when we finally meet your man, he convinces me you're telling the truth.''

FIFTEEN MINUTES LATER, Carlos had been dropped at the plane with Grimaldi. The pilot had smiled good-naturedly as he pulled back his shirt to show Carlos the stainless-steel .357 Magnum pistol beneath it. Carlos got the message. He dropped into a seat at the rear of the plane, and settled in for the duration.

"Now," the Executioner said as they pulled away from the airport once more. "What's your man's name, and where do we find him?"

"His name is Benito," Pollard said. "He's the assistant night manager at the Lima train station." He glanced down at his watch. "He should just be coming on the night shift by the time we get there. He has computer access to the records of all train tickets purchased throughout South America. One of the things that makes him valuable."

"Point out the way," Bolan said, and began following Pollard's directions.

Known as the City of Kings, Lima, Peru, was one of the most typical Spanish cities in the western hemisphere. The Chevy Blazer made its way past massive plazas featuring historical buildings that dated back to the viceroyalty. They sped down tree-lined boulevards that led them past elaborate churches and opulent homes in the fashionable residential districts.

The railroad station stood just behind a huge palace. From here, travelers embarked for the highland interior of the country. The smell of the nearby Rimac River was thick in their nostrils as it flowed past nearby, with its colonial stone bridge serving as the unofficial dividing line between the old area of the city and the new. The river smell was overpowered, however, by the scent of the train engines as Bolan pulled the Blazer into the parking lot outside the station. "Let's go," he said, and reached for the door.

"Just a second," Pollard said.

Bolan stopped with his hand on the door handle.

"Are you planning to just go in and get him?"

"You know a better way?"

"Not right offhand, but there's a problem."

Bolan waited.

"Like I told you, Benito's the assistant manager. But they have a new night manager. And the last time I spoke with him, Benito was suspicious of the man."

"What do you mean, suspicious?" Platinov asked.

"He thinks the man might be a plant. From the Peruvian government."

"Why would they place an agent in charge of the station?" Platinov said.

"Benito thinks they may have begun to suspect him. The Shining Path connection."

Bolan took a deep breath. Another new wrinkle that would have to be overcome. "Have you ever made contact with him here before?" he asked Pollard.

"A time or two," Pollard said. "I never liked to. And neither did he. Usually we met—"

"This is not a *usual* situation," Platinov said, interrupting. "And we must all sometimes do things we don't like." Her words were punctuated with a surly smile. She turned to Bolan. "How do you want to do this?"

Bolan paused, thinking. If he was sure the man could be trusted, the ideal plan would be to send Pollard in alone. But they had no proof that Benito even existed, and if the former CIA director's story was all just an elaborate lie, he'd be out the back door of the station as fast as his legs could take him. On the other hand, if he and Platinov both went with Pollard, and this new manager really was a government plant, it was bound to raise his eyebrows. Especially when they took him away from his job, which they were going to do.

The soldier turned and looked at the dark brick of the train station as he continued to contemplate the situation. He could go in with Pollard but that would look almost as bad as all three of them. Two men were always more suspect than a man and a woman. On the other hand, if he sent Platinov, there was the likelihood that he wouldn't see either of them again. The Russian woman could have the former CIA director out the same back door and on his way to Moscow before the Executioner even knew they were gone.

Bolan turned back to the back seat. "Describe this Benito," he said.

"About five foot eight, I guess," Pollard said. "Hispanic, of course. Medium build. No facial hair. Normal haircut. He'll most likely be wearing a light-colored sport coat with an open collar. No tie. At least that's the way I've always seen him."

The soldier shook his head silently. There would be hundreds of men in the station who fit that description. "Does he have an office?" he asked. That would narrow it down.

"Yes, and sometimes he's in it and other times he isn't. He moves around the station a lot of the time." Pollard could tell what was going through the soldier's mind. "I'd say you've got a fifty-fifty chance he'll be there, but you're going to have a hard time finding him if he isn't. If I don't go in, that is."

Bolan didn't answer. He still hadn't yet made up his mind as to the best course of action.

He continued to stare at Pollard but studied Platinov, across the Blazer's seat from him, out of the corner of his eye. He could tell by the expression on her face that the Russian woman was pondering the problem just as he was. One of them had to go in with Pollard, but she didn't want Bolan stealing the man any more than he wanted her to do the same.

Before he could speak again, Platinov said, "I need to speak to you. Privately, please." She nodded outside the car.

Bolan turned to her, nodded and opened his door. He circled the Blazer as Platinov got out on the other side. The windows were rolled up but they took a few steps away from the vehicle—out of Pollard's earshot—anyway.

Marynka Platinov looked up into the soldier's eyes. "We have reached that point we have both been dreading," she said.

Bolan nodded.

"Our missions no longer coincide, and we can no longer trust each other."

Bolan looked down at her. As beautiful as she was, he forced his mind to stay on the job.

Platinov sighed. "I am confused," she said. "I am torn. I already have killed my own people for you."

"They weren't your own people," the Executioner said. "They were Russian Intel, all right, but they'd sold out. They were tied up in this whole black-market round-robin."

"Yes," Platinov said. "But I didn't know that at the time I pulled the trigger."

Bolan didn't answer. She was right. She had thought her fellow Russians were as interested in doing their duty as she was when she killed them, and she had killed them anyway. To help him.

Platinov's eyes fell to the ground for a moment, then returned to his. "There is no good answer to our problems," she said. He could tell she meant more than just how to get Benito out of the train station. She also meant how she felt about him. "But for now, the best of the bad answers is for me to go in with Pollard. The two of you will look too suspicious to this new manager." She paused and drew in a deep breath. "You have my word I will return."

The Executioner nodded. His instincts told him she would keep that word of honor. "How about *after* you bring Benito back out?" he asked.

Her eyes grew harder once more. "After that, I can make no promises," Platinov said.

Bolan studied her face, again pushing his personal feelings away. He would trust her. He knew he could be wrong, but at this point he had no other choice. "Then you go with him," he finally said. "Try to get Benito alone with Pollard, and get your story straight. You can pose as friends or relatives and tell his supervisor Benito's had a death in the family." He paused. "The story is still going to draw suspicion if the new manager really is a plant, but it's the best we've got at short notice."

"Are you going to wait here?" Platinov's tone made it clear she didn't believe that was very likely.

Bolan shook his head. "I'll follow you inside but stay away." He smiled. "You never know when a plan might fall apart and you need backup."

The statement brought a hearty and sincere laugh from Platinov. "Yes," she said. "I'm sure that's the reason you want to come along." She stared into his eyes again. "I won't break my word."

Turning back to the vehicle, she opened Pollard's door. "Let's go," she said.

Pollard gave the soldier a quick worried look. He didn't seem convinced being sent off with Platinov wouldn't find him on his way to Siberia but he didn't speak.

Platinov and Pollard started toward the station. Bolan gave them a thirty-second head start, then followed. Ten feet from the vehicle, he saw a discarded railroad ticket receipt and bent to pick it up. He carried it in his hand to further his cover as he followed the two into the brick building.

The Lima railroad station was busy twenty-four hours a day, and early evening was one of the busier times. Men, women and children hurried along the rails to catch trains to the outskirts of the city, deeper into the country, or to the other myriad nations of South America. Other passengers, their journeys complete, disembarked down the steps as their trains pulled into the station. A female voice speaking Spanish over the loud speaker rarely rested as it announced both arrivals and departures.

Bolan trailed Platinov and Pollard along the concrete to the side of the tracks, passing a variety of food, news and souvenir stands. They came to a glass door leading into what was obviously the station offices, and Platinov glanced over her shoulder. A mischievous grin covered her face.

The Executioner stopped, turned sideways, and pretended to study the ticket receipt in his hand. The Russian woman's smile had said it all. She knew he couldn't follow beyond this point without making it obvious he was with them. And that meant for the next several minutes, she and Pollard would be out of his sight.

If she was going to find that back exit, now was when she would do it.

Bolan waited. There was nothing else to do. Yes, Platinov had given him her word. But which of her loyalties took precedence in her mind? Her word or her mission? Few agents lost sleep over lying to operatives from other countries.

There was another reason the Executioner had decided to trust the Russian woman, and it held more weight with him than anything she could have said. Behind all the tough professionalism on the outside, Marynka Platinov was a deeply caring woman. He didn't think she was any more interested in seeing South America nuked by the Shining Path than he was. She'd want to carry out her mission, and take Pollard back to Moscow. But she'd want to end the threat in Peru first.

Five minutes went by. Then ten. Bolan didn't question what he had done or the chance he had taken. Calculated risks were often part of the game. He had made the right decision under the circumstances. Much of that decision, true, had been based on what he knew about Platinov's character, and there was always the chance that he'd misjudged her. If that turned out to be the case, it meant he would chase her to the ends of the earth.

It didn't.

Fifteen minutes after they'd entered the office area, Platinov, Pollard and a man fitting the description Pollard had given of Benito emerged. Benito didn't look happy. In fact, he looked terrified.

Bolan let the three pass, then fell in behind them and returned to the Blazer. Benito got into the back seat next to Pollard as Platinov took the passenger side again and the Executioner returned to the wheel.

"I am ruined," Benito whined behind him as Bolan started the engine. "You are my aunt and uncle? And my grandmother has died?" In the rearview mirror Bolan saw him shaking his head in dismay. "You are too young to be my aunt!"

he practically screamed at Platinov. "And neither of you is even Hispanic!" As he pulled away from the station, Bolan saw tears forming in the man's eyes. "My manager is probably on the phone this very minute," he said in a choking voice. "At the very least, I will lose my job."

Platinov turned to face him. Her eyes were hard and tough once more, and so was her voice as she said, "That is nothing to worry about, little nephew. By the time this is over, you will likely be dead and not need a job."

7

Ramone Lopez lifted the small soft-sided suitcase from the baggage rack and descended the steps leading off the train. The hot humid air hit him before his feet touched the ground. He looked up and down the tracks, seeing only several rotten wooden benches that served as the Pias train station. Thick jungle surrounded the clearing where the train had stopped. Not far from here, Lopez knew, lay Peru's famous jungle park—Rio Abiseo National Park. The park boasted more different species of animals than any other area in the world. Lopez took in a deep breath of humid air. It burned his lungs almost all the way to his spine. Staring off into the dense vegetation, he saw the half moon casting an eerie glow down over the trees, vines and leaves.

Lopez turned his attention back to the benches. They were deserted except for one lone shadowy figure. The figure rose to his feet and started toward the Gypsy.

Lopez waited as the man walked toward him. At the same time, two dozen other men came climbing down from the train. These men were hard-looking cases, most of them dirty and unshaved. They wore the baggy peasant clothing of Inca Indians, but occasionally a gust of wind blew the loose cotton shirts against their bodies, exposing suspicious bulges. Most of them carried suitcases. But the suitcases, Lopez knew, didn't contain clothing. They hid rifles, shotguns and other weapons.

These men were what they appeared to be—gunmen. Shining Path gunmen.

The Gypsy waved a hand, motioning the men to assemble along the tracks. Individually or in pairs and a few trios, the gunmen had boarded the train at different stops on the way to Pias. The Shining Path gunmen had mixed with the other passengers without so much as the smallest of nods of recognition toward Lopez or each other. Even as hard as they looked, they hadn't stood out among the other men on board the train, many of whom appeared just as grim.

But now, Lopez knew as he watched them drop to the ground, so many men whose very ambience bespoke violence getting off together at this isolated stop were bound to draw the attention of the train's personnel and the other passengers. He chuckled softly to himself. It made no difference. Not now. Even if someone reported the fact to the Peruvian authorities, he and these men would be long gone before officers could arrive to investigate. They would be hidden far into the jungle, where none of the lazy Peruvian police would care—or dare—to follow.

The man from the bench stopped a few feet from the Gypsy and extended his hand. "Señor Lopez," he said. "I am Miguel Caranza. It is my honor to finally meet you."

Lopez gripped the man's hand and stared into his eyes. Caranza was the current leader of the Shining Path. They had become acquainted over the phone after Juan Ortega had made the introduction, and up to now they had dealt with each other only through that means of communication. So far their arms-smuggling shipments had been small-time—at least compared to what they were about to do. For business of this magnitude it was to both of their advantages to meet face-to-face.

Now Lopez studied that face. Inca. Hard, weathered, with the look of a peasant. But also containing sharp, penetrating eyes that bespoke intelligence. Caranza had indeed proved intelligence, as well as cunning in his decisions so far.

The Gypsy reminded himself that such intellect bore watching.

Lopez looked around at the surrounding jungle. "You have come alone?" he asked.

Caranza shook his head. "No, I have brought an escort party. I thought it better if they waited out of sight. Everything possible has been done to insure security." He glanced up at the train.

Lopez nodded silently. That was good. He had done the same on his end. The men who had accompanied him on the train hadn't even known their final destination until they had seen him preparing to get off at Pias. Other members of the Shining Path, who would join them at the encampment the following day, were only now learning that they were to go to this station at Pias. When the Russians arrived, Lopez would act as liaison between them and Caranza until the deal had been completed. Then carefully selected members of the Shining Path would spread out across the South American continent, clandestinely planting the backpack nukes at previously chosen sites. As soon as the devices were in place, the governments of the cities where the bombs had been hidden would be contacted. Each would pay according to the capabilities Lopez had determined they possessed after a careful economic study of each nation.

The thought brought a silent laugh to Lopez's heart. From those who have to those who need, he thought. Perhaps he was a socialist at heart. On the other hand, he hadn't picked any poverty-stricken targets, so he supposed he was also a good capitalist businessman at heart.

Lopez planned to stay with Caranza and his men until the money had been collected. He would have to do so in order to collect the money to pay the Russians and get his own broker's fee. Still gripping Caranza's hand, he glanced past the man into the jungle. The remote habitat they were about to enter and this waiting period were not something he looked forward to. On the other hand, his fee of one hundred million dollars was worth a little discomfort.

The other men from the train had congregated just behind where Lopez and Caranza stood. The train whistle blew, sounding lonely in the jungle night. Lopez looked up through the small window at the engineer, and saw that the man's eyes vere wide. Indeed, it did look like a pack of Peruvian *bandidos* had just exited his train. The engineer didn't look at all ad to be leaving as the engine pulled away.

Not until the lights of the train were completely out of sight lid other shadowy forms begin to emerge from the jungle. Greetings between old acquaintances were made and hands vere shaken as the men from the jungle joined those from the rain. A few brief freedom-fighter slogans were shouted into he darkness.

Lopez grinned, unseen in the darkness now that the train's lights had vanished. Freedom fighters. They could call themelves whatever they liked; he knew what they were. Terrorsts. And while he had done nothing but broker the deal hrough which the Shining Path could either extort money or plow half of South America to kingdom come, he didn't lie o himself. He, Ramone Lopez, was a terrorist, too.

The suitcases that had come down from the train were now ppened, and assault rifles, machine guns and other weapons— he prizes of earlier smuggling operations Lopez had mediated—appeared in the moonlight. A half-dozen pack mules ad been led by the Shining Path men who emerged from the ungle, and these men helped those from the train tie the rest of their luggage to the animals' backs.

"Shall we go?" Caranza asked when the ropes had been secured.

Lopez nodded. "How long will it take?"

Caranza glanced at the mules. "Three, perhaps four hours with the animals," he said.

The Gypsy fell in just behind Caranza as the Shining Path leader switched on a flashlight and led the way from the train stop to a small path leading into the jungle. Lopez didn't know exactly where they were going, but a three-to-four-hour walk sounded fine. He needed some exercise after being cooped up n the mountain retreat for so long.

As he found his stride behind the Shining Path leader, his mind returned to the thought he had had earlier—the irony of errorists calling themselves freedom fighters. He supposed

such appellations softened the knowledge that they killed in
nocent men, women and even children as they fought for tha
freedom. And while he didn't try to justify his own activitie
in the same way, he was smart enough to know he rationalize
them just the same.

The path grew increasingly narrow as the train station dis
appeared behind them. As parrots protested above his head
and thousands of other forms of wildlife chattered and scat
tered to the sides of the path, Lopez let his thoughts continu
to drift. Caranza and his men were about to receive nuclea
bombs that had formerly been the property of the Soviet Un
ion. Members within the group would then plant the bomb
in various South American cities. He was responsible for th
transaction. That meant he might soon be just as responsibl
for the deaths of thousands, if not millions of people if th
extortion money wasn't paid.

Lopez continued to follow the beam of the flashlight ahea
of him. So how did he rationalize it all, he asked himself
Simple. Extortion was just another form of stealing. An
Christ had given him, as a Gypsy, license to steal.

They came to a spot in the path too narrow for the heavil
laden mules. Several of the men hurried forward with ma
chetes, widening the way. Lopez continued to mull the situa
tion over in his mind as he waited. Yes, extortion was a forn
of stealing and he had license to steal. But how about mur
der—mass murder—that occurred during the theft process
Had Jesus Christ granted Gypsies that authority, as well?

The men with the machetes finished chopping, and the pro
cession started through the night once more. No, Lopez ha
to admit, he had no authorization to murder. On that, he wa
on his own. But the thought brought another silent chuckle t
his chest.

Ramone Lopez knew that the legend of Christ and th
Gypsy woman wasn't true, yet he had operated on it all hi
life. And it wasn't really that big of a step from theft to mur
der. In any case, what did it matter?

One way or another, he suspected he was on his way to hell.

And the fact that he didn't give a damn turned his chuckle to a loud laugh that brought quizzical stares from the men walking close enough to hear him.

THE HUMAN BAGGAGE the Executioner had picked up along the way on the mission was getting heavy. In addition to Pollard, he now had Pollard's informant—Benito—to keep an eye on. At the same time, another eye had to be trained on Platinov herself to make sure she and the former CIA director didn't suddenly vanish and then surface in Moscow. And he suspected he was about to go toe-to-toe with South America's most ruthless terrorist organization.

Bolan glanced over his shoulder as he parked the Blazer in the parking lot next to the airplane hangar. Just outside, Grimaldi waited in the Learjet with Carlos, the engines already warmed up. The soldier, Platinov, Pollard and Benito got out of the Blazer and started toward the plane. According to what Benito had told them on the way to the airport, he had indeed found out where the Russian black market was preparing to deliver the nukes. The problem was, it was deep within the jungle in the Peruvian province of Mariscal Caceres in San Martin. The nearest place Grimaldi could land was Trujillo.

And Benito had learned something else. The small backpacks had already arrived by ship, and been successfully offloaded, in Peru. They were on their way to the site, and would be there within a few hours.

Bolan glanced from Benito to Pollard as they walked. Everything the CIA man had told them so far had proved to be true, but that still didn't mean his overall story was legitimate. He could have had Benito set up all along as a backup in case American agents found him. He could have paid off Benito earlier, provided him with this elaborate Shining Path story and instructed him to back it up when he was taken into custody. Benito might even now simply be preparing to follow through with the hoax by leading them on a wild-goose chase to buy Pollard time in which the former CIA director could devise another plan of escape. Bolan reminded himself of two things. First, Hugh Pollard was a professional clandestine agent, and therefore quite capable of pulling off an intricate conspiracy of this nature. And second, it had been a similar foul-up between the CIA and FBI that had given him the chance to escape Washington in the first place.

As they reached the plane, Grimaldi opened the door. "More baby-sitting?" the pilot asked, immediately recognizing Benito for what he was.

"I haven't decided yet," Bolan said as he pushed Pollard and the Shining Path man onto the plane. He turned to Platinov. "Get these two situated in the back with your friend," he said. "I need to discuss something with him." He nodded toward Grimaldi.

Platinov's radar went up.

Bolan shook his head to answer the unasked question. "No, we're not getting ready to cut you out," he said. "I just need to work out the logistics of how to get where we're going."

The Russian woman's face filled with suspicion.

Bolan stared down into her eyes. "You gave me your word at the train station," he said. "You kept it. I'm giving you my word now."

Platinov stared him in the eyes. Slowly, she nodded her head, then stopped. "I made it clear that my promise held good only until we got Benito out of the train station."

"Yes," Bolan said. "You did."

"Well?" Platinov asked.

"Well what?"

"What about later?"

"No promises later."

Platinov understood, and accepted. She turned to the back of the plane to keep an eye on the two informants.

Bolan slid into the seat next to Grimaldi. "The site where the nukes are supposed to be delivered is near Rio Abiseo National Park," he said.

Grimaldi understood the problem immediately. "No way," he said. "Closest place I could land would be Trujillo."

"That's what I figured," Bolan said. "What are the chances of getting a bush plane or chopper?"

"How soon do you want it?"

Bolan smiled at his old friend. "Yesterday would have been good. The nukes are on their way there now."

"You know, you sure don't make things easy for those of us who work with you, Striker," Grimaldi said, grinning back.

"Nobody ever said life was easy, Jack."

Grimaldi reached forward to the rechargeable cellular phone that had been mounted next to the steering gear. Tapping in a few numbers, he glanced over his shoulder at his passengers. They were all watching intently. As the number dialed through, the pilot turned back to Bolan. "Want this on speakerphone where you can hear it?" he asked.

Bolan glanced at the people in the back. "Yeah," he said. "But use one of the hello lines."

Hello lines, whose name came from the neutral way they were always answered, were hardly unique to Stony Man Farm. Every police department, military intelligence and civilian agency that employed undercover and covert operations had them. They were a method by which field agents could contact their bases in the presence of unauthorized people. They could also be given to targets, with the voice on the other end playing to part of shill in the ongoing game.

Grimaldi immediately reached forward, cutting off the call he had just made before it could be answered. He tapped in a new set of numbers, and the sound of ringing came over the speakerphone. A moment later Barbara Price's voice said, "Hello?"

Bolan glanced over his shoulder to see that Platinov was listening. "We're in Lima," he told Price, not identifying her by name. "We need a bush plane or chopper. Do we have immediate access to anything close by?"

"Are you on a speakerphone?" Price asked. The fact that

he hadn't said her name as he usually did hadn't escaped the Stony Man Farm controller.

"Right. Plenty of guests around."

"Let me check with our man," Price came back just as generically.

Bolan waited. The "our man" whose name Price hadn't said was Aaron Kurtzman, the same computer wizard who had tracked down the fingerprints for him and Platinov earlier. Now Kurtzman would run the Executioner's question through his magic machines and determine the location of the closest suitable aircraft.

A few minutes later Kurtzman came on the line himself. "Closest thing we can get—legally—is going to take you four hours."

The Executioner knew he meant an aircraft that they would have to outright steal. Not that it would be the first time he had commandeered a plane that didn't belong to him, and not that it would bother him to do so again for a greater good, but it could create problems that would result in delays. Besides, there was an easier way into the jungle.

"Four hours is too long," Bolan said. "Okay, forget it for now." He nodded to Grimaldi.

Grimaldi disconnected the line. "You've always got one other alternative," he said.

"I was just thinking about it."

They could parachute to the site. He and Platinov had jumped together before, so that was no problem. He supposed he could leave Pollard with Grimaldi but he hated to do so. Agents from all over the world were looking for the CIA man, and while there was no better pilot in the sky, and he was more than just an adequate man with a gun, he was still only one man. The bottom line was that Pollard would be safer if the Executioner kept the man with him. And Bolan knew from the CIA man's file that he was jump qualified.

Bolan nodded through the Lear's front window at the runways in the distance. "Get takeoff clearance, Jack," he said.

Grimaldi had flown the Executioner too many times to question an order. He lifted the radio mike and requested permission from the tower as Bolan strapped the seat belt around his waist. As they taxied toward a runway, Bolan turned in his seat. "Benito," he said. "You ever jump out of an airplane before?"

"What?" the man asked in astonishment. "Why would anyone—"

Platinov was seated next to the man and she elbowed him in the ribs. "He means do you know how to parachute, you idiot," she said.

Benito shook his head silently, then suddenly stiffened as he realized what Bolan was proposing. "No," he said through clenched teeth. "And I don't intend to learn now."

A hard smile covered Bolan's face as Grimaldi guided the jet off the ground and into the air. "I'm afraid you're going to have to, Benito," he said.

Several moments went by during which the Lear gained altitude and the people on board remained silent. Then, as the jet leveled off in the sky, Benito's voice, small and quiet, drifted through the plane. "I won't do it," he said softly. "Regardless of how much money you offer me."

Bolan looked at Grimaldi.

The pilot grinned.

Bolan unsnapped his seat belt and moved to the back of the plane. "I guess you misunderstood me," he told Benito. "I'm not offering you any money to do it. You're going to do it for free."

Benito shook his head violently back and forth. "No," he said. "There is no reason for me to jump out of this plane. You don't need me to go with you. I have told you all I know, and I can't help you further on the ground."

"I realize that," Bolan said. "That's not why I'm taking you with us."

"Then why?" Benito pleaded.

With one swift, smooth movement, Bolan drew the Rad from its Kydex sheath on his belt. Held in the ice-pick grip, three inches of dagger blade gleamed under the interior lights of the plane. Benito's eyes widened as his eyes fell to the steel.

But the soldier didn't stop there. He wanted to make his point, and he used the point of the Rad to make it. Thumbing the opening stud, the Rad's blade grew from three inches to seven and changed automatically to a saber grip. "The reason you're going with us," he said in a soft voice as he pressed the tip up under Benito's chin, "is that for all I know you're lying to me. And if you are, I'm going to cut your throat. Do you understand?"

After another moment of remaining as frozen as an iceberg, Benito shook his head. "I understand," he whispered in a squeaky, mouselike voice.

"You see, Benito," the Executioner said, "I'm operating completely from instinct. I have been ever since I met your friend here." He nodded toward Pollard.

Pollard's face betrayed no emotion. He was either telling the truth, an Oscar-deserving actor, or didn't care if Benito lived or died.

Turning his attention back to Benito, Bolan continued. "Like I said, I still have no concrete proof that this whole Shining Path story wasn't hatched in advance as a backup plan for Mr. Pollard here. If I find out it was, I still can't kill him—he's got to go back to the U.S. to get things cleared up." The Executioner moved the knife blade slowly in and rested the edge against the skin of Benito's throat. "But I can kill you. And I will." He watched the man's reaction closely. If Benito was lying for Pollard, now would be the time when he admitted it.

But he didn't. Benito's eyes closed. Sweat began to roll down his cheek, and his Adam's apple bobbed up and down beneath the edge of the Rad.

Platinov smiled. "I saw an American antidrug commercial on TV several times," she said. "It didn't go exactly like this, but similar." She paused, straightening dramatically and touching the front of her neck. "This is your throat," she said.

Her forefinger suddenly made a slashing movement across her flesh. "This is your throat after being cut. Any questions?"

"She's right, Benito," Bolan said. "This is your last chance to tell the truth. The nukes, the Shining Path, this jungle encampment—is it real or just a story you two concocted? Keep in mind that if you lie, I'm going to find out. Then...." Bolan turned the Rad slightly and dragged the flat of the blade across Benito's neck in a motion similar to what Platinov had done with her finger.

The cold steel against his skin made the man shiver as if he'd been dropped suddenly into an icy lake. "I have told you...the truth," Benito managed to squeak.

Bolan folded the Rad, replaced it in the sheath on his belt and turned back to the front of the plane. Behind him, he heard Benito whine to Platinov. "But...I don't know how to use a parachute!"

The Executioner could almost see the sarcastic Russian face as Platinov answered the man. "Don't worry," she said. "I will tell you what to do. In fact, I will give you the crash course."

BEING TOLD by Benito where the encampment was located was one thing. Actually finding it from the air was another.

Although he had learned several days before that a purchase of nuclear weapons was in the making, Benito hadn't been told where to meet until a few minutes before Platinov and Pollard had appeared to whisk him away from the railroad station. And even then he had been given only general directions. The voice on the other end of the phone had identified himself using a Shining Path code number, then told him simply to go to the railroad stop in Pias. From there he was to start up the path north of the village into the jungle. Shining Path men would be stationed along the route. They would watch him, and other members searching for the camp, long enough to determine that they weren't spies. When they were convinced, they would pick him up and escort him in.

The soldier shrugged into his parachute. The encampment

had to be fairly close to the path. At least within a few miles. But how were the Russians bringing the nukes in? According to Benito, the path he'd been instructed to follow was a man-and-mule-only route. Would the black marketeers be bringing nuclear weapons overland through the jungle by mule? If so, they couldn't be large devices—at least by nuclear standards.

Even one of the smaller nukes known as backpack models would be more than enough to wipe a city the size of Lima off the map.

During the flight, Bolan, Platinov and Pollard had raided the lockers bolted to the sides of the jet and changed into camouflage jungle fatigues. Platinov had doffed her clothes with her usual immodesty, and Bolan had watched the expression it brought to Pollard's face. The former CIA director might be getting older but he wasn't dead. Carlos, who would stay on the plane with Grimaldi, had watched the beautiful Russian woman with even more voyeuristic enthusiasm than he had exhibited for the porno magazine back at his house. Benito was too scared to pay attention. He had turned into a barely breathing zombie. He hadn't even reacted when Platinov took his clothes off of him, then re-dressed him in cammies.

Bolan turned in his seat now to see how Platinov and her charges were getting along. The Russian woman had slipped the straps of her chute over her shoulders and was helping Benito into his. Benito stood as still as a statue, his normally olive-skinned face gone a sickly gray. Bolan studied the man's eyes—fear had driven his mind back into itself. There was every chance in the world that he'd freeze in the air and forget to pull the rip cord. And there was no static line available on the plane.

The soldier moved to the rear of the plane as Platinov finished cinching Benito's straps. She frowned as she, too, studied the man's faraway gaze. Then she turned to the Executioner. "Do you want to do it or do you want me to?" she asked.

Bolan knew what she meant. Someone was going to have

to jump tandem with Benito to insure that his rip cord got pulled. "Whichever one of us does it," the soldier said, "I think more promises are in order." He shot a quick glance at Pollard, who appeared to know what he was doing as he rigged his own chute on his back.

The woman nodded. "The one who doesn't go with Benito agrees not to run off with Pollard," she said. "Okay on my end."

"It's a deal. Neither of us steal Pollard. At least during the jump."

The soldier turned back to the front of the plane. Once again he felt he could trust the Russian agent. But only until the appointed time of the agreement ran out. "How long, Jack?" he asked.

Grimaldi glanced at his controls. "Two minutes," he said. "I can still drop lower and see if we can locate it from the air if you want."

Stony Man's top flyboy had made the same offer earlier and Bolan had declined. "No, the problem's still the same," he told Grimaldi. "As thick as it is down there, they've got a better chance of spotting us than we do them. We'll jump over the train station at Pias. From there, we'll have to find it on our own." He moved to the rear of the plane once more, passed Platinov, Pollard and Benito and opened another of the lockers. From inside, he pulled two Heckler & Koch MP-5 submachine guns. He slung one over his shoulder and handed the other to Platinov. A pair of web belts holding extra 9 mm subgun magazines went around each of their waists.

"I have only my squeeze-cocker," Platinov said, patting the H&K P-7 holstered at her waist. "Do you have an extra backup pistol?"

Bolan waved to the gun locker. "Take your pick," he said.

Platinov looked through a variety of handguns inside the locker, finally pulling out a Colt Woodsman .22 with a sound suppressor threaded into the barrel.

"How about me?" Pollard asked. "You going to give me a weapon?"

Bolan stared hard at the man. He had gambled that the former director was telling the truth so far, and nothing had proved that he wasn't. On the other hand, nothing had proved that he was. Giving him a gun now, under these conditions, might mean both he and Platinov took bullets in the back somewhere in the jungle.

So the Executioner ignored the question and moved back to the front of the jet. Thirty seconds later he opened the door. Grimaldi slowed the aircraft in the air but the wind still whirled through the plane, beating his hair against his forehead and making enough noise that he had to shout to be heard. "You're first!" he yelled to Platinov. "Then Pollard. Benito and I'll bring up the rear!"

Platinov had tied her own hair back into a ponytail. Now, it thrashed around into her eyes like a bullwhip. The soldier wasn't sure if it was her hair or his words that brought the new frown to her face. "Any reason why Pollard shouldn't be going *before* me?" she shouted above the noise. It was clear that she realized that once she was out of the plane, Bolan could simply leave her in the air and fly on with the former CIA man.

"Yes, Dr. Platinov, there is," Bolan yelled back. He glanced from Pollard to Benito. "If anybody gets hurt from the jump, I want you already on the ground and ready to help. That's the reason. The only reason. You have your medical bag?"

Platinov looked at him suspiciously for a moment, then tapped the backpack she wore beneath her chute. A second later she disappeared beneath the door frame. Pollard gave her ten seconds, then followed.

Benito was still frozen in place. He was too far gone to resist when Bolan grabbed him by the belt and jumped.

The wind caught them as they left the jet, shooting them up above the plane rather than allowing them to drop. They paused for a moment, suspended in midair, then started down as the jet flew on. It was at that moment that Benito suddenly came out of his trance. And like a drowning man irrationally fighting a lifeguard trying to save him, he began to struggle.

Benito wasn't strong, he wasn't tough and the punch he landed on the Executioner's jaw wasn't that hard. But it came unexpectedly, and while Bolan didn't lose his grip on Benito's belt, the force of the blow was enough to snap the cheap leather that encircled the informant's waist. Bolan was left holding the man's buckle. And before the soldier could reach out and grab him again, Benito drifted away from him like an astronaut in a space movie.

A sudden gust of wind caught the lighter man and shot him twenty yards away from Bolan. The soldier watched Benito plummet in a parallel descent, his arms and legs flailing wildly in the air. But, Bolan knew, the man's panic might be his only chance of salvation. He wasn't intentionally spreading his limbs to slow his fall like a trained jumper might, but the effect was partially the same.

Turning his head toward the ground, Bolan extended his arms above his head like an Olympic diver. With the least possible air resistance now, he began to drop faster toward the earth. His only chance of saving Benito, he knew, was to get beneath him, then angle over as he slowed his own descent speed. He glanced over to the frantic man as he passed him in the air, then looked back to the ground.

It could be done, he knew. The question was whether it could be done before they were too low to make use of the chutes.

Bolan let himself fall twenty feet below Benito, then spread his arms suddenly like an eagle unfurling its wings. His rate of descent slowed suddenly, and he began to angle toward a spot beneath Benito. He couldn't have misjudged the fall by more than half a second. But that was all it took to glide past the man and miss him.

Benito fell suddenly below the Executioner once more.

Bolan turned in the air, face to the ground again. Below, he could see the massive patch of green jungle racing toward him. He would have one more chance. As he picked up speed again, he took a deep breath. Directly beneath him, he could see Benito still thrashing his arms and legs in the air. Screams of terror drifted up to the soldier.

What seemed like minutes could only have taken seconds. Gradually, inch by inch and then foot by foot, the gap between the two men abated. Bolan looked back and forth from Benito to the ground. It was impossible to judge now how much time he had left. Should he abandon the rescue and pull his own rip cord? As the void between the two men continued to close with excruciating slowness, Bolan considered the situation. If he fell to his own death he couldn't stop the terrorists. Should he trade this life beneath him for the thousands who might die without his help? He didn't know. He knew only that he couldn't allow Benito to plummet to the earth without doing all he could to save the man.

He was still too high to clearly see the ground when Bolan's outstretched left hand found Benito's dark hair. Entwining his fingers in the oily mess, he jerked himself downward and at the same time brought the Peruvian up. His right hand reached for the man's rip cord and jerked.

The chute opened and Benito went sailing back up above him into the sky.

Bolan spread his arms, angling to the side. All of his efforts would be wasted if his own chute now tangled with the other man's. He gave it a count of five, then looked up to see that he was roughly ten feet to Benito's side. Not an ideal distance for safety between canopies but it would have to do. He was out of time.

With a quick tug, Bolan jerked his own rip cord. The chute shot out of the pack and overhead, and he felt the straps beneath his arms bite into his flesh. His shoulders felt as if he'd been tied to a medieval torture rack and were being ripped apart. For a moment he seemed again to hang weightless in space. Then the Executioner's head struck something solid. What actually hit him, he didn't know.

All he knew for certain as he closed his eyes was that he was suddenly very tired.

THE FIRST SENSATION he felt when he woke was the heat of the blinding bright light in his left eye. The heat moved to his other eye for a moment, then went away quickly. But white glows remained in both of his pupils.

Bolan blinked his eyes as the sharp slivers of pain suddenly shot through his head. He felt hands on his face, and when his eyelids opened once more he saw two faces leaning over him. Both belonged to Marynka Platinov. Two faces. Two noses. Four eyes. And if he were not mistaken, all four of those eyes had tears in them.

As if from far away, he heard her voice. "Can you hear me?"

Bolan nodded his head, and a thousand needle-tipped daggers drove into his skull. He closed his eyes once more. When he opened them the two faces had merged into one. But he had been correct. Tears streaked Platinov's cheeks. In her hand he could see a small flashlight.

"How do you feel?" the woman asked quietly.

"Like someone hit me in the head with a baseball bat."

"Your head struck a tree limb," Platinov said. "Your chute opened but you were too close to the ground. You didn't get its full benefit." She dropped the flashlight somewhere out of his sight.

Bolan tried to sit up but the pain threw him back. He took a deep breath. "What about the others?" he asked.

"Pollard is fine. Benito...I don't know."

Bolan blinked several times as his vision continued to clear. "What do you mean you don't know?"

"He came down somewhere over there," Platinov said, pointing into the jungle. "Pollard has gone to look for him."

Bolan frowned and his tightening skin brought new pain to his head. "You let him go?"

Platinov looked perturbed. "What did you want me to do?" she asked. "Leave you and go after him myself? I couldn't care for you, baby-sit Pollard and go hunting for Benito at the same time."

"You took a chance that Pollard would bolt."

"We've been taking chances with that man, and each other, for the last two days," Platinov said. "I am tired of it. Pollard's story is either true or it isn't." She reached into her backpack which lay on the ground next to him.

Bolan watched her pull out a small vial and syringe. She stuck the needle into the vial and began filling it.

"What's that?"

"Something for your head. I have already stitched it while you were unconscious."

Bolan's hand moved automatically toward his head. Platinov reached up and grabbed it. "The stitches are in the back," she said. "Don't touch them." For a moment her voice sounded more like an irritated-but-caring mother than one of the world's best clandestine agents.

The pain in his head was still excruciating, but his mind was clearing. He looked back to the syringe. If Platinov wanted him out of the picture so she could take off with Pollard, she now had the perfect opportunity. Just give him enough morphine to put him back to sleep.

Or kill him.

Platinov finished filling the syringe, then caught the Executioner's gaze as she started to inject him. "Don't be silly," she said, reading his mind. "If that was what I was going to do, there was no need to waste a needle. I could have left with Pollard right after you struck the tree." She smiled down at him. "Do you need another of our short-term promises?"

"It wouldn't hurt," he said.

Platinov placed a hand across her heart. "I swear I am not giving you anything which will kill you or knock you out so I can run off with Pollard," she said. "Right now, anyway. Boy Scout's honor."

Bolan nodded his head. The movement brought on new pain and he stopped. But the pain couldn't keep him from saying, "Want to extend that promise for the future?"

"No," Platinov said.

Bolan let her jab the needle into his arm, and began to feel better almost immediately. As soon as she'd finished, he said, "You'd better go find Pollard and Benito."

Platinov looked up and around. "Why?" she asked. "Pollard has been gone over an hour. If he has decided to run from us, it is too late to find him now."

"I've been out for that long?"

Platinov nodded her head.

Bolan felt the drug begin to shoot through his system. Gradually, the fire in his head went away completely, but he still felt dizzy. Taking it slow, he sat up. He was also mildly nauseated—maybe from the tree limb, more likely from the drug. He knew that would go away, too. It was hardly the first time in his life the Executioner had been knocked cold.

"You feel like getting to your feet yet?" Platinov asked.

Bolan nodded. Slowly, he stood. Only now did he finally take notice of the fact that they were in a small clearing. Very small. In fact, it appeared that he had created the clearing himself with his fall. Recently broken limbs and vines lay both around and above him. As he found his balance, he was surprised to find that except for the slight burn of the stitches in the back of his head, he felt almost as good as new.

"What did you give me?" he asked.

"Demerol," Platinov said. "You feel all right?"

The soldier nodded his head and this time it didn't hurt.

Platinov had started to speak again when they heard footsteps in the foliage to the side. Both of the MP-5s were on the ground but the Desert Eagle and Platinov's H&K jumped suddenly into play. A second later Pollard's voice said, "Don't shoot. It's us." Both his and Benito's faces, appeared through the vines. They stepped into the small clearing.

"Where did you find him?" Platinov asked.

Pollard laughed. "Hanging from a tree a few hundred yards east," he said. "Unconscious."

Platinov stepped forward to examine him. "Did you hit your head, too?" she asked.

Benito didn't answer. His eyes fell to the ground.

"No." Pollard grinned. "I already checked him. He passed out from fright."

Benito's eyes rose and filled with embarrassed anger. He looked to Bolan. "You are bound and determined to get me killed, aren't you?" he said.

Bolan shook his head, still amazed that the pain was gone. "No," he said. "You've done your job and been through enough. You can take off. Where's the path?"

"About fifty yards that way," Pollard said, pointing.

"Follow it to the train stop," the Executioner said. "A train should come by sooner or later."

Benito shook his head. "I don't think so," he said.

Bolan frowned. "Why not?"

"Because I have come this far," Benito said. "Besides, you need me."

"How do we need you?" the Executioner asked. "And you've played both sides of the fence for twenty years. How do we know we can trust you?"

"The only way to find the camp is to get back on the trail and follow it until you come across the Shining Path men who are waiting."

"I think we can find the path without your help," Platinov said sarcastically.

"I'm sure you can," Benito said. "But they will see you before you see them. And they will kill you the minute they do. None of you look Inca to me, and you won't to them, either."

Bolan suddenly understood what Benito had in mind. And it wasn't a bad idea at all.

"If I am with you, it will cause them to wonder," Benito went on. "It will mean they will at least try to find out who you are before they kill you."

"What good will that do?" Pollard asked. "We still don't look like candidates for membership in Shining Path."

"No." Benito smiled. "But all of you speak Russian."

What Bolan had realized a moment earlier suddenly dawned on the faces of Pollard and Platinov. "It could work," Plati-

nov said. "If you aren't trying to double-cross us." She
glanced to Bolan, then back at the man. "Like he just said,
how do we know we can trust you? What's in this for you?"

"If Shining Path finds that I led you this far, they will kill
me," Benito said. "And if I go to the train station, they will
find out. Someone will be watching it, and they will wonder
why I am going that way instead of to the camp." He looked
at all three of them, and the anger grew stronger in his eyes.
"That is what is in it for me. My life. I don't like it, but at
this point you appear to be my only hope. As I am yours."

Bolan lifted the two MP-5s from the ground and handed
one to Platinov. Behind him, he heard Hugh Pollard clear his
throat. When he turned, Pollard looked him in the eye, then
glanced to Benito, then back again. Pollard cleared his throat
once more to make his meaning clear.

The former CIA director could have easily escaped when
he went to find Benito. He hadn't. He had brought the man
back. He had proved himself.

The Executioner drew the Beretta 93-R and handed it to the
man. "We'll get you better equipped after the first Shining
Path men we come to," he said.

Pollard smiled. "Then let's get started," he said. "I'm
ready to get this over, get home and help put William Brookings's ass behind bars for the rest of his life."

Pollard had come across the path leading into the jungle as he searched for Benito. He led them back there now. Bolan was about to take the lead when Benito reached up and took his arm. "It will look strange if I am unarmed," he said.

The Executioner studied the man. As both a member in good standing with the Shining Path and Pollard's informant, he had burned the candle at both ends. Which end was on fire now? Could he be trusted now with a gun? Bolan didn't know. He did know the man was right—when they finally encountered the Shining Path men waiting to pick up the other members of the terrorist group who were coming in today, an unarmed Benito was bound to create suspicion.

Drawing the Desert Eagle, he handed it to the man.

Benito took the big .44 Magnum in both hands and looked down at it. "What do you shoot with this thing?" he asked. "Elephants?"

"No," Bolan said in a low, threatening voice. "Just men who lie to me."

Benito caught his drift and nodded. He stuffed the Desert Eagle into his waistband. Looking up again, he said, "It will also look better if I lead the way."

"So do it," Bolan said.

Benito smiled nervously and stepped around him.

"Remember I'm right behind you," Bolan added as they started forward once more. He lifted the MP-5 and tapped the barrel gently into the informant's kidney for emphasis.

Benito took the lead and the Executioner dropped back a

few steps. Just behind him walked Marynka Platinov with Hugh Pollard acting as rear guard. In the trees overhead, orange-breasted parrots fluttered their wings. Occasionally, a chestnut-headed duck quacked as it flapped across the sky. Lizards of all types scurried away in fright as the intruders' footsteps disturbed their sleep, and at one point the soldier saw a spectacled bear watching them from several yards away in the foliage.

But it wasn't the eyes of the species-endangered bear that Bolan began to feel on him as they continued to follow the path north. The longer they walked, the more the Executioner could sense that they were being watched. Finally, as they made their way over a series of broken stones and around a bend in the path, Benito let out a short gasp in front of him. Bolan took another step around the curve.

And came face-to-face with four heavily armed men.

All of them gripped AK-47s in their hands. Hand grenades hung from makeshift assault suspenders, and more were stuffed into the pockets of their loose-fitting peasant garments. Three of the men also had pistols stuffed into wide leather belts. Two wore wide-brimmed straw hats, the other pair had their long jungle-damp hair tied back with colorful lengths of cloth. Their rifle barrels were pointed toward him and Benito.

Behind them in the jungle, the Executioner heard the metallic thuds as more rifle bolts were pulled back and allowed to slide home, chambering rounds. He looked over his shoulder to see another quartet of armed, and similarly clad, men behind Platinov and Pollard. These men also carried AK-47s, and now they used the barrels to prod the former CIA director and the Russian woman forward.

A tall wiry man in front of Bolan did step forward now. He had long black hair which fell almost to his waist. A red bandanna had been tied across his forehead, and cold black eyes— reminding Bolan of the eyes of a shark—were set deep within a face almost the same texture as the leather gear he wore. He frowned at Benito and said simply, "Who are you?"

"I was summoned here," Benito said calmly. He spouted

off a series of code numbers in Spanish, and the taller man's frown eased somewhat. "You are here to guide me into camp, I assume?"

"Who are they?" the man's rifle barrel rose slightly to indicate the three Caucasians behind the Hispanic.

"Russians, of course," Benito said. "I met them only a few minutes ago. They are part of the group bringing in the delivery."

The tall Indian was clearly not convinced. "I see nothing in their hands," he said suspiciously. "Except personal weapons."

"The shipment isn't with them."

"Then why are they here?" the tall Shining Path man demanded. "We weren't told that any of the Russians were coming this way."

Bolan stepped forward. "You weren't told for a reason," he said in Spanish with a heavy Russian accent. "I see the distrust in your eyes, and I can't blame you for that distrust. There is much at stake. Can you blame us for our own distrust? Can you blame us for taking our own precautions?"

The Executioner could see in the black eyes that the story made sense to the man. Although the fact that it made sense didn't mean the Shining Path completely believed it. Its logic meant only that it might be true, not that it was.

The tall Inca spoke slowly, enunciating each word clearly. "We will take you into camp," he said. "But we will take your weapons first."

Bolan shook his head. "No," he said. "We'll follow you but we will keep our weapons. We won't use them unless you force us to do so."

A moment of indecision was portrayed on the tall Inca's face. Then, slowly, he nodded. His gaze shifted to Platinov and he eyed her from head to toe, the lust in his eyes barely concealed. The other men around him didn't even try to hide their desire. One of them even licked his lips. The Executioner had little doubt that the men in back of them would be having

the same sort of reaction to their rear view of the beautiful
Russian woman.

The tall man with the red bandanna turned and started off
through the jungle with his three companions. Bolan, Platinov,
Pollard and Benito fell in behind them. The four men who had
come up from their rear stayed there as the procession continued to follow the path north.

The Executioner estimated they had gone between a mile
and a half and two miles when they left the path and began
making their way through the dense growth. It was clear from
the recently cut vines and leaves that these men had come this
way earlier. But the jungle grew back almost as quickly as it
could be cut down, and they broke out machetes to help them
along. Without the means to help in the extrication, Bolan,
Platinov, Benito and Pollard followed the footsteps of the men
in the front, sandwiched in the middle by the rear guard.

The going was hard, and after an hour the leader called out
for a break. The Shining Path men broke out canteens and
plastic water bottles but offered none of it to the newcomers.
Bolan and Platinov dropped to sitting positions on the ground
with Pollard and Benito close by.

"Do you suppose any of them speak Russian?" Platinov
called out loud enough for all to hear. A few of the Shining
Path men turned to look at her, but it looked as if they had
been attracted simply by the noise, and didn't understand the
words.

"There's no way to be sure," Bolan answered in the same
language. He studied the hard faces of the men who had turned
toward her voice. No, he saw no signs of comprehension; however that didn't mean none of them understood. Lowering his
voice until it was barely above a whisper, he said, "We're
going to have to take them down before we reach the camp."

"Why not simply let them lead us there?" Platinov asked.
"We could walk right in as if we belonged and then open
fire."

The Executioner shook his head. "There'll be too many of

them. Especially if the real Russians have already arrived with the nukes.''

"*I'm* a real Russian,'' Platinov said, smiling.

"Real Russian black marketeers,'' Bolan amended. ''We'll be better off moving in quietly.'' He continued to watch the Shining Path men. Even the ones who had turned at the initial sound of their voices seemed to have lost interest now.

"Well, speaking of quietly, we have no idea how far we are from this camp,'' Platinov said. ''Gunfire doesn't carry as far in the jungle as it does in the open. But it carries. You have any thoughts on how to get rid of them without alerting the camp?'' She glanced quickly around. ''There are eight of them. That's four apiece.''

Bolan nodded silently. ''There's no other way,'' he said. ''You've got the Woodsman with the sound suppressor. Pollard has my Beretta.''

The former director had been close enough to listen to the conversation. Now he leaned in and whispered in Russian, his voice sounding mildly irritated. ''I'm not as young as I used to be,'' he said. ''And I was probably never as good as either of you. But I can shoot your damn gun. Unless you want me to give it back and go play shuffleboard in the nearest Peruvian nursing home while you do it all.''

Bolan shook his head. ''You draw a weapon right now—even to hand it to me—and they're likely to shoot us all where we sit,'' he said. ''Even if they don't, they're going to wonder why we're trading guns. They'll know something's about to go down.'' He cleared his throat, then continued. ''Just be ready to shoot.'' He turned back to Platinov. ''I'll have to use my MP-5 as a club. And my knife. The problem is going to be getting them close enough together in a small enough group. It'll alert the camp just as well if they fire rather than us.'' He paused once more, thinking. ''We need a distraction of some kind.''

The mischievous grin crept across Platinov's face once more. ''Leave that to me,'' she said.

Before Bolan could ask what she had in mind, the leader in

the red bandanna barked out orders to move on. Grumbling under their breath, the Shining Path men got up off the ground. Their machetes began hacking away once more.

Platinov fell in next to Bolan. They had taken no more than a few steps when he noticed that her hand had ridden up to her fatigue blouse. Quickly and deftly, Platinov unbuttoned the top three buttons of the blouse. Through the opening, the Executioner could see bare skin. She wore no bra.

Bolan had seen the Shining Path men leering at Platinov earlier, and so had she. He knew what the beautiful Russian woman had in mind now, and if anything was going to draw all of the men's attention at once, that would do it.

They trudged slowly through the thick vegetation as the machetes did their work. The soldier had to hand it to her. Marynka Platinov was no slut, but neither was she a particularly modest woman. She knew what worked for her, and she made the most of it.

A few steps later, Platinov jerked at his side, let out a short scream and stumbled. "My ankle!" she cried out in Spanish. She took another stumbling step—long enough to make sure she had all eight of the men's attention—then fell against a tree. Her blouse accidentally caught on an outstretching limb as she twirled clumsily around. She finally caught her balance with her back against the tree's trunk.

The tree limb had ripped the fatigue blouse the rest of the way open. As Platinov ground to a halt, an expression of astonishment and embarrassment covered her face. She looked down at her open shirt as her naked breasts bounced in the air.

Bare-breasted women always have an effect on men. But when those breasts are bared with no warning and out of a normal environment, the effect increases a hundred-fold. Now, added to the tension and stress under which these men were already operating, the impact was electrifying.

The men of the Shining Path froze.

Bolan grabbed the barrel of his MP-5 with both hands and brought it around like a baseball bat across the face of the nearest terrorist. He heard a crunch as the folding stock pulverized cartilage. The man's face literally caved inward. Swinging the weapon back to the other side, Bolan shifted one hand to the receiver and jammed the weapon at a man with a wispy goatee. The blunt end caught the Shining Path man in the throat, and a grinding, gravelly sound issued forth as his larynx split.

In his peripheral vision, the Executioner saw Platinov draw the sound-suppressed Colt Woodsman. She pulled the trigger twice, and a short stocky terrorist fell to the ground, clasping his head. Slightly to the side, he saw Pollard draw the Beretta. But the former CIA director had spent the past ten years behind a desk, and now the sound-suppressed weapon went flying from his fumbling fingers.

Bolan suppressed a groan of disappointment as he took two running steps to the side, toward a Shining Path man wearing white peasant pants and a torn black T-shirt. As he drew the MP-5 back as a club once more, it seemed to catch in the air. Twirling, he saw that another of the terrorists had snagged the sling with one hand. The man's other hand was fumbling to find the pistol grip of the AK-47 slung over his own shoulder.

The Executioner dropped his left hand from the MP-5 and continued the tug-of-war with his right. The Rad came out of its sheath in an ice-pick grip. He stepped in, a thrusting backhand aimed at the Shining Path man's throat. Three inches of steel disappeared beneath his chin on the left side of the man's throat. Bolan ripped the blade backhanded across the skin, and blood shot forth from the severed arteries.

More quiet coughs sounded in his ears, and Bolan turned back in time to see Platinov sending .22-caliber rounds into the torso of a terrorist with a chest the size of a redwood tree. The tiny rounds slowed the thick man but didn't stop him. With a roar of rage, he sprinted toward her. His AK-47, dangling from its sling across his back, appeared forgotten as he raised his machete over his head.

The man Bolan had meant to strike before the MP-5 had been snagged now raised his own Kalishnikov rifle. He stood four feet to the Executioner's rear as Bolan whirled back around to face him. But he had carried the AK-47 with the safety on, and now, under battle stress, he forgot to take it off. The mistake cost him his life and gave the Executioner his.

Thumbing the Rad open to its full seven-inch length, Bolan lunged. The big knife's blade penetrated the terrorist's thin peasant shirt and sank to the handle in his heart. The man's eyes opened wide in surprise.

Bolan pumped the knife twice, widening the wound and increasing the shock. A volcano of crimson shot from the man's chest. The Executioner stepped to the side, out of the spray.

The big man with the machete had reached Platinov, whose back was still against the tree. He was bringing the twenty-inch blade down over his head at her face.

The Russian woman continued to send .22-caliber rounds into the Shining Path man's thick chest until the last possible second before finally stepping out of the way of the machete. The razor-edged blade missed her head by less than an inch. It sank into the trunk of the tree with a loud thud.

The muscular terrorist reached up with his other hand, frantically trying to free the machete from the bark. His own massive strength had been his downfall—the blade was firmly wedged. Before he could rip it free, Platinov stepped in and jammed the Woodsman into his ear. She pulled the trigger.

The low-caliber round didn't even exit the big man's head.

Whatever it did inside his skull caused him to fall to the ground like a felled oak. On his back, his eyes stayed open, staring sightlessly at the sky.

Bolan twirled once more. Platinov's ripped-shirt-ruse had succeeded in getting the men to all take a few steps forward in the hope they'd get a better look at her breasts. He could see now that they hadn't been grouped close enough. Even after all he and the Russian woman had done, two of the men still stood. Both had recovered from the initial shock of the half-nude woman, and then the secondary surprise of the unannounced attack. Now they were raising their AK-47s.

In the corner of his eye, the Executioner saw Platinov take aim and place a well-sighted round between the eyes of the nearer of the men. The man flew to his back on the ground. But the slide on her Woodsman locked open.

The final terrorist stood a good thirty feet away. Even now, he was raising his AK-47 and searching for the sights. The Rad still in his fist, Bolan shot toward him, knowing even as his legs pumped beneath him he wouldn't make it in time. Even if the terrorist hurried his shot and missed, the roar would alert the Shining Path camp in the distance.

The Executioner cursed softly under his breath. It had seemed to be the best decision at the time, but he saw now that giving Pollard the Beretta had been a mistake. Had he had the sound-suppressed weapon now, it would have been an easy shot.

Bolan dropped the Rad as he ran and raised the MP-5 from where it was still slung around his chest. No, he wouldn't reach the terrorist in time to use the knife. So if a shot that would alert the camp had to be fired, it might as well be one that saved his life rather than took it.

The Executioner had already taken up the short trigger slack on the subgun when he heard two soft coughs to his side. The final terrorist let his hands fall from his rifle, clutched his chest, then dropped to the jungle floor among the tangled leaves and vines.

Bolan turned to the side.

Hugh Pollard had found the Beretta he had dropped earlier. He now held it in both hands. A thin wisp of smoke rose through the air from the end of the suppressor.

BOLAN WOULD SOON LEARN just how close they had been to the Shining Path camp. And how lucky they were that no shots had been fired to alert the rest of the terrorists to their presence. But first, as soon as he had Platinov, Pollard and Benito picking through the bodies of the dead men for weapons and other useful equipment, he stepped into the jungle ninety degrees north of the direction they had been headed.

Their Shining Path escort hadn't followed a straight line as they took them toward the encampment, and he had to assume it to be another attempt to slow any pursuit that might have learned of their existence. Now, one of the machetes in hand, the Executioner cut the path looking for a sign. He found it just south of where they had all taken the break and the escape plan had been formed.

Recently cut vines and still-green leaves covered the ground where the Shining Path men had come from the camp the day before. The Executioner followed the sign that led him to another narrow path a quarter mile later. He stopped briefly, considering the situation, as the hot and humid jungle air sent sweat pouring down his face to soak the collar of his shirt. He had to be close. Otherwise, the trampled undergrowth—which acted almost like an arrow pointing forward—wouldn't have been there. With even more caution, he crept forward through the foliage, avoiding the path itself but navigating a parallel course ten feet away.

After what he estimated as another eighth of a mile, Bolan suddenly came upon a drop in the jungle floor. A valley area, filled more with large boulders and stones than greenery, lay below. Dropping to his belly, he crawled out of the jungle to the edge of the ridge.

From his new vantage point, the soldier could see that the valley had once been the site of some ancient quarry. Crude instruments had cut many of the stones, probably forming them into images of whatever pagan gods had been worshiped by the tribes of the day. But the quarry had been abandoned hundreds, if not thousands, of years ago. Now, here and there, green blades of life had sprouted in the areas where the stones had been moved. Small versions of the foliage behind Bolan now struggled to grow around, and within, the rocks.

None of which was what caught the soldier's eyes. What was of paramount interest lay on the other side of the quarry. The area had been cleared of growth to form a clearing, and perhaps two dozen canvas and nylon tents, of various sizes and shapes, had been set up. The Shining Path base was crude and temporary, consisting only of the tents and a large smoldering fire pit in which gray ash and an occasional flickering spark could be seen. The camp had obviously been designed to be struck as soon as the shipment of backpack nukes arrived, and even now, at one of the far corners of the camp, several of the terrorists were tearing down tents.

Bolan squinted across the quarry. Heavily armed men, all seemingly cut from the same mold as those they had just battled less than a half-mile away, moved about the camp. Although a variety of weapons was present, AK-47s were by far the favored rifle. But the Executioner wanted—needed—to see more, and rolling to one hip he unzipped the binocular case on his belt and pulled out a pair of Zeiss binoculars. Pressing them to his eyes, he watched.

Many of the men, he counted forty-eight in all, moved about the camp performing mundane tasks. Some lounged around the fire pit. Others were playing cards in small groups. But they all had one thing in common—they were just passing the time. They were waiting.

And Bolan knew what they were waiting for.

Every so often, a tall slender man with a drooping black mustache appeared in the soldier's view. Unlike the rest of the Shining Path men, he wore faded blue jeans, a white shirt and a thick leather gun belt. On his right hip Bolan could see a holstered Vektor CP-1 pistol. Made in South Africa, the Vektor was state-of-the-art in handguns. Bolan seriously doubted it had come from any of the earlier Russian black-market shipments to the Shining Path. But what was even more interesting was the seeming contrast of the high-tech weapon and the modern gun belt and holster with the rest of the man's attire. He wore a bright red sash just above the belt and, although it was hard to be certain, when the man turned sideways he appeared to carry something shiny in the fold of the sash. That something was thin and curved. If he had been forced to guess, Bolan would have put his money on the fact that what he had

seen was the curved tail of a folded Spanish *navaja*. The
ratchet knife had been the weapon of choice of Gypsies along
the Mediterranean for centuries. If it was indeed a Spanish
navaja he saw now, the Executioner had to assume that this
man was the Spanish arms broker acting as go-between for
the Russians and Shining Path.

Bolan squinted into the lenses as the man in the sash approached another man. They spoke briefly. The second man
was more traditionally dressed in the dirty white cotton shirt
and pants. He was also obviously in charge. The soldier had
seen several of the other terrorists approach him as they went
about their business, and their body language bespoke defer-
ence. He and the Spaniard discussed something, nodded their
heads and then went their separate ways.

But only for a moment.

The Executioner was just about to drop the binoculars when
the distant sound of helicopter blades sounded. He looked up
as the rest of the men all hurried toward the fire pit at the
center of the camp and tilted their eyes skyward, as well. Their
feet pounding through the ashes sent more sparks glimmering
through the gray, and a few seconds later, a chopper appeared
in the distance above the thick jungle. It began descending as
it neared the camp.

Bolan dropped the binoculars to the encampment below. He
now saw why the men had been striking the tents at the far
corner of the camp—they had cleared a landing pad for the
helicopter. Turning the binoculars to the sky again, Bolan
watched the chopper reach the camp and hover over it as the
men below scurried to get the last obstacles out of the way
for the landing. He studied the helicopter through the lenses
as he waited. It bore no markings of any kind. He wouldn't
have expected it to. But then it didn't have to be marked. He
knew it belonged to the Russian black marketeers. And he
knew what it contained.

Enough nuclear explosives—all compressed into tight little
easily transported packs—to blow a dozen South American
cities off the face of the earth.

The chopper finally descended, its skids setting down onto the ground perhaps twenty yards from where the men stood around the fire pit. Three men stepped out of the bubble, hunching beneath the blades as they walked forward. They were obviously of Caucasian descent rather than Peruvian, with light ruddy complexions and big shoulders under the epaulets on their khaki bush shirts.

Both the Shining Path leader and the man wearing the Vektor and *navaja* walked forward to meet them. They all shook hands. A moment later one of the Russians stepped back up into the chopper and handed something down to the man in the red sash.

Bolan dropped the binoculars from his eyes, replaced them in the case on his belt, and scooted back away from the ridge on his belly. He had seen all he needed to. The Russian on the chopper had handed the first of the backpack nukes to the Shining Path leader.

Hugh Pollard had indeed been telling the truth.

And if the Executioner didn't act fast, South America would pay the price.

PLATINOV, POLLARD and Benito had stripped the dead Shining Path men of all useful items by the time the Executioner returned to the spot where he'd left them. In addition to the MP-5, H&K and Colt Woodsman, Platinov had added an AK-47 to her arsenal. Pollard had another of the Kalishnikovs and a pair of Russian Makarov pistols. Benito had found his own rifle and a Tokarev. He handed the Desert Eagle, butt first, back to Bolan.

All three sat at rest as the Executioner emerged from the jungle. Platinov rose to her feet when she saw him and lifted yet another of the Russian assault rifles from the ground. She extended it to him. "I checked all of them out as best I could without test firing them," she said. "We've got the ones which appeared to be in the best shape."

The soldier had already taken his Beretta back from Pollard, and now he accepted the AK-47 and slung it over his shoulder.

"You found the camp?" Platinov asked.

Bolan nodded. He gave them a quick summary of what he ad seen, then said, "A helicopter with the nukes just arrived. watched them start unloading." Moving to Benito, he looked own at the smaller man and said, "You've earned your freeom. Take off."

Benito looked up at the Executioner, puzzled. "Where?" e asked.

"Go back to the train station," Bolan said. "It should be afe now." He indicated the dead Shining Path men on the round around them.

Benito shook his head. "How do we know these were the nly men?" he asked. "And I already told you what they'd lo to me if they found out I led you here."

Bolan shrugged impatiently. "Suit yourself," he said. "Come with us if you think your odds are better." He turned o Platinov, then dropped down to a squatting position between er and where Pollard sat. He pulled the Rad from its sheath, nd opened the big folder. With the blade, he cleared the veeds and other jungle growth away from a spot in front of im to reveal the damp bare dirt. "We're here," he said, taping the Rad's point into the earth. He lifted it slightly, and noved it a couple of inches away from the spot he had indiated. "They're here." Then, dragging the tip of the knife lightly back toward him, he stopped it again and said, "Right ere is a valley. Looks like an old stone quarry. I watched hem from this point." Again he moved the knife to indicate he vantage point from which he'd observed the encampment. 'And here is where the chopper set down." The Rad moved gain to show the spot at the corner of the camp where the ents had been cleared away for the landing.

"So, what do you want to do?" Platinov asked.

"The quarry is a death trap," the Executioner said. "We an't cross it without exposing ourselves and being seen." He ifted the Rad, then tapped spots to each side of the point he ad marked as the encampment. "But I don't want us shooting ach other in a cross fire, either." The knife moved to the far

side of the dirt map. "I'm going to circle around through th
jungle to here," he said. "And come in from the rear." H
glanced up at the woman and saw her eyes frowning down
the dirt. "You circle the quarry, too. But stop here. Come i
from this side."

Platinov nodded both her understanding and approval of th
plan.

"What about me?" Pollard asked. "Come in on the oth
side?"

The Executioner shook his head. "No. We'd still have th
cross-fire problem." He tapped the spot at the edge of th
quarry where he had watched the encampment earlier. "I wa
you here, Pollard," he said. "Where I was. With your rifl
Your job is to take out the chopper. You'll be shooting at a
angle away from Platinov and me."

"And what's the best way to do that?" Pollard asked.

"Clip the blades off the top," Bolan said. "It's more su
than trying to disable the engine. And even if you took o
the gas tank, they might get a few miles out of it before
went down. Besides, there's a smoldering fire pit down ther
It's quite a ways off, but with a hole in the tank and the rig
gust of wind...I think you see my point."

Pollard nodded. "The blades," he said.

"You won't be that far away," Bolan said. "It should b
an easy shot, but no matter what, I don't want that helicopte
capable of getting into the air again. You understand?"

The former CIA man's eyebrows lowered quizically. "N
really. I thought you said you saw them unload the nukes."

"I said I saw them *start* to unload," Bolan corrected. "A
ter the first one came off and I was sure what it was, I cam
back here. There wasn't any time to waste. Whether they'v
already taken the backpacks off the chopper, or whether th
Russians are just using the one to show the Shining Path me
how they operate, and the rest are still on board, I don't know
But I don't want to take the chance of those things getting i
the air and away from us again."

To his side, the Executioner heard Benito clear his throat. Bolan, Platinov and Pollard turned toward him.

"I think I've changed my mind," the informant said. He rose to his feet. "I'll be taking my chances on the train, I believe." He turned and started back in the direction from which they'd come.

"Benito," Bolan called out, stopping him.

The informant turned back. "Yes?"

"When you get back to Lima, go back to being a simple assistant train depot manager. If you don't break your connection to the Shining Path, I'll hear about it." He tapped the Rad on his belt with a forefinger. "You got that?"

Benito understood. The lump that went down his throat was the size of a baseball. He nodded his head, then turned and disappeared into the thick green jungle.

Bolan swiveled back to the other two. "Any questions?"

"Yeah," Pollard said. "I should be able to cut the blades off that chopper with a few well-placed shots. What do you want me to do then?"

"Help us," Bolan answered. "Fire down into the camp at anyone who moves."

"Except us," Platinov added. She turned to the Executioner. "It sounds like we'll need some help. You said you counted close to fifty men?"

"Give or take a couple," he said. "I might have missed a few."

Platinov sighed. "So, that's only about twenty-five well-armed men apiece that we're preparing to attack. Maybe we should alert them so they can get some reinforcements and make it fair?"

"The odds aren't in our favor," he agreed. "But I don't see any other choice. We don't have time to call in reinforcements."

"What about an air strike?" Pollard asked.

Bolan shook his head. "They've got nukes down there," he said. "They could activate one or more and decide that if they've got to go, everyone else might as well, too. And it's not just us I'm worried about. There are several indigenous tribes within range.'' He turned his attention back to Platinov. ''You've got your Woodsman,'' he said. ''I've got the Beretta. First thing we do before we attack—'' he glanced quickly to Pollard ''—and before *you* start shooting at the chopper, is take out as many as we can, quietly. Pick the easiest targets first. Men on the perimeter. Other targets who won't quickly be spotted and alert everyone else to the fact that they're under sound-suppressed fire.'' He paused and drew in a deep breath. ''We can bring down the odds that way.''

The beautiful Russian agent looked him in the eye. ''How long do you think it will be before they realize what's going on?'' she asked.

''Not long,'' the Executioner said. ''Seconds. When that happens, we shift to the big guns.'' He patted the stock of the AK-47 slung over his shoulder.

Platinov grinned and shook her head. ''If you were anyone but you,'' she said, ''I'd tell you to go take a flying leap off that quarry.''

The Executioner rose to his feet. ''My guess is it'll take me a half hour to circle the camp. You and Pollard will be in position before that. Keep low, keep out of sight and wait on me. Platinov, your signal to start is when you see me drop the first man. Pollard, you don't fire until you hear the first non-suppressed round, regardless of who it comes from.''

Pollard's head moved slowly up and down. ''What if the chopper starts to leave before that?'' he wanted to know.

''Then take it out regardless. Under no circumstances is that helicopter to get airborne.''

''But what if you and Platinov—?''

''Under no circumstances,'' the Executioner emphasized. ''If that leaves us hanging out in the open, that's just too bad.''

''Okay,'' Pollard said.

''Any other questions?''

Platinov looked down to the ground, then back up. ''No questions,'' she said. ''But I think it's time to update some promises.''

Bolan knew what she meant. During the confusion of the battle that was about to ensue, either of them could circle back, snag Hugh Pollard and be gone with him before the other knew what was going on. "Okay," he said. "I won't if you won't."

"I won't," Platinov said. "The promise holds until the nukes are secured."

The Executioner nodded his agreement.

Pollard shook his head and smiled. "It's so nice to be wanted," he said. "And even fought over."

Without further words, they started off toward the encampment.

THEY ENTERED the dense jungle growth once more. Behind her, Marynka Platinov could hear Hugh Pollard's footsteps. As far as she was concerned, the man had proved himself. She now thought he was no traitor to his country partly because of his actions, and the help he had given them since they'd found him. But another reason was the fact that Belasko now trusted him. And she valued his judgment. More, perhaps, than anyone she had ever known. More, perhaps, than even her own judgment right now.

It didn't matter whether or not Hugh Pollard had actually sold out the United States. Platinov had been assigned to find him, then take him back to Moscow for debriefing. Grabbing a former CIA director for interrogation would be, in the intelligence community, the equivalent of striking gold. She would probably be promoted to general, and she would become a legend within Russian Intelligence.

A vine whipped toward Platinov's face, but her catlike reflexes allowed her to duck under it. Behind her, Hugh Pollard wasn't as quick or lucky. She heard it lay into bare skin with a snap, and a quiet oath issued forth from the CIA man's lips. She walked on.

Ahead of her, Belasko had stopped for a moment, staring through the thick foliage. They must be nearing the quarry. But after a moment's hesitation, his own machete sliced through a vine hanging down in front of him and he moved on.

So, Platinov wondered, what was she to do? She knew she wouldn't break her promise to Belasko any more than he would break his to her. Neither of them would attempt to steal the former CIA director away until after the nukes had been secured and the threat that South American cities would be destroyed was over. But what then? Would Belasko and Pollard suddenly be gone? How did Belasko feel about her? Did he return her feelings? She didn't think he would allow himself to do so. At least not until he had completed his own mission and returned Hugh Pollard to the U.S.

Which was why Marynka Platinov knew that while she was a great clandestine agent, Belasko was even better; the best, by far, that she had ever known. Not only would he never allow his personal feelings to interfere with his mission, but he wouldn't even question it as she was doing now.

Belasko stopped again, peering ahead through the jungle, and Platinov felt a certain anger replace the warmer feelings she had been experiencing. Her indignation wasn't directed toward the man she saw in front of her. He was just doing his job. The anger she felt in her heart as she, too, stopped to look through the foliage, was directed toward herself. Yes, he was doing his job without letting his personal feelings get in the way. Why couldn't she?

The soldier turned back to them and held a finger to his lips for silence. Then, moving in closer to her, he motioned the CIA man to step forward and join them.

"Ten feet ahead," Belasko whispered quietly. "We'll break out of the jungle. Hugh, you'll have to belly-crawl to the edge. Make sure you stay hidden until the firing begins. But remember, under *no* conditions is that chopper to get off the ground."

The former CIA director nodded.

Belasko turned to Platinov and hooked a thumb to one side. "You go that way," he whispered. "You'll have to stay far enough inside the green to keep from being seen. But edge out close enough to find the best vantage spot for your Woodsman." His eyes fell to the pistol holstered on Platinov's hip. "I'd go for head shots if I were you."

"I agree." Platinov stated.

The big man nodded, then turned and disappeared into the jungle in the opposite direction from which he had pointed her. Platinov watched Hugh Pollard take a few steps forward, then drop to his face and make his way out onto the rock formation leading to the valley ahead. She turned and began working her way in a circular path around the quarry.

Platinov walked quietly, concentrating on her feet and what they were about to step on with each footfall. This was no time for a sprained ankle or a snapping stick that might alert the Shining Path men in the distance. But it also forced her mind away from Mike Belasko. Somewhere below the surface, on a more primordial and emotional level, Marynka Platinov knew he was still in her thoughts.

Roughly fifteen minutes later, Platinov guessed she had passed around the quarry and drawn adjacent to the tents Belasko had described. She began angling forward, out of the thick branches and vines, finally dropping to her knees when she saw blue sky through the leaves. She knee-walked a few steps farther, then reached out, pulling a branch back slightly to peer past it.

She had estimated well, and ahead, in the valley below, she saw the tents of the Shining Path men. Beyond the temporary shelters, alone in an open area at the corner of the encampment, stood the helicopter. The pilot still sat behind the controls. Shining Path men—none of them fitting the description Belasko had given of either the leader or the Spaniard—sat around the camp. Some of them played cards while others were engaged in some game involving dice.

The Russian woman dropped the branch, moved a few feet farther to get behind a tree, then sat on the jungle floor to wait. She continued to watch through the foliage.

Ten more minutes went by with nothing out of the ordinary happening. She still had not seen the Shining Path leader or the Spaniard, and had to guess they were out of sight inside one of the tents. Which one? She couldn't be sure. She had seen one of the men take two bottles and several glasses into the largest of the tents near the middle of the camp. If she were betting, she would place her money on it. She had to guess that the final details of the exchange were being worked out even as she waited for Belasko to position himself.

One of the men playing dice threw the tiny speckled cubes, then cursed loudly while the rest of the men in the game laughed. The man who had lost said something else too low for Platinov to hear, then stood and started walking away from the game. He passed the tents and the helicopter, and moved to the edge of the clearing. He faced away from Platinov but she could see his hands moving in front of him as he unzipped his pants. A few seconds later, a stream of urine arced away from him through the air.

Then, suddenly, for no apparent reason, the urinating man dropped to his knees and fell forward, facedown, into the puddle he had created.

Platinov turned her eyes toward the rear of the encampment where she knew Belasko had positioned himself. She saw nothing in the dense jungle. But another man—just inside the clearing—had been carrying a bucket of water along the perimeter. He suddenly tripped and fell forward, the water spilling ahead of him and the bucket rolling to a halt ten feet away. The man hadn't hit the ground hard, and anyone watching would have expected him to rise to his feet and look around in embarrassment at his clumsiness.

But he didn't. He lay where he had fallen.

Platinov drew the Colt Woodsman from her holster. The rest of the men in the camp were either involved in the games of chance or lounging around in twos and threes, talking. There were no more single targets to take out who weren't likely to be noticed. But there would be, as Belasko had predicted, several seconds of confusion during which the men hadn't yet figured out what was happening.

Those were seconds during which they had to cut down the enemy force as much as possible.

Marynka Platinov raised the sound-suppressed Woodsman and extended the barrel out of the jungle. With no place better to start, she lined the sights up and let them fall on the face of the man who had taken the dice from the earlier player. Just before she pulled the trigger, she saw him roll. The dice came to a halt and he shouted in glee as he grabbed for the money on the ground in front of him.

The irony of the man winning wasn't lost on Platinov. A part of her was actually happy he had won. His final thought would be pleasant.

9

From where he knelt just inside the thick jungle, Bolan had a clear view of the open flap of what was obviously the Shining Path command tent. Through the binoculars he could see the wooden table set up in the center of the canvas room. Seated around that table were the Spaniard, the man he had seen earlier who appeared to be the leader of the Shining Path and the Russians he had watched get off the chopper.

In the center of the table sat a rectangular object somewhat bigger than a shoe box. The simple camper's backpack from which it had been removed had been dropped under the table and now rested between the feet of two of the men.

The Executioner had already carefully searched the rest of the camp with his field glasses, and this was the only nuclear device, or backpack, he had seen. Which told him his earlier guess had been correct. The Russians had only unloaded this one to use as a demonstration model in order to educate the Shining Path men in the activation process. The other nukes were still on the helicopter. He glanced to the chopper now. The engine was off, and the bird was at rest. But a pilot sat waiting to take off at a moment's notice.

Behind the men at the table, leaning forward for this mini-course in nuclear activation, stood a dozen more Shining Path men. These men, Bolan knew, would be the ones sent out to plant the devices. These were the men who would activate the timers on the nukes to murder hundreds of thousands, if not millions, of innocent people.

The Executioner shifted the binoculars slightly, aiming the

lenses over the tent and past the rock quarry on the other side of the camp. At the top of the ridge, he saw Hugh Pollard's head move slightly. He took in a deep breath, wishing the CIA man hadn't had quite so many years behind a desk since his field experience. Pollard's job was simple—wait until he heard gunfire, then take out the chopper. He should have stayed completely out of sight until then instead of peering over the ridge where he might be seen. His cue to action would be heard, not seen, and he was taking stupid chances by allowing any part of his body to come into view.

Bolan dropped the field glasses and quickly surveyed the camp. The men outside the tent were passing the time with various games of chance and other commonplace activities. None of them seemed to have noticed the head at the top of the ridge, and the Executioner let his breath out in relief. Swinging the binoculars sideways, he scanned up and down the jungle where Platinov would be. He spotted nothing. But he knew she was there.

The Executioner paused briefly, thinking about the beautiful Russian woman. He didn't know if she was in love with him, but she was certainly acting like a woman in love. Actually, she was showing the signs of a woman fighting a battle inside herself *not* to love him. She was smart, and regardless of how she might feel, she knew the complications such a love would inevitably bring with it. Perhaps the real question, he mused, was how did he feel about her? He respected her—of that there was no doubt. And there was no denying the strong physical attraction.

Bolan stared through the lenses at the trees in which he knew Platinov was hidden. So, how did he feel about her? It was simple. Another place, another time, another life perhaps, but the Executioner was nothing if not a realist. There was no sense wasting time dreaming about what wasn't going to happen. He couldn't afford to.

Replacing the binoculars in their case once again, the Executioner drew the Beretta. He double-checked to make sure the sound suppressor was tightly threaded into the barrel,

checked the magazine and the chamber for the subsonic 9 mm
rounds that would "cough" from the weapon almost silently
and flipped the selector switch to semiauto. His mind hadn't
completely left Platinov, however, and now he wondered if
she would keep her promise not to try to run off with Hugh
Pollard during the upcoming battle. Yes, she would. She had
kept her word so far. But Bolan reminded himself that neither
of their promises extended beyond getting the nukes out of
the hands of the Shining Path. From that point on, if yet another mutual agreement wasn't made between the two of them,
it would be open season on the former CIA director.

Turning his attention back to the camp, Bolan saw one of
the men who had been playing craps suddenly rise and walk
away. He watched the man pass the tents, then the helicopter,
and come to a halt at the edge of the camp. The helicopter
almost blocked his line of sight, but he could still see the man
as he began to urinate. The Shining Path terrorist stared off
into the jungle, his head barely visible to the side of the chopper's glass bubble.

It was time to start evening the odds for the upcoming battle, and this was as good a place to start as any. Steadying his
aim against a tree, Bolan lined the sights up on the side of the
man's head. Slowly, he pulled back on the trigger, taking up
the slack. The Beretta jumped lightly in his hands as it sent
out a sound-smothered round that entered the man's head just
to the side of the ear. He fell to the ground.

Bolan had barely squeezed the trigger when another man
suddenly appeared in his field of vision just inside the clearing.
Less than ten feet away, he strolled along the edge of the
jungle carrying a bucket of water and whistling softly. The
Executioner froze as the man passed. As soon as he had, the
Executioner moved the sights to send another quiet 9 mm
round drilling into the back of his head. He, too, fell to the
ground just outside the trees.

Looking back to the crap game in the clearing, Bolan saw
the man who had taken the dice player's place suddenly pitch
forward. Thinking he had simply lost his balance, the other

men seated and squatting on the ground around the game burst into laughter. A split second later, another of the Shining Path gamblers hit the dirt.

A poker game had been in progress on the other side of the camp, and the Executioner now turned his attention that way. Platinov had obviously picked out the dice players as her targets, and there was no sense duplicating her work by sending his own rounds into the same men at whom she was aiming.

Bolan had taken out three of the card players with as many shots by the time the men at both games realized they were under silent fire. The time when silence was an advantage had ended.

Jamming the Beretta back into his holster, the Executioner swung the AK-47 from the sling across his back. Flipping the selector switch to full-auto, he sent a steady stream of 7.62 mm Russian rounds into the men still playing poker. One by one, they began to fall in death as he cut a figure-eight back and forth from one end of the game to the other. Some of his rounds passed through the bodies, flying on to strike the gray ash in the fire pit and send twinkling glimmers of fire dancing through the air.

From the side of the jungle, the Executioner heard another AK-47 begin. Glancing that way, he saw the leaves fluttering at the edge of the clearing as Platinov's rounds cut through them. He still couldn't see her.

As he turned back to the camp, slow semiauto rounds from yet another of the Kalishnikov rifles began to explode on the ridge above the quarry. Bolan's eyes rose that way. He could now see Pollard from the waist up, lying in the prone position as he fired down at the helicopter. Bolan turned quickly to check out the results. So far, the blades were still intact.

Platinov had neutralized all but three of the men in the crap game before all hell had broken loose. But now, these three dived for their own AK-47s. The other men around the camp had produced rifles, as well, and now sent barrages of bullets into the jungle toward both Bolan's and Platinov's positions. Bolan fired one more full-auto burst, nearly cutting a tall reed-

thin Shining Path man in half, then dropped to all fours and
crawled ten feet to the side. Return rounds flew over his head,
slicing through the foliage where he had been only seconds
before. Ripped leaves and stubby pieces of vine flew through
the air to rain over his head and back.

Taking up a new position, the Executioner stared out of the
jungle for a second before he fired again. Pollard hadn't
stopped blasting away from the ridge. Still, the helicopter
hadn't been touched. And even now, the pilot was turning over
the engine to warm it up. Bolan frowned, wishing now that
he had given the sniper assignment to Platinov. Pollard was
less than a hundred yards away, and the shot—even aiming at
the relatively small rotary blades—should have been a cinch
for anyone who even knew what rifle sights were for.

The Executioner cut loose with another series of fire, dropping a Shining Path man who had a long knife scar across his
face, and another who sported a thin, wispy mustache and
goatee. From the side of the jungle, Platinov's AK chattered
on, as well. She had shifted her position, too, moving farther
away from Bolan.

Glancing back at the ridge, the Executioner saw Pollard
swing his rifle away from the helicopter and begin firing down
into the camp. Bolan's jaw clamped tightly. What was happening? What was Pollard doing? Was he seized by panic?
The former CIA man knew he was supposed to take out the
chopper first, and he knew how important it was. Why was
he deviating from the plan?

For a brief moment, the Executioner once again questioned
Pollard's loyalties. Had this all been a ruse on his part?

The Executioner was about to try to move into position to
destroy the helicopter himself when a trio of Shining Path men
fell victim to panic. With banshee-like cries of rage and fear,
they suddenly sprinted directly toward where Bolan squatted
at the edge of the jungle. He was forced to turn his thoughts
momentarily away from the chopper, swinging his AK-47
back around at the men. He pulled back on the trigger, and
the rifle exploded with a burst that took the man in the lead

in the chest. A wide-brimmed straw sombrero went flying from his head as he fell to the ground like a rock. The Executioner moved his weapon slightly to the side and pulled the trigger again, trying for another quick burst. But the magazine had run dry, and the rifle bolt locked back open empty after the first bullet left the barrel.

The lone round, however, was enough to drop the second man in the sprinting trio—it sailed through his heart and out his back, ricocheting off the stones in the quarry on the other side of the camp. The final man of the kamikaze attack still ran forward, screaming, and sending a wild spray of gunfire into the jungle all around the Executioner.

With no time to slam a new magazine into the AK-47, Bolan let the rifle fall to the end of his sling. Hours, months and years of muscle memory jerked the Desert Eagle from hip leather. A massive .44 Magnum round exploded from the Israeli-made handgun, slamming into the forehead of the final suicide gunner. The Shining Path man was thrown a full five feet back onto the grass.

The Executioner holstered the Desert Eagle. Leaving the empty AK-47 where it hung, he twirled the H&K MP-5 around and into play. He turned once again toward the helicopter. He had heard the engine start only moments before, and now he saw the blades beginning to whirl as the chopper prepared to take off. Glancing up past the quarry, he saw that Pollard was still shooting down into the camp. Not only that, he didn't appear to be shooting at any of the Shining Path men. He rounds were all directed into the empty tent which was closest to the ridge.

For a second the Executioner was tempted to aim his MP-5 at the ridge. He would have to deal with Pollard later. Right now, there was no time. Lining the H&K's sights up on the spinning chopper blades, he was about to pull the trigger when another hail of fire drove him to the ground once more.

The Executioner crawled through the undergrowth as bullets split the limbs above his head. The remaining terrorists had estimated his position once more, and were sending every round at their disposal in that direction. They were "spraying and praying" but they knew his general location, and sooner or later one or more of the shots would find him. He had to get out of there. In the meantime he heard the chopper's engines rev louder. It was almost ready to leave the ground.

Bolan had crawled twenty yards, and left the return fire several feet behind him, before he rose high enough to see the action once again. When he did, he saw the men who had been inside the command tent come sprinting out. The ones dressed in peasant garb came first, and the Executioner sent a series of bursts from the MP-5 to drop five of them. However, by that time the remaining Shining Path gunmen had his position yet again, and another bombardment of rounds forced him down. He crawled back in the direction he had come from, trying to get closer to the chopper. Again, when he looked up, he saw men exiting the tent. This time, it was the Russian black marketeers, and he held the trigger back on the H&K, dropping two of them. Then other rounds—he had to assume Platinov's—took out the final Russian. But the terrorists still standing had been waiting for him to surface again, and their return fire came faster this time.

The Executioner saw the Spaniard and the Shining Path leader exit the tent as he hit the ground beneath this new storm of lead. He scurried along the ground, again rising to fire. The enemy had anticipated his movement this time, and rounds shot past both of his ears almost as soon as he'd raised his head. He aimed the MP-5 at a spot between the shoulder blades of the Shining Path leader as he and the Spaniard raced for the chopper. The Shining Path man turned a cartwheel in the air as the heavy rifle rounds split his spine. The other man, the Spaniard, ran as the Executioner ducked under the return fire once more.

The Spaniard had boarded the helicopter by the time Bolan was again in position to fire. As he raised his head, he saw Platinov emerge from the jungle and sprint across the camp. The AK-47 jumped in her hand with every step. He also caught a glimpse of Hugh Pollard, still on the ridge. The former CIA director seemed to have remembered his orders, and was directing his fire at the chopper once more.

Several of the Shining Path men now deserted, dropping their weapons and fleeing into the jungle. Platinov caught several of them in the back before they reached the trees. As he shouldered the MP-5 again, Bolan saw the Spaniard swing himself on board the chopper. The Executioner sighted down the barrel at the revolving blades atop the craft.

Just as he was about the pull the trigger, he caught a glimpse of a Shining Path man directly behind Platinov. The terrorist had played possum on the ground as the Russian agent raced past him. Now, he rose to a kneeling position and took aim to shoot her in the back.

Bolan stepped from the jungle into the clearing and swung the H&K's barrel past Platinov. The Russian woman saw the move, and for a moment she must have thought he was about to break his promise and shoot her. Her AK-47 came his way. As the Executioner's bullets flew past and to her rear, she spun around to see where they'd gone and watched her would-be killer drop in a pool of his own blood.

Platinov had turned back now, and she looked as if she was about to speak but the Executioner turned back to the helicopter and saw that it was now ten feet off the ground. The Spaniard was holding on to the doorway with one hand as he leaned out of the chopper and fired the Vektor with the other. Bolan twirled the MP-5 toward him and cut loose with a trio of rounds. The helicopter had risen another five feet when the Spaniard fell out to the ground.

Bolan could still hear Hugh Pollard firing away from the ridge. The former director wasn't shooting much better than he had earlier. Several holes appeared in the body of the helicopter, then one round struck the glass bubble and spiderwebbed outward. The bullet missed the pilot, and did little other visible damage to the aircraft. As the Executioner tilted the H&K upward, he saw another of Pollard's rounds skid across the chopper's roof, taking some paint but nothing of value with it.

As the helicopter continued to rise, Bolan zeroed the MP-5 in on the blades. A hard smile twisted his lips as the front sight fell on the whirling target and he viewed it through the rear O-ring. The chopper was still in range, he had a clear shot at the blades and he couldn't miss at this distance. He pulled the trigger.

And heard a click. Only then did he realize that he'd fired his last rounds at the Spaniard.

Bolan's MP-5 dropped to the end of the sling. But his heart dropped even further. Even as he jerked the Desert Eagle free from his hip again, he watched the helicopter rise higher into the air. The angle of trajectory changed, and now the body of the chopper blocked any shot he might have had at the blades. The pilot, too, was out of sight—covered by the bottom of the helicopter.

The Executioner cursed quietly under his breath. He could fire at the gas tank or engine and hope for the best, but his odds of success had just dropped like a Las Vegas gambler at the sudden end of a winning streak.

The Executioner's jaw tightened. He had never been a quitter, and he didn't intend to start now. Raising the hand cannon in his fist, he lowered his eyebrows in concentration as he estimated the angle that might—just might—send the big Magnum rounds drilling through the bottom of the helicopter and into the pilot. He was starting to squeeze the trigger when a final round came from high on the ridge, and the chopper—now thirty feet high—suddenly stalled in the air.

A moment later Bolan watched it come plummeting straight back down to earth.

He turned to the ridge.

Hugh Pollard stood at the top of the ancient rock quarry, his AK-47 held over his head in victory.

THE SHINING PATH camp looked as if an invading army had struck. It had. A small army of two, backed up by a sniper. But an army nonetheless.

Bodies of dead Shining Path men littered the grounds. Bolan

kept the Desert Eagle ready as he used his other hand to drop the empty magazines from both the AK-47 and MP-5 and insert fresh loads. Not until both weapons were chambered did he reholster the hand cannon.

With the AK-47 now aimed out over the carnage, the Executioner took stock. He estimated no more of than a half-dozen men had escaped into the jungle. They were no longer a threat, and could be easily picked up later by Peruvian authorities. The rest of the men who had planned to blow up a dozen cities in South America lay dead on the ground.

All but two.

As he walked cautiously farther out of the jungle, Bolan saw a body stir ten feet from where Platinov stood, taking her own inventory of the scene. The woman didn't hesitate. A lone 7.62 shot from her AK-47 and the man's head exploded.

That left one.

It wasn't the pilot. Through the fractured glass of the helicopter, Bolan could see the man. His sunglasses hung from one ear, and his head drooped at an awkward angle from his neck. Blood soaked his entire neck and shoulder area. It was still pumping faintly out of the wound. The pilot's eyes stared ahead. He hadn't blinked since the chopper had hit the ground.

The body of the helicopter was now riddled with holes. Most of the windshield had been shot away by Pollard's wild rounds, and only splinters of glass still clung to the frame.

Bolan took a final glance across the grounds, assuring himself there were no more Shining Path men faking death, before starting toward the chopper. Ten feet away, the Spaniard lay in a twisted mess where he had fallen from the rising craft. Both of his legs had been broken, and jutted out from his body awkwardly. As he drew closer the Executioner could see the man's chest heaving up and down as he gasped for air. One of the .44 magnum rounds had struck him in the right frontal deltoid muscle, nearly ripping his arm from his shoulder. The other had entered the Spaniard's chest, pierced a lung and dyed his white shirt a cardinal red. A frothy red foam bubbled from the hole with each breath for which the man struggled.

Coming to a halt next to him, Bolan saw the Vektor lying on the ground thirty feet away. He leaned down and ripped the *navaja* from the man's sash, keeping the AK-47 trained on his head. "Who are you?" he asked the man.

The Spaniard looked at him through cloudy eyes. "*Gitano*," he said.

"*Gitano* means 'Gypsy' in Spanish," the Executioner growled as he pocketed the *navaja*. "I asked you who you are, not what."

Before the dying man could say more, Hugh Pollard appeared at Bolan's side. "Damn Russian sights were off," he panted. "I couldn't hit jackshit."

The Executioner glanced at him. That explained it all. Pollard hadn't tried to avoid his duty. The sights on his rifle had been out of alignment. There had been no opportunity to test fire the weapon, and the former CIA man wouldn't have recognized the problem until he'd missed the first few easy shots. When he had, he'd used the nearest tent to mark his rounds in order to learn where the bullets were actually hitting in relation to his sight pattern. Then he'd applied "Kentucky windage"—adjusting his aim accordingly and returning his fire to the chopper.

It had taken a long time—almost too much time—but the former CIA director had finally hit his target. But on his way to finding it, it appeared he'd fired at least two magazines full of 7.62 mm rounds. Now, as the odor of cordite blew away in the gentle breeze, the faint smell of gasoline filled the Executioner's nostrils. He looked back briefly at the chopper. It had more holes in it than a golf course, and at least one of Pollard's rounds must have found the gas tank.

Bolan turned back to the Gypsy on the ground. "I asked you who you are," he said again.

The Gypsy shrugged and the movement sent a choking shiver through his chest. More pinkish foam spumed from the bullet hole. He glanced down at his chest, saw that he was dying and decided there was no sense in lying. "Ramone Lopez," he sputtered, his voice filled with pride.

Platinov had moved in to join them. Bolan turned to her. "Go check the chopper," he said. "Make sure the other nukes are still on board."

The Russian hurried to the helicopter, peered inside, then turned back and nodded. "They are here."

"Tell me about your American CIA connection," the Executioner demanded of the man on the ground.

Lopez smiled, then actually laughed, which sent even more tremors through his body. "William Brookings?" he said. "He's not here."

"I can see that," the Executioner said impatiently. "But he *was* your man?"

"Yes," the Gypsy said softly. "Brookings. He's back in Washington by now, though." He turned his head painfully and squinted at Pollard to Bolan's side. "You are Pollard?" he asked.

"I am," Pollard said.

The Gypsy started to laugh again, thought better of it and made do with a grin. "You are a fool," he whispered.

"It's not me lying on the ground dying," the former CIA director countered.

"No," spluttered the Gypsy. "But soon it will be. If there's anything left of any of us."

"What do you mean?" Platinov asked.

The Gypsy didn't answer, but the smile widened and became even more evil.

What he meant suddenly hit Bolan like an anvil in the face. Turning, he raced toward the command tent where he had seen the nuke on the table. He hadn't noticed it from a distance, even through the binoculars, but now he saw a small digital timing device attached to the bomb by two wires. Red numbers were visible on the timer's screen. And they were changing with every second.

1:04:01...1:04:00...1:3:59....

The Executioner took in a deep breath. The backpack nuke had been activated. It had happened as he had feared it might if they called in an air strike. When Lopez, the Shining Path leader and the Russians had realized they were under attack, they had activated the nuke and set the timer. They had planned to escape in the helicopter with the rest of the bombs, and let the rest of the Shining Path men be damned.

The Executioner pivoted on the balls of his feet. "Platinov! Pollard!" he yelled through the tent flap. "Get in here!"

The urgency in Bolan's voice brought the two running. Platinov was first through the opening. "What?" she said, then stared down in horror at the timer.

Her eyes answered the question Bolan would have asked her. No, she did not know how to deactivate it.

Pollard was only a few steps behind. His face went blank, and he shook his head in disbelief. "After all this..." he said, letting his voice trail off and answering the same question.

The Executioner turned to Platinov. "Take him and get out of here," he said.

"Where?" Platinov asked. "We have an hour. We can never get far enough away to—"

"Maybe you can't, maybe you can," the Executioner said. "But you've got to try. Go on. Take him and go. It's what you've been wanting anyway."

The woman stared up at him, and unless his eyes were playing tricks on him, the Executioner saw a tear in the corner of one of her eyes.

"Just go! Do it!" Bolan almost shouted. He pushed her out of the tent so hard she almost fell.

Pollard looked down at the device on the table. He was truly between the devil and the deep blue sea. If he stayed, he stood a good chance of turning to vapor in a little over an hour. But if he went with Platinov, and she took him to Moscow...

"Go with her," the Executioner said. "At least you'll be alive."

Pollard evidently agreed, deciding to face the devil he didn't know rather than the one he did. He turned out of the tent and he and Platinov began running across the camp.

The Executioner turned back to the timer. His eyes followed the lines connecting it to the small nuclear device. The nuke itself was enclosed in a vinyl-covered box and looked no more dangerous than a stereo speaker. Near the bottom, he could see a half-dozen Phillips-head screws holding the sides to the base. Pulling a small multitool out of his pocket, he went to work on them.

He glanced at the timer as, one by one, the screws came out—1:01:07…1:01:06…

Bolan checked the base for trip wires, then lifted the frame away and set it next to the bomb on the table. He stared down into a multitude of wires and other components he didn't recognize or understand. For a brief moment, he wished for the help of either Gary Manning of Phoenix Force or Gadgets Schwarz from Able Team—an explosives expert and an electronics genius, respectively, and both well educated in the nuclear field.

"If wishes were horses," Bolan muttered under his breath. No amount of wishing was going to make either of the men, or any other nuclear expert, magically appear in the Peruvian jungle. He was on his own.

He turned to the timer once more—59:43…59:42….

The Executioner continued to study the device. Activating such a device was simple—just set the timer and push a button. That was what the Russians would have been showing the Shining Path men. But deactivation was a whole different story. Not only was this outside his area of expertise, but any number of booby traps could also have been installed. His best guess was that cutting one of the wires leading from the timer would stop the countdown. The other, he had to assume, would set the nuke off immediately if severed. That gave him a fifty-fifty chance.

If he was right. He couldn't even be certain that either wire he cut wouldn't immediately send a mushroom cloud up over the jungle.

As had always been his practice, the soldier made up his mind quickly. He still had the better part of an hour left, and he would put it to good use. He would study the device from top to bottom, end to end, over and over. Perhaps some clue would be spotted. Perhaps he would suddenly see the nuclear bomb in a different light and understand how to confidently disarm it.

Perhaps a miracle would happen.

Bolan straightened up, rolled up the sleeves of his shirt, then bent over the table once more. No, a miracle wasn't likely, but he saw no point in feeling sorry for himself or anyone else who might be within range of the bomb. Such inaction wouldn't do any good whatsoever. No, he would take advantage of the time he still had. And if he still hadn't come up with a better solution when the clock hit ten seconds, he could cut one of the wires and see what happened.

If he was wrong, he'd never know it. However, waiting as long as he could would give Platinov and Pollard the maximum time to escape. Would it be enough?

He doubted it. But it might.

The seconds continued to tick away. Seconds became minutes as the Executioner continued to stare at the backpack nuke from every possible angle. He traced wires from their origins to their ends, and back again. He learned nothing he hadn't learned during the first fifteen seconds after he'd lifted the vinyl covering off the bomb.

Finally, the Executioner looked over at the timer and saw he had a little over a minute left. He drew the Rad from the Kydex sheath on his belt but left it closed. The wires leading from the timer to the bomb weren't thick. Three inches of edge would be more than enough. He had no need for the additional leverage the seven-inch blade would give him.

With thirty seconds left, Bolan reached down and separated the two wires. Which one? It didn't matter. They were both black, looked identical, and one was as good a guess as the other. It was like playing roulette. The Executioner took a deep breath.

0:17...0:16...0:15...

Bolan allowed his mind to drift for only a few seconds. It raced back over time, covering his long career and his family—his parents and sister had been dead so long now. He thought briefly of Johnny, his sole surviving brother, then his thoughts turned to the other men and women who had become his new family.

The warriors of Stony Man Farm. Jack Grimaldi, Barbara Price, Hal Brognola. Able Team. Phoenix Force. Aaron Kurtzman and his computer crew. The blacksuits, and all the rest.

0:11...0:10...0:09...

It was time.

A strange calm fell over Bolan as he grasped the wire closest to him and lowered the knife blade to it. If it was his time to go, it was his time to go. Nothing could change that. His only prayers were that Platinov and Pollard were far enough away that they didn't get vaporized if he chose the wrong wire.

0:06...0:05...0:04...

Bolan waited until the red digital readout said 0:02 before leaning down and severing the wire cleanly in half. The timer stopped dead in its tracks. Another second went by, and then a tremendous, deafening boom sounded in his ears.

The Executioner stepped out of the tent and felt the wind on his face. Just past where the Gypsy now lay dead, he saw the helicopter in flames. The pungent odor of gasoline filled the air.

Turning, Bolan looked across the campground and saw the gray ash of the fire pit twirling in tiny dust devils. Sparks from the smoldering fire danced within the ashes and looked like children's sparklers on the Fourth of July.

Bolan smiled as he started back toward the path.

HUGH POLLARD WAS SITTING on one of the benches at the train station when the Executioner got back to Pias. He was alone. A white envelope was visible sticking out of the breast pocket of his jacket. He reached up and pulled it out as Bolan walked forward.

"From her."

Bolan stuck the sealed envelope in his breast pocket. "She didn't try to take you with her?" he asked.

The former CIA director shook his head. "No," he said. "In fact she told me to stay here and wait on you."

"Where'd she go?"

Pollard shrugged. "Eventually, back to Moscow would be my guess, he said. "She took off down the tracks, anyway."

"When?"

"As soon as the time had run out and it was obvious you'd been able to deactivate the nuke," said Pollard, holding up his wrist to show Bolan his watch. He glanced back in the direction Bolan had come. "We weren't far enough away, were we? If you hadn't figured it out, I mean?"

"No," Bolan said.

Pollard shook his head in awe. "You know," he said, "I'm not too sure, but what all this has given me is religion." After a pause he asked, "What was the explosion we did hear? It came right about the time we figured the nuke would go off. Scared the living shit out of me, and I'd bet Marynka, too, although you'd have never known it to watch her."

"The helicopter tank blew up. The wind had picked up and must have blown a spark over from the fire pit."

Pollard burst out laughing. "Great timing for it," he said. "I guess the God I've started believing in has a sense of humor."

"Seems to," Bolan said.

"The other nukes okay?"

"I'm no expert, but they aren't like dynamite. Fire won't set them off." He walked over to the pay phone and tapped in a number. As he waited for it to ring, he said, "In fact, the meltdown will probably render them inoperative. In any case we'll have men in there by then to pick up the pieces."

A moment later Jack Grimaldi came on the line. "Hello, Striker," he said.

"Guess we'll have to find our way to Trujillo so you can land," Bolan told him. "Want to meet us there?"

"If that's what you want," Grimaldi's voice came back. "Or we can do it the easy way. While you were playing games in the jungle, I came up with a helicopter." Only then did

Bolan notice the flapping blades in the background on Grimaldi's end. "Where are you, Striker?"

"Back at the train stop. How far out are you?"

"Give me ten minutes," the ace pilot said. "I know waiting isn't in your nature, but sit and relax, okay? You might even want to catch a nap—I just talked to Stony Man and Hal said something about getting you back to the jet as soon as possible. Sounds like you'll be heading for Bosnia before the night is out." Grimaldi chuckled softly on the other end of the line. "No rest for the wicked, you know."

Bolan disconnected the call and took a seat on the bench next to Hugh Pollard. During the mission, he had gone from believing Pollard was a traitor to his country to respecting the man as a true patriot willing the risk his life for the United States, and the world. Pollard wasn't in the same league as Marynka Platinov when it came to field operations. but he had done his best. And he had shown that he was still adequate, and able to think on his feet.

"You ready to go home?" Bolan asked the former CIA director.

Hugh Pollard grinned from ear to ear. "Am I ever," he said. "And now I can't wait to testify in court. I can't tell you how much I'm going to enjoy seeing William Brookings behind bars." He looked as if he might have wanted to keep the conversation going, but when Bolan pulled the envelope from his pocket, the former CIA man coughed nervously and stood.

"Er, I've got to go take a leak," Pollard said. His eyes fell to the envelope, then he looked off to the side, his eyes on the ground. "Take your time." He turned away and hurried off down the tracks.

Using the Rad as a letter opener, Bolan slit the envelope open. Inside, he found a single page of white paper. The note was brief. It had been written in bright red lipstick.

"One last Americanism from me: the big one that got away."

It had been signed with a kiss from lips wearing the same lipstick.

Bolan smiled as he heard Grimaldi's chopper blades nearing in the distance. As Grimaldi began to descend Bolan watched him and waited. His thoughts were no longer on Marynka Platinov. He would think of her during the quiet moments. Instead he was already wondering what was waiting for him in Bosnia.

Don't miss the action and adventure of Mack Bolan on these titles!

DON PENDLETON's

MACK BOLAN®

#61472-1	CONFLAGRATION	$5.99 U.S.☐	$6.99 CAN.☐
#61471-3	KILLSPORT	$5.99 U.S.☐	$6.99 CAN.☐
#61470-5	EXECUTIVE ACTION	$5.99 U.S.☐	$6.99 CAN.☐
#61469-1	VENGEANCE	$5.99 U.S.☐	$6.99 CAN.☐

(limited quantities available on certain titles)

TOTAL AMOUNT	$
POSTAGE & HANDLING	$
($1.00 for one book, 50¢ for each additional)	
APPLICABLE TAXES*	$ _____
TOTAL PAYABLE	$ _____
(check or money order—please do not send cash)	

To order, complete this form and send it, along with a check or money order for the total above, payable to Gold Eagle Books, to: **In the U.S.:** 3010 Walden Avenue, P.O. Box 9077, Buffalo, NY 14269-9077; **In Canada:** P.O. Box 636, Fort Erie, Ontario, L2A 5X3.

Name: _____

Address: _____ City: _____

State/Prov.: _____ Zip/Postal Code: _____

*New York residents remit applicable sales taxes.
  Canadian residents remit applicable GST and provincial taxes.

GOLD
EAGLE®

GSBBACK2

When all is lost, there's always the future...

JAMES AXLER

DEATH LANDS®

THE SKYDARK CHRONICLES Book III

Shadow Fortress

The Marshall Islands are now the kingdom of the grotesque Lord Baron Kinnison. Here in this world of slavery and brutality, the companions have fought a fierce war for survival, on land and sea—yet the crafty baron still conspires to destroy these interlopers. They cunningly escape to the neighboring pirate-ruled Forbidden Island, with the baron's sec men in hot pursuit...and become trapped in a war for total supremacy of this water world.

Available in September 2001 at your favorite retail outlet.